Wild Words
Volume 6

Wild Words Children's Book Festival,
c/o The Reading Room,
Bridge Street,
Carrick on Shannon,
Co. Leitrim,
Ireland.

+353 (71) 96 71580

www.wildwords.ie

Published by Leitrim County Council Arts Office.

www.leitrimarts.ie

ISBN: 978-0-9576189-6-1

Edited by Helen Carr.

A collection of writing by young people produced as part of the Wild Words Children's Book Festival, Carrick on Shannon, Co. Leitrim.

Introduction

By Helen Carr

When Leitrim County Council decided to run a competition inviting young writers aged between fourteen and eighteen to submit their work to be considered for publication, they probably couldn't have foreseen that, six volumes later, the annual Wild Words book would still be going strong. The number, quality and variety of entries just continues to grow, year on year. This year, there were over 350 entries from young people all across Ireland – narrowing them down to the sixty one included here was no small task!

I'm delighted to have been involved with Wild Words – assessing the submissions and choosing which should be included in the book – since the very beginning; this time of year has become a favourite of mine as I look forward to seeing what young Irish writers have to say about their lives, interests and beliefs.

As I've come to expect, this year's collection once more offers a huge breadth of themes, subjects and genres – there's humour, fantasy, vividly evoked historical pieces, stories set in warzones, and others set closer to home, work looking at family relationships, back at childhood, or forward to old age. There are well-crafted crime stories; lyrical expressions of friendship; poetry and prose about love of all kinds, about bullying, feeling different and working out just who you are. Interestingly, in the year that poet and award-winning Young Adult author, Sarah Crossan, becomes Laureate na nÓg, Wild Words contains a greater proportion of poetry than ever before.

Ireland is undergoing a remarkable period of change; during the 2015 Marriage Equality referendum and this year's referendum on repealing the 8th Amendment, young people were to the fore, campaigning, raising awareness and becoming politically engaged. Some of the spirit of this changing Ireland (and of the openness stemming from Hollywood's #metoo movement) shines through in this collection, in prose and poetry where young writers explore their lives in modern Ireland and speak up for equality – for all races, sexual orientations and genders. Alongside this, many of these young writers use their writing to go beyond their own experiences and put themselves in others' shoes. There's a line on the power of reading in the film *Shadowlands* that rings very true to me: 'We read to know that we are not alone'. I feel that the writing in Wild Words is reaching out to the world, and introducing itself; read it to realise that none of us are alone.

Helen Carr

June 2018

Helen Carr has worked in publishing for twenty years and is Senior Editor with The O'Brien Press. She has worked with many Irish children's and YA authors, including Judi Curtin, Sarah Webb, Kim Hood, Alan Nolan, Erika McGann, Ger Siggins, Ruth Frances Long, Chris Judge, Nicola Colton and Sarah Bowie. Helen has also reviewed books for many publications, including The Sunday Independent, Inis magazine and BookFest and regularly speaks at publishing events and on panels.

Contents

Memories

By Emer Minish, age 15.

We're storing memories,

Like memory cards in a camera.

Left alone, but always there for when we want to view them again.

Although sometimes we miss details,

Like a camera when it is set to capture single photos.

But someone else will have trapped a different moment of the same event.

I don't see it all,

But once put together, we see it all.

Constellations

By Emmie Hanlon, age 14.

Ever since I was a little girl, I loved the constellations. Before Granddad died we used to watch them together. He taught me the names of all of them. I used to go to his old log cabin every Saturday and stay with him while Mum and Dad went out. He'd read me old books about ghosts and stars, occasionally flowers, just stuff like that. He was always quoting his favourite authors, Tolkien and Dickens, mostly. Somehow, Granddad had the perfect famous quote for any type of situation. He always knew what to say, almost like he had some sixth sense.

The day he died, we were all there at the hospital, me, Mum and Dad. Granddad was lying there in the hospital bed, IV tubes sticking out from his arm. In all the time I had known him, Granddad never looked old... but on that day, he looked like he had been around for thousands of years. Mum was crying relentlessly into Dad's shoulder as Dad rubbed her back comfortingly. Dad looked angry at... well angry at everything. I knew this was hard for him, Dad has never been the crying type, he was more aggressive in his grief. I was just... looking at Granddad, holding his wizened hand, waiting for something, anything to happen.

Breathing heavily, Granddad turned to me and grinned weakly, "You better not let them bury me in some god-awful suit."

I giggled a little bit at that, "Old knit jumpers and holey socks it is then."

Mum looked up at my chuckles and glared at me, face red. I shrugged it off. I didn't really feel guilty. On the day he was diagnosed, Granddad and I had promised each other that if the worst were to happen, we wouldn't make it harder on each other, and to be honest, I didn't want to spend my last moments with him crying over something I couldn't change.

Granddad looked up at Mum's disapproving look and calmly stated, "There is nothing in the world so irresistibly contagious as laughter and good humour. Don't blame Lily for trying to make this easier on me, Julie."

Mum huffed a little, nodded as Dad patted her shoulder reassuringly. Mum never really got Granddad's quote habit and used to complain about it a lot.

I smiled to myself at the quote, "Dickens…" I thought. "Nice quote Granddad."

He grinned again. He opened his mouth to speak, paused as the heart monitor sped up. Rapid beats, making every single one of us go pale.

"Guess I'm nearly outta time then," Granddad chuckled. I shook my head a little then. I had so many things I wanted to say, I knew Granddad probably wanted to speak, he always said he wanted to make some grand ending speech and now it was finally time.

He looked at dad, "You better take care of my girls." Dad nodded solemnly and Granddad chuckled, "And loosen up a bit! Always so serious… If more of us valued food and cheer and song above hoarded gold, it would be a merrier world." Dad nodded again and smiled. He loved Tolkien too. Granddad laughed again at Dad's sudden change in demeanour.

He looked at Mum next, she was crying again. "My sweet Julie… you always were a little crybaby, weren't you?" Mum hiccupped, blushing as she tried to stop her tears. "Heaven knows we need never be ashamed of our tears, for they are rain upon the blinding dust of earth, overlying our hard hearts. I was better after I had cried, than before— more sorry, more aware of my own ingratitude, more gentle. Don't refuse to cry, Julie. Don't reject what makes you, you." Mum nodded, letting her tears flow and smiling at Granddad.

Lastly, he turned to me, "Last but not least, our little Lily flower." I smiled at him, a couple of stray tears leaving my eyes. "The pain of parting is nothing to the joy of meeting again, my Lily."

At his words, I broke my carefree persona a little, "B-but what if we never do meet again?"

Granddad smiled a little, "We will." He squeezed my hand, "Have a heart that never hardens, and a temper that never tires, and a touch that never hurts."

3

I laughed a little, "Nice one."

Granddad smiled, "Thanks… Lily."

He sank back into the pillow and closed his eyes, sighing heavily. "Oh, and one more thing," We all looked at him in anticipation. "I left my will in the drawer in my bedroom. You should look for it… later." Dad nodded grimly. Granddad closed his eyes again and a nurse rushed into the room as the heart monitor went still.

That night we went back to the log cabin. I spent half the night on the roof, looking up at the constellations. All of them had a story, a place, not like me. Granddad had left me his old telescope, our old books and even a little black notebook with his favourite quotes written in it. The biggest thing he had left me wasn't mine until I was much older, though. A sum of money, enough to pay for any college I would ever want. I already knew my first choice, Lakewood University of Art."

Granddad had been the one to buy me my first easel and complying with his request, I painted a very sloppy version of the Pegasus constellation. It was so hideous I had nightmares for a week. Granddad laughed his head off and in an embarrassed rage, I vowed to get better at painting and I realised art was something I actually enjoyed doing. From there, I researched different colleges and universities and, of course, Lakewood's was my first choice. Not only was it beautiful, with abundant forests and other plant life, it was incredibly prestigious and infamously difficult to get into. So, of course, being me, I chose one of the hardest art schools in the world to get into.

After about two hours of just staring up at the sky, Mum made me get down from the roof. I lay awake in bed for a long time thinking a lot about Granddad and about what I would do without him and I made some decisions. I was going to work harder at the things I loved, like art. I really wanted to get into that college and if I was going to get accepted I would need an impressive portfolio. I was going to become more responsible, actually take control of my life. Learn how to take care of myself. Make Granddad proud.

I didn't cry that day. I didn't cry at the funeral. I wore my promise to him like a badge. No tears, no sorrow. No making it harder on anybody. I blocked off all vulnerability and distracted myself from grief with other things. Over the next couple of years I became a bit of a workaholic. All work no play. I painted and studied all the time, I learned how to cook, clean, even pay bills and things like that. I got accepted into Lakewood and moved into the city where it was situated. Even then, I couldn't stop. I was tied to working and churned out one lifeless painting after another, distracting myself from grief and never taking any time to rest, but there was one indulgence I allowed myself.

Outside my little apartment there was a small park near the lake from which Lakeside got its name. In the middle of it there was a gazebo with a plethora of mahogany benches surrounding it. An elderly homeless man had been sleeping in the gazebo for as long as I had lived in the city and a professor at Lakeside had told me that the man had just appeared there one day and taken up residence in the park. Nobody knew where he came from, if he had family. He was just… there.

One day, I bought some food at the fish and chip shop by the park and brought it to him. He was sitting on a bundle of dirty blankets and seemed to be reading some kind of tattered, old book.

I cleared my throat, "Um…Hello?"

The man looked up at me. His face had deep wrinkles and was covered in grime and dust. He looked familiar, but it was hard to tell where I might have known him from.

"Yes?" He had a scratchy voice, deep and gravelly.

I looked at him and hesitantly handed him the brown, greasy paper bag, filled with vinegar-soaked chips and a cheeseburger. "Uh… I thought… I thought you might be hungry."

He looked in the bag and smiled, "Y'know you are the first person here who has given me anything."

"That's not fair," I stated firmly, "It's not your fault that you're…"

The man chuckled, "I'm homeless, kid. You can say it."

I blushed at his reply and fidgeted with my hands. "What's your name?" I blurted out, nervously.

The man thought about it for a moment, "Hmm… I'm…Pictor."

I wrinkled my nose. "Pictor? Like the constellation?"

He shrugged, "Sure."

I looked him over. "Where did you live before here?"

Pictor started devouring the bag of chips, "Around, I guess. Want one?"

I shook my head no and glanced down at my watch. "Oh! I'm going to be late if I don't leave now! I'm really sorry, but I have to go…"

Pictor looked at me. "Come back tomorrow, kid."

I looked at him in shock, "What? Why?"

He smiled, "You're good company. Besides, you probably want to ask me more questions."

I nodded at that, "I suppose you're right. I'll be back tomorrow, with more food."

So the next day I went, and I kept going back day after day. I got to know Pictor a little better, though he kept most of his life a mystery. I still didn't know where he came from or why he came here, but I enjoyed his company and it was the only time during the day, apart from sleep, that I relaxed. During this time, I found myself thinking more about Granddad. "This is what he would have wanted, right?" I thought to myself, "He would have wanted me to do well and work hard…" The more I thought about him, the harder I worked. I stayed up even later than I already did. I got up earlier, wrote and painted twice as much as before. I drank an extremely unhealthy amount of coffee in order to stay awake and gained dark circles like bruises under my eyes.

Pictor began to notice. We were discussing art one day and in the middle of my rant about Picasso, he pointed out my weary expression. "You alright, Lily?"

I nodded, brushing my limp hair out of my face listlessly. "Yeah… why do you ask?"

He looked uncomfortable. "You look like you haven't slept in weeks."

"I'm fine."

I tried to continue our conversation, but Pictor kept bringing it back to my obvious exhaustion. "Look, Lily, don't try to lie to me. I know you. Please just tell me what's wrong."

Tired and irritated, my reply to his concerned questioning came out sharp and cruel. "Look, I'm fine. Just shut up about it already! We barely know each other, really. You're just some homeless guy, prying into business that doesn't concern you."

He stared at me in shock. I immediately felt terrible and yet... I felt liberated, free almost. I never let my frustrations out. I used to, with Granddad before... and then it clicked.

"Y-you... I know why you were so familiar now."

Pictor raised his eyebrows at me, looking disgruntled, though I could hardly blame him. "You remind me of my... of my Granddad." I buried my face in my hands, grief, almost like a knife, finally flowing through me. I cried for the first time in years and Pictor smiled gently. "I'm sorry. I'm s-so so sorry." I sobbed.

"It's okay Lily... you haven't done anything like this in a while have you?"

I shook my head, tears still flowing. "I don't know what I'm doing anymore, Pictor... I'm so scared..."

"Don't be scared, my little Lily flower..."

My eyes widened. Only Granddad called me that. I jolted my head up and gazed at him astonished, "Granddad!?"

Pictor smiled. "I told you we'd meet again."

I shook my head in shock, "B-but how?" He chuckled and patted my hand. "That doesn't really matter right now, Lily. What matters is why you're doing this to yourself."

I dropped my gaze from his piercing green eyes. "I… wanted to make you proud…" Granddad tutted a little bit. "You know I'm already proud of you, Lily. There's another reason, isn't there."

I looked back up at him, confused. "I don't know…"

He looked at me intently. "Look at all this, Lily. Why do you think this is happening?"

I thought about it for a moment. "I… haven't… I haven't dealt with you being gone properly. I distracted myself… instead of dealing with my feelings."

Granddad nodded, smiling. "And that's why "Pictor" was here. To help you deal with this. I'm never really gone, Lily. I'm always here… somewhere."

I smiled through my tears, a thought occurred. "You have to leave, don't you?"

He nodded gravely. "I'm not alive, Lily. But that doesn't mean I'm gone."

I nodded. "I know that now."

"Good." Granddad got up from the ground, smiling once again, before turning to leave the gazebo. "Oh… but one more thing…"

Weeks later, I stood, smiling on the stage of Lakewood's yearly art convention. Judges staring up at me, I beamed as I whisked the curtain off my painting and Granddad's final request. A beautiful painting rested on the easel, a rendition of the constellations and the most brightly shining being; Pictor.

The Accidental Rescue of Lucio

By Emma Flannery, age 15.

One thing I've noticed, when I introduce myself to people: they always get excited when they hear I'm a god. They think I'll be able to – I dunno – make new universes, or be everywhere at once, or see the future, or something.

I can't do any of that. I'm a god of geese. Well. Other stuff too, but mostly geese. And I don't have a cool temple, either. I don't even have a house. Most nights I hide under a bridge, or something.

So, yeah. Lamest god ever.

Most of the other gods don't like me. Like, they never invite me to stuff. Usually that annoys me. But last Halloween… I didn't mind last Halloween.

They had some big convention, because apparently some chosen one who was going to change the entire multiverse forever was coming of age, or in big trouble, or impossible to find, or something. I don't know. No one invited me.

So, I was just chilling out. Under my bridge. Alone. While all the other holy deities hung out, and ate grapes, and talked about important destiny stuff. And I mean. I was cool. Totally.

I heard footsteps, tromp-tromp-tromping over my bridge, and I didn't do anything, because who am I, a Billy Goat Gruff? Except then they stopped, like right overhead, and then I got annoyed, because how is a god meant to mope with some mortal just hanging out on their bridge?

Except that then I heard something that sounded like they were climbing onto the parapet, and then I kind of panicked, because I thought, you know, they were gonna commit suicide or something. So I came out of hiding, and started to fly up.

(I'm a god. I can fly. And yes, it is the BEST. Anyway.)

9

I was about halfway up when we smashed into each other. So, all of a sudden I have this flailing kid in my arms and I'm like I didn't sign up for this, and then I'm like well okay, I'm immortal, I should be okay, I need to protect this guy.

I hit the water first, and it hurt. For a minute everything was really confused, but then I came back up and I could see the guy struggling and splashing for air. So I grabbed the back of his hoodie and dragged him to shore, and while he hacked water into the dirt, I got some godfire going. (It's normal fire. It's normal fire, I don't know why we call it godfire. Goddamn egotistical deities.)

So I turned around, and took a good look at the guy, and I got this big shock. I mean… I dunno, I was expecting some middle-aged bankrupt business dude, you know? This guy was young, really young. Like sixteen at absolute most. And he looked really sweet. Duck fluff hair, big puppy eyes, pouty lips. Although the pouting might have been because he was about to burst into tears.

'You saved me,' he said, and I could hear them coming. Like, any second, he was gonna start bawling. So I nodded.

'Why?'

And there they were, big ugly sobs, shock and misery and pain all in one. And then I felt absolutely awful.

'Um. I didn't want you to die?'

'I wanted to die! Why do you think I jumped off a bridge?'

And I didn't know what to do. So I did the thing I always do when I feel bad, because if it works for me, it might work for him, right? So I clicked my fingers, and then we're both in this farmyard. He screamed, and that woke them up.

The geese came stampeding out of their house, and I felt my heart soaring, because my babies. They gathered around me, honking, and I cleared my throat. The kid was staring at me.

'Everyone,' I said, pointing at him, 'this is… um…'

'Lucio,' the kid said, dazed.

'Lucio. Lucio needs cheering up. Everyone be nice to him.'

And they knew exactly what to do. My little leader, Miss Mama Goose, settled herself in Lucio's lap, and everyone else clucked gently, rubbing him with their heads and their wings.

And for a moment, I was scared, cause what if he didn't like them? What if I was wrong?

But then, this wondrous expression came over his face, and the tears stopped. And I could see this kind of peace settling over him. And we just kind of sat there, and it was great.

'So...,' Lucio said after a while. 'Uh... what's the deal with you and the geese?'

'I'm a goose god.'

'Oh. Okay. Is that how... you know... the flying and teleportation and stuff?'

'Yeah. Can't do much else, though.'

'And why... why were you under a bridge?'

'I live there.' I caught his look. 'Don't judge. Cutbacks. Not every deity gets a temple... or followers... or invites to – to god stuff...'

'I'm not judging.' He looked down, fidgeted. 'It's... kinda cool. Geese. And stuff.'

So we stayed there, and petted the geese, and leaned back and looked up at the sky.

And he started talking, after a while, and I didn't stop him, because it was important.

He told me about his family. His mother, politely interested in him. His stepfather, who was kind, but eternally busy. The endless stepsiblings, most of whom despised him. The brother he idolised, dead six months. The brother he had just wanted to see again.

I learned about his friends. The lack of them. The grades, falling and falling. The part-time job, endless hours for table scrapings. His life, the burden that had gotten too heavy for him to carry.

And I told him some stuff too. About being a god but not really and not having much non-geese friends and living under the bridge. And then Lucio said we could be friends with each other, and I was totally down with that.

So that's why I didn't mind not being invited to the god-conference thing. They could keep their chosen one. I had a friend, like an actual friend, and not an I'll-tolerate-you-because-I'm-taking-pity-on-you friend. So that was great.

Gran

By Ellie Keaveney, age 14.

"Thanks be to God," the thirty mass attendees sang out as Fr. McMahon finished his Sunday morning preaching. As all left the church the Gregg was still sparkling after being visited by Jack Frost the night before.

"Ah Nuala, I haven't seen ya this ages!"

Mrs. Foxe was always looking for someone to chinwag with. If something had happened within a five mile radius of the church she knew about it. I was convinced that inside the little navy handbag she carried on her shoulder was an FBI badge!

"Did ya hear? They're finally clearing all those cranes and what not from the quarry. Oh 'twas an awful shame they put a stop to that business, 'twould've brought a bit of money to the area!"

Gran wasn't much of a gossiper apart from when the discussion of bringing money into our little village was brought up. Her hunched back would straighten. Her tired old eyes would awaken, it was mind-boggling.

"But sure Nancy ever since all them EU regulations came in sure this place has failed a sight and 'tis a shame really." "Oh, and did yam' hear poor auld Mrs. Lynam's brother's wife is after dying. Down near Birr I think they lived."

And there it was every Sunday morning after mass. Every conversation ended up with someone's relative's spouse passing away. I helped my elderly grandmother into the car amongst the hum of a football match wafted through the morning air. As Gran and I returned home to our dull cottage at the back of the hill we could see the workers starting to remove the machinery from the quarry. Dust fragments swirled through the worksite like a sand storm in the Sahara. The sound of trucks driving over gravel poisoned the silence and still of the Irish countryside. Ever since I'd been around nothing had ever happened at the quarry, it was just an eyesore in the vibrant green grass of the hills. Although it was dull and mundane the big lump of rock held a sense of intrigue and mystery.

I sat in Gran's little old fridge of a house contemplating how ridiculously predictable my life was when the phone rang.

"Rose Mulligan, this is Dr. Sweeney from the Galway Clinic calling about Nuala's test results."

Gran had lung cancer and had finished her last round of chemotherapy about six months ago. She was once a vibrant woman but now withered and frail, these tests were going to tell me if Gran was better or not.

"Oh yes, this is Rose. How were the tests?" "I'm afraid they are not as we had hoped Ms. Mulligan. I'm sorry but there is nothing else we can do to help your grandmother"

A teardrop trickled through my lashes, meandered before crashing on my lips. I tried to talk back into the phone but couldn't

"Well, um, Th…Thank you for ca…calling."

I couldn't find the courage to tell Gran that night. I hadn't even accepted it yet. After all her fighting nothing had come of it. I broke the news to her the next day as she sat in her leather armchair. In her right hand she held a cup of tea, in the left two plain rich tea biscuits. She placed them down as I walked closer to her. I took her little withered hand in mine.

"Gran, the test results came back."

"And how were they, dearie? Is my cancer gone?"

"I'm sorry, Gran, there's nothing else they can do, it's not going away."

She tried her hardest to hide how heartbroken she was, but I could tell she wanted to cry every tear she possibly could. I could see in her hazel brown eyes the pain she felt. The next week she wasn't herself as if part of her had died already.

Sunday after Mass the village was chaotic! Neither Gran nor I could figure out why. Garda cars, sirens, average pensioners frantically gossiping over the mystery. Mrs. Foxe was nowhere to be seen to update Gran and me about the news as she usually did.

"Did ye hear? The workers have found the body of a man up at the quarry; they can't tell who it is. Only bones left I heard."

I couldn't get my head around it. A murder? Freak accident years ago? How did nobody notice until now? No one around here really knew how to deal with drama. After all, the most exciting that had happened until now was the church being repainted. The entire village was in total shock. Everyone was told to stay close to the village in case they needed to question anyone about the case, but nothing seemed to happen over the next three days. The prospect of a murderer on the loose around kept me and probably everyone else up at night. Never mind Gran, who would leave her bedroom light on during the night out of sheer terror. A blanket of mystery covered the village separating us from the outside world; I decided that I had to figure out what was really going on.

I drove five miles away from our house to arrive to what was called the Garda station despite the fact that it looked like a shed. The warm scent of coffee attempted to overthrow the stale smell of dampness. Sat at the desk was an overweight man who looked to be in his mid-fifties. His hair as white as snow. His belly hanging over his belt.

"Hello my name is Rose Mulligan and..."

"Get to the point! Does it look like I've got nothing to be doing?"

Well to be honest it looked as though he had just awoken from a slumber, he had nothing on his desk, his computer was turned off. By the looks of things he really did not have anything else to do.

"I was just enquiring about the body found in the quarry; my grandmother and I have been told to…"

"Have you got any evidence?"

"No, but I'd be open to helping with the case; I have lived in the area all my life and my grandmother is one of the oldest in the village, we know everyone we could help greatly."

"This is a very serious case Ms. Mulvihill"

"Mulligan."

"Ms. Mulligan and if your grandmother is as old as you make out would it not be in your best interest to be taking care of her instead of causing me trouble?"

I left the station without another word. How rude? Thinking he had any superiority over me? I'd say I knew more about solving a murder case than he did. I could feel the heat coming from my scarlet red cheeks when I returned to my tin wagon. I turned the keys signalling the engine to start and made my way home to Gran's.

"Nothing," I sighed as I opened the kitchen door and threw my handbag on the kitchen table. I looked over to Gran on her armchair. Her face was as pale as Snow White, her eyes limp. She lay still, quieter than usual.

"Oh, Rose, I don't feel too well."

"Do you want me to make you a cup of tea?"

"No, really not well Rose. Will ya ring Dr Sweeney?"

There was definitely something... something seriously wrong; you would have to drag Gran to the hospital if she was hit by a bus. I rang the doctor in panic, but to no avail, he was too busy with appointments. She seemed to be in another world, wouldn't drink, eat. Nothing. I was terrified that the police officer was right; I should have been taking care of Gran instead of heading into town. She fell asleep, but I stayed by her side ensuring she was okay. Raindrops trickled and meandered on the window before crashing at the bottom.

"Rose, Rose!"

She frightened the life out of me. Awoke me from my slumber of guilt and worry.

"Fr McMahon is surely nearby, see if he'll call"

"And Gran, what in the world will he do?"

"He'll bless me and… and I'll get better."

And good auld Gran was back – still weak as a kitten, but had full faith that Fr McMahon, a middle-aged man, would be able to cure her.

When the miracle man himself arrived with a knock on the door Gran instantly perked up; making a right liar out of me. Her hazel brown eyes regained their twinkle. A pink hue returned to her once blue lips. Maybe Fr McMahon really had cured her?

"Rose will ya be a good girl and make myself and Fr McMahon a pot of tea?"

The good cups came down from the dusty top shelf. The dainty little blue china cups only ever appeared when the priest or our third cousins once removed all the way from the amazing unknown world of Dublin came to visit.

"Father, have you any idea what's going on at the quarry? Have they found the people responsible?"

"To be honest, Nuala, I'm staying out of it, you wouldn't want to be interfering with all those detectives."

"You're very right."

Gran lifted her wobbling hand gripping her little dainty china cup, a plain rich tea in the other as she always did but she still seemed quite frail. It pained me to know that she probably wouldn't be around to find out who committed the crime even if she did tell the priest she wanted to stay out of it.

After he left Gran sat I front of the television mesmerised by the six 'o clock news. I sat day dreaming in the kitchen shrouded in boredom. On the wall hung a photograph of myself and my father whom I hadn't seen since I was eleven years old. After my mother died, he left and had never returned. As if he had disappeared from the face of the earth. No phone calls. No letters. I had always presumed that he couldn't handle the grief of losing Mum, but in that moment something in my brain clicked. I thought of the headline: "Body of man in his Fifties, estimated to have died twelve years ago".

It could be him.

"Gran, Gran! What if it's Dad they found? What if he didn't leave us and move away, he was in an accident?"

"Now, dearie, I know you miss your father but don't be completely ridiculous!"

"Gran…think about it!"

I could see the rusted cogs in her head turning as she tried to figure out if I was right or had totally lost my sanity.

"Y'know girl, you could be right!"

Gran sat beside me, both of us attempting to come to terms with our discovery. We had no way of proving that it was him, simply just a gut feeling. We had no witnesses. No evidence. Nothing. The Gardaí wouldn't listen to anyone unless they had hard evidence. I turned to look at Gran, biting her lip in deep concentration.

"I'm going to prove that that man is my son or at least find out who it is if it's the last thing I do!"

"But Gran how will we prove it's him, they won't listen to anyone, especially us women?"

"If we go to them and tell them the story they might."

"We may go to the quarry itself because that gombeen in the station will send us away within the space of two seconds!"

The next day we arrived to the quarry to a greeting of detectives deep in thought trying to uncover the missing piece of their puzzle. The sun peeked out from behind the hill reflecting on the ripples in the rock pools. Glimmering, shining, a blinding beauty brightening the dull grey of the quarry. I asked to see some evidence but was quickly turned away. I sat back into the car beside Gran who the decided to take things into her own hands. She carefully climbed out of the passenger seat car and with quite a frightening stare marched over to the group of detectives while I rushed behind.

"Excuse me; I see you have dismissed my granddaughter even though we have a story that could help your case!"

"I'm sorry we cannot give the discovered evidence to the public ma'am"

"I think that the corpse found was my son and I would like to see the evidence to determine if it is him or not!"

"I'm sorry, there are no exceptions!"

"I cannot sit in my house wondering for the rest of my life never knowing what happened to my son!"

I had never seen Gran as cantankerous since my cousin broke her good serving dish! No matter how hard myself and my eighty-nine year old grandmother tried to get our point across they wouldn't believe us. We retreated to our miniscule abode to drink tea and find some evidence. Dad was a doctor and so we decided to call all the hospitals in the area and see if there was any trace of an Enda Mulligan. Absolutely nothing. We searched a missing person's website to eliminate it being anyone else. Everything we did kept pointing us back to Dad however there was still a foggy blur over the whole case and unfortunately; we didn't have a flashlight to guide us through.

Gran and I continued to search for evidence to prove that it was Enda for the next week. Gran even skipped knitting club on Tuesday and cards on Thursday night to improve our private investigation. Gran always wanted something big before she made her way to the God she had spent almost every minute of her life worshipping; now she finally had her one last mission. Our project had given her a spring in her step, a smile as bright as the midday sun to her face and hope, hope that she, in her eighty-ninth year, could make a difference. However her battle with cancer was forcing her health to persistently deteriorate. Each day the battle was getting tougher and her body was running out of ammunition, until one day it did and her body started giving up on her. We were both getting ready to bring our evidence to the quarry when she began making her way to heaven. Her face grew pale, her eyes dreary, her lungs refusing to work despite her hearty willing it. The piercing sound of the ambulance grew louder, more persistent as they brought us closer and closer to the last room Gran would see.

They wheeled her away on a trolley when we arrived at the hospital. I sat in the waiting area surrounded by screaming children, worried forty-year-olds and a handful of old age pensioners reading today's paper. I sat shrouded in my own misery and worry attempting to come to terms with the fact that Gran probably wasn't going to make it. If she was gone, I would have nothing, my only purpose in life until now was minding Gran. My parents were gone; all my childhood friends had spread their wings and flown far and wide.

"Rose Mulligan, if you would like to follow me?"

I followed the young man with a turquoise green nurse suit down the dull beige corridor to where Gran was. She lay motionless on the bed, wires and machines keeping her alive. I took her withered hand in mine, tears streaming down my face

"Gran it's me, Rose."

"Oh, dearie, sure I know you well."

"It's okay to let go y'know, I'll be fine."

"Oh I know you'll be fine it's just..."

"What Gran?"

"I'll never be able to prove that goon at the quarry wrong."

"Gran, you are just something else!"

I laughed for a moment, providing a brief respite from my sorrows. Beep. Beep. Beep. Medical machines reminding me of the short time I had left with Gran.

"Rose, promise me you'll prove that man was your father, the poor man deserves some dignity."

"I love you, Gran."

"I love ya too, dearie."

And just like that she was gone. Her closed eyes never to open again. Her lips never to experience her favourite taste of tea and Rich Tea biscuits. A shadow of sorrow hung over me as I drove home in the pouring rain. All I wanted to do was lie on the couch, watch re-runs of programs from five years ago, drink tea and cry but instead was greeted by a house full of relatives I hadn't seen since the last funeral. All accompanied by trays of triangular sandwiches and shop-bought iced buns. Although they were trying to help, I just wanted to be alone in my pit of misery.

For the next two days I sat in the dark, cold good room as Gran called it listening to an endless amount of 'sorry'. I shook hands with strangers and long-lost friends until it was finally time to say goodbye to my grandmother, whom I adored, mourned, loved and had the happiest of memories with. During her final time the church, I sat staring at the multi-coloured stained glass window. A beam of light through the darkness shone only on her coffin, as if it were her leaving for good, her spirit floating to the beyond.

Enveloped in loneliness I sat in Gran's armchair seven days later when the phone began to ring.

"Hello, this is Rose Mulligan."

"Ms. Mulligan, my name is Philp Harris. I am a detective looking into the case at the quarry and I believe you have evidence or may know who it is?"

"Oh…um…Yes, I have reasons to believe that the man found was my father-Enda Mulligan. I don't have much proof but…"

"Anything is helpful Ms. Mulligan because between us, we really have nothing at the moment"

At last there was someone willing to listen to me! We agreed to meet the next day at the station and maybe run a DNA test. I spent the rest of the day putting all my research together to prove for once and for all that Gran and I were indeed right.

After what felt like an hour of me persuading Mr. Harris that the mystery man was my long-lost father he decided that we should do a DNA test to prove I was right. I followed the detective down a grey corridor to a cold room. I had to give a sample of my spit and wait for a machine to tell me the news. My heart raced, my fingertips shaking. I was curious, yet terrified. Mr. Harris came back into the room ten minutes later.

"Rose, it's a DNA match, the man they found is your father."

"Thank you, you have no idea how much this means to me and would've meant to my late grandmother."

"Your help in this case will not be forgotten, Rose."

He smiled and shook my hand apologising for the hardship I had gone through to get to this place.

I lay in bed that night staring at the twinkling stars of the midnight sky as I always did. Missing my mother, father and mostly Gran before drifting off into a deep slumber. Through a hazy mist I could see a field of lavender, a scent so fresh and soothing. I heard Gran's voice, whispers of heaven, as if she were there. She appeared wearing her favourite white dress and took my hand; a touch so tender and familiar I almost thought it was reality.

"Well done, dearie, you've done yourself proud girl."

"I don't know what to do, Gran, I have nothing, nobody."

"Rose, move on, start again. You've done enough for this town and family."

"I don't know how Gran, I still don't know what happened to Dad."

"Let go, spread your wings. You will find the answers on your journey and I will be with you all the way."

Suddenly Gran was gone and I was staring at the swirling stars in darkness once again. Although Gran was gone I finally knew that the secret to life wasn't having all the answers, but learning to live without them. It was now my time to let go, with Gran by my side, always.

The Future

By Ruby Delaney, age 14.

They say to know a generation,

you must look to what they think

about the future.

What is there, then, to say

about my generation

Who look to the future –

A thing that to you was

a beacon of hope and opportunity –

And see nothing but

Darkness.

A world where no one –

not least those meant to protect us –

Can be trusted;

Where corrupt governments are the norm

And no one, not even your children,

Is safe.

You might say that we lack hope,

I say, no, you lack change.

Are these dystopias we read about

Much worse than the world we live in?

"Think of the children,' you cry ,

Yet children die in your very schools.

"Stop being greedy!" you yell,

And still more tax cuts for the rich.

"What would you know?" you scream.

Let me tell you what we know:

We know when governments are corrupt,

We know when children are not safe,

But most of all,

We know how to rebel.

Nothing Came

By Aoife Devlin, age 15.

"BEST OF LUCK to our u16 boys who begin their DIVISION 1 league campaign tonight at home vs. St. John's at 6pm. GET OUT AND SUPPORT THE LADS. Also, our u16 girls get their league campaign underway when they go to CT Gaels at 6:30pm."

"Our minor boys lost 4-14 to 2-04 to a very strong Curry side in DIVISION 1 yesterday. Hard luck lads, you're a great bunch of lads; we'll go again, lads.

In other news our u14 girls beat favourites Tourlestrane and Calry to qualify for Féile finals after extra time."

PLEASE NOTE CHANGES:

Ladies' game has been changed to 9am on a Sunday morning to accommodate minor boys training at 11.

***

Conversation at the breakfast table had taken an abrupt turn for the worse. The argument over who needed to be taken where and at what time was turning steadily vicious.

"For the last time, Mum, training WILL be over at nine sharp, the boys train after us and the coach kicks us out ten minutes early because they boys need to stretch."

"Okay, then, but I still can't collect you until 9:30, dear. Your brother has swimming, then soccer, then Pilates. Really, darling, I can't be expected to bring you everywhere. I have a son as well, you know."

"I've noticed," I scowled, shooting a death glare at the spoilt, entitled little brat sitting opposite me.

"So it's settled then?" Mum asked sceptically. "You'll wait the half hour?"

"Yes, Mum," I said, the energy for any sort of argument draining out of me.

"HARD LUCK TO OUR SECOND YEAR BOYS WHO LOST THEIR LAST QUALIFYING MATCH TODAY TO TOUGH OPPOSITION. In other news, congratulations to the senior girls team who won their all Ireland semi final today."

"Okay, girls, here's the deal," Mr Young said, sounding bored. "I know that we're in the All-Ireland Final, but I see no reason to change what seems to be working for us so far. I won't be training you after school, so see that you get in club training and um... eat well."

"Would one training session do us any harm?" I asked confusedly. "We need to work on our kickouts."

"Sorry girls, I just don't have the time." He replied. "Tomorrow evening I normally would, but I've to train the second year boys."

"BUT SIR, THEY'RE OUT!" we yelled in frustration. "Yes, but I have to get a start on next year, maybe you can take it on yourselves to train a bit together. Now, that would show real initiative..." he said, his sentence trailing off as he walked away.

The girl power DOVE ad was playing on TV. I sat, slumped on the couch watching the paid actors play girls who succeeded in sport. They didn't seem to have a problem with resources. Or ridiculously early trainings because the boys were playing later. Or respect. Or heart. I had been playing sport for so long that I had nearly gotten used to the endless second-place scenarios whenever the opposite sex were involved. Even the lack of Facebook support was starting to get to me, though.

Maybe I should quit? I wondered. Become a cheerleader or take up some other sport dominated by women. No. I'd keep going. What would I have to complain about if I didn't have sexism in the GAA? My phone beeped. It was a family WhatsApp message. A photo of my brother playing on the main pitch. I'd never played on the main pitch. He was six years my junior and he'd already accomplished it.

I opened my laptop and clicked into my Gmail. In my drafts were twenty-seven unsent emails to anyone who was anyone associated with power and Gaelic football. I could send them, I thought. I hadn't composed them well, though. They were long rants every single one of them. If I sent them they probably wouldn't even be read. I went to click the 'x' button. My computer froze. It often did that. I waited around five minutes and tried again. I stopped. I stared. I blinked and then I blinked again. All the emails had been sent.

That night I persuaded myself that it wasn't such a disaster. It would be bad, but maybe it wouldn't be all bad. Maybe someone would listen. Maybe something would change as a result of my little accident. I fell asleep dreaming of making something change.

The next day I waited for a reply. There were twenty-seven emails sent so I assumed that at least fifteen would reply. When none came that day, I decided to give them the benefit of the doubt. I would give them a week before I judged them completely. Nothing came on day one.

Nothing came on day two.

Nothing came on day three.

On day four I got a reprimand from some women named Kathleen warning me to ask someone who cared.

Nothing came on day five.

On day six some man named Ben told me it was nothing to do with him.

Nothing came on day seven.

Nothing came any day after that.

And to be honest, I wasn't even surprised.

Hope Springs Eternal

By Grace Daly, age 15.

I crouched down further into the cold, damp corner, cradling Nadia in my arms, wishing the ground would swallow me whole. A stray tear meandered down my face, dropping ungracefully on her greasy hair and I held my breath. I could feel her shaking beneath me, and her frantic heartbeat pounding against her tiny chest. Whimpers erupted from the room as a tall, dark haired man burst through the steel door, scanning the room full of vulnerable, scared women, choosing his next victim. A woman let out a strangled cry as he roughly grabbed her by the arm and gave a feeble protest, only to be smacked hard in the face. We all turned our heads. They came and went every day, rarely bringing back the women they took.

I relaxed only slightly when I heard the door slam. Guilt instantly invaded me as I realised I was hoping, praying to god that it would be someone else, anyone else other than Nadia and me. Could you blame me?

I felt her frail body beneath me begin to move and I recognised it as an attempt to turn around to face me. I'm not sure was I ready to see her face. To see the hope and faith she still had in me to get us out of this place. How long had it been? I had lost count. Long enough for me to be able to recognise every individual whimper or cry from the sixty plus women and children in here.

Nadia eventually managed to manoeuvre her frail body around to face me. Despite the lack of food and water, she had still managed to retain her baby face. Round chubby cheeks, dark, wild eyebrows, and long, dark, slender eyelashes that failed to cover her astonishingly beautiful bright-green forest eyes. She was beautiful, and for that I feared for her.

"It stinks in here," she mumbled, her voice barely reaching a whisper.

I almost smiled at her innocent comment. Almost. Because the truth was, she was right. The smell was vile. Any possible combination of pee, vomit, blood or fuel. I racked my brain for a response. Normally, I would bypass responding to the statement at all and just tell her stories of what we were going to do once we reached 'the safe land'. Although I had told her similar stories before, she would allow herself get lost in the dream world every single time. Close her eyes and imagine herself, running around with her new friends, going to school, coming home to a meal. I envied how she was able to let herself go like that, let herself believe. She had that spirit though. The one that would see the good or positive side to anyone or anything.

But today, today I just couldn't. I didn't have an inch of energy left in my body to even think up a story. So I settled on a hum of agreement. Strangely, she seemed content with my vague response and rested her head on my shoulder and not long after, I began to hear the faintest snores vibrating off her.

My thoughts flitted back to the day we left. The day we set out on a journey to escape the misery of this war. This was certainly not what we had hoped. The sun was starting to head down in the west, dropping the temperatures by at least five degrees. Everyone welcomed the coolness, myself included.

All at once, a loud ear piercing noise vibrated off the walls and an artificial light filled up the room.

"ALL WOMEN WITH CHILDREN UNDER THE AGE OF 11, HEAD TO THE BOAT THAT HAS JUST DOCKED. WAIT IN AN ORDERLY QUEUE OR THERE WILL BE CONSEQUENCES," a loud, strong, authoritative voice shouted out through a rusty, broken speaker in the left corner of the room.

I gasped. It felt as though I could breathe again. And breathe proper fresh clean healthy air at that. At last. This was our opportunity. This was our chance to get the life we finally deserved. Nadia and I.

After months in this tiny, cramped, vile smelling shed, we finally were getting what we came for. What we paid for.

I stood up abruptly, adrenaline rushing through me. I was no longer tired. I would be the first person on that boat and the first person off. As I stood, I felt my muscles cramp painfully; it had been awhile since I had stood. I welcomed the ache. The once silent room was now filled with excited murmurs, pleas, whispers, moans. I would have been scared only for the fact that I knew I would be in a completely different country by next week at most. I remembered the promise I gave to my mother as we left home, oh, she would be so proud of us if she could see where we were headed.

An angry gun shot rang through the air bringing me back out of my fantasy. I remembered the orders and walked to the boat, still carrying my dazed and confused girl in my arms. The sky was almost dark, the sun still managing to stretch a few of its golden rays into the dark blue sky. The moon was now visible with a few stars accompanying it. We trundled along down to the beach where the boat would be docked. The sand beneath my feet felt like heaven on earth. I dug down, letting my toes get consumed by the cool, soft, white powder. The air, hung damply around us, wrapping itself around and clinging on. As we near the shoreline, I could smell the strong salt scent from the water. My heart stuttered a little as I noticed the small dingy boat that we would be travelling on. There was no way we could all squeeze ourselves into that. Especially not with the other groups of women stumbling towards us carrying their loved ones. And would it even last? It was plastic, and it was covered in tape.

"This is the boat that will take you to Europe."

Hope fluttered through me despite the weak and unreliable method of transport.

"From there, you are on your own." He lowered his voice into a more serious tone. "Do not speak your language, wear your native clothes or practise your religion. Follow these rules and you'll be fine, blend in. You are going to be living in Europe, so act like a European," was the man's advice. He looked tired and annoyed, with heavy dark bags beneath his eyes and dishevelled hair.

His voice sounded hoarse and bored. How many boats had he sent off already this week? Did they all make it across? Everyone knew not everyone made it across. A cold shiver ran down my spine.

Our group began to slowly shuffle towards the boat, excited murmurs bouncing between us, as we carefully stepped in. Nadia, now fully aware of what was going on, squeezed my hand tightly, nervousness, excitement, worry and curiosity seeping from her. She bounced up and down, trying to see if there was still room for us.

Adrenaline kept the tiredness and cold away and as the mother and two daughters before us stepped inside the boat, I could feel tears brimming. I swallowed down a sob of joy and stepped inside. The plastic floor wobbled beneath my feet. I assisted Nadia in and we sat down together. It was uncomfortably tight, my knees digging into a woman's back in front of me and my back squashed up against the side of the boat. Not many words were spoken, but I knew everyone was thinking of the exact same thing. Suddenly, the engine roared to life, an annoying, loud buzz, and Nadia's hands shot up to cover her ears, her face scrunched up in a ball. Honestly, I didn't mind. I would put up with anything to get to Europe. I managed to loop my arm around her and gave her a quick peck on the head. She gave me a full-watt beam in return. We both were excited as each other.

As we set off, I turned back and thought of the country I grew up in, where most of my loved ones still lived, where my childhood belonged to. I waited for feelings of regret, longing, fear, homesickness, but no emotion stirred, I felt no guilt for leaving. There was nothing left here and everyone knew it.

That's the one thing all of us strangers on this boat had in common. The only thing we were leaving behind us was war, bombings, hunger and depression.

The sky was pitch black now, the stars illuminating the darkness. The moon created a magical pathway of light across the still water with our boat adding a soft yet consistent ripple in it. The cold, bitter air swept across our faces and somehow managed to seep through our tightly compacted bodies. We sat in complete silence, the sound of the engine loudly humming away. A serene and peaceful atmosphere settled over us. Everyone lost in their own thoughts.

An hour or so later the wind began to strengthen, arousing the waves. Its strong current tossed us back and forth. The smell of fuel now wafted around the boat, its vicious scent making my stomach churn. The boats continuous rocking didn't help. As the wind picked up, the waves viciously pushed and shoved the boat, spraying water on us. Nadia glanced up at me, her eyes a storm of confusion and worry. I gave her a weak smile, and turned away before she saw the panic in my eyes. Was this boat strong enough to hold through a storm? Still no one spoke, but dread and hysteria swarmed the air. The sky cried out and waves of ice cold water now pounded in on us. Scared voices shouted out in question of what to do. One woman took charge and began to scoop as much water as she could out of the boat with her hands, making a tiny dent in the litres of water pouring in. We all followed suit, too panicked to think for ourselves. I could hear Nadia's scared voice, but I couldn't tell what she was saying. Instead, I grabbed hold of her tiny wrist with my free hand and vowed to myself not to let go. There was a loud ringing in my ears that I couldn't shut out and I choked on the sudden burst of water that sprayed in. I looked all around me, children were crying while imitating their mother's attempts to keep the water out.

Waves crashed relentlessly into the boat and despite everyone's best efforts, the boat was being consumed by water at an alarming rate. My breathing grew shallow. I held onto Nadia's arm as a thought sprang into mind. No one knew how to swim.

The ocean's water crept up the boat, with one end completely submerged, eating it with every second. I grabbed Nadia and hoisted her up into my arms, holding her tighter than I should. Panic coursed through my body and my heart hammered against my chest. What could I do? There wasn't any room to take a step backwards. Suddenly, I felt a push at my back and I hurled forward, with Nadia still in my arms and plunged into the water. I gasped as the pain consumed me. It was like a thousand needles were piercing into me all at once. I opened my eyes underwater, instantly regretting it. My eyes burned and my whole body felt as if it was on fire. Even underwater, I could hear Nadia screaming, crying for help. Somehow, I still had my grab on her and dragged her up towards the surface.

We both gasped for air, struggling frantically to stay afloat. Her black hair was covering half her face and her skin was as blue as the ocean. Waves thrashed into us, making it impossible to consume air rather than water. We must have stayed like that for minutes, our energy totally focusing on staying afloat. As a wave dropped, I caught a glimpse of the sunrise. Its orange, pink and yellow glow illuminated the sky. Too beautiful for such a tragic moment.

After a while, I could feel my energy tiring. Although we were still holding hands, I only caught glimpses of Nadia, when the waves decided to be kind. I struggled to fill my lung and black dots were dominating my vision. My legs felt weak as my body begged to give in. The oceans current felt like sandpaper against my raw skin

Holding onto Nadia was the only thought I could manage to keep in my head.

A heavy wave crashed down onto me, but I didn't have the energy to fight it. I felt myself being tossed and thrown underneath. My lungs were screaming and begging for air, they were on fire. My mind was hazy, vision going black. I was being submerged into blackness. Nothingness.

A blazing white light shone directly at me. I willed it to stop. My throat felt too raw and scratchy to speak up. Every part of me ached and all I wanted to do was to curl up and sleep. Without warning my stomach lurched and I puked pure sea water. My head throbbed as I rested my back off a wall. I heard soft murmurs around me, but I couldn't make out what they were saying. As I opened my eyes, I was stunned to see two male, white doctors around me. They were both similar with blond hair and green eyes. One was short though, the other tall and broad. Both of them stood with their backs to me, not noticing my return. I was in a small room, an emergency room by the looks of it. Without warning, the memories of yesterday came flooding back. The boat, the waves, the water, Nadia??!

I looked around frantically and before any consideration, I hopped out of the bed and ran towards the door. My head complained, but I had only one thought on my mind. One person on my mind. I received a shock when my eyes adjusted to the scene around me. I was on a massive ship, full of women, children and men, crying, shouting, calling, talking, and praying. I instantly recognised some of the women I had travelled with and immediately started calling out Nadia's name. At first my voice sounded small and weak, but I forced myself to shout louder. She wouldn't hear me over the crowd. She would be so scared right now. I was the only person she knew on this entire ship and I had abandoned her. Although I got the feeling this ship did save me, us, I still wouldn't trust anyone with my baby sister. Once I found her I could tell her. Tell her that finally, we were safe. We could live the life we were promised. I grinned. I could imagine her giddy smile, the excitement in her eyes, that sparkle. I ran down three floors vigorously checking each one while willing my inoperative, overtaxed body to continue searching. I felt dizzy from the lack of air as I reached the bottom floor. My eyes took a minute to adjust to the darker setting.

My blood turned cold. As cold as the bitter water. Ice in my veins. Tears burned in my eyes and I started to shake. Her small frail body lay there among other bodies. White as a ghost. That usual spark in her eyes, gone. I dropped to my knees and I begged and screamed. This couldn't be happening, couldn't be real. How? How had I let this happen? What about her future, her school, her friends? What am I going to do without the only joy I had left? Memories flooded to my head of her sweet smile, her gorgeous laugh, and her beautiful eyes. Her body was ice cold to touch. I cried and cried and cried. My eyes burned and felt raw. I felt sick to the stomach and had to run to the edge of the boat and heaved up everything. My throat burned as I sobbed. The tears wouldn't stop coming. I had never felt so much emotion in my life. Guilt, sadness, anger, pain, fear, hatred. Why had this happened to her? How could I let this happen? She was too young, too innocent, too much of a beautiful soul. I looked over my shoulder at her body. My throat tightened, as more tears threatened to fall. My eyes stung, my ears rang and the aftertaste of my vomit burned in my throat. I stumbled over to Nadia, dropped down to my knees and held her precious hand in mine, rocking back and forth, whispering about the life she would have had.

The Offer

By Finn Doherty, age 15.

Alan stepped off the bus and onto the busy city street. He pulled out his wallet and glanced down. All that was left was a tenner and some loose change. That was his budget then. A tenner.

He hurried into the little café with a fading red door. It was warm inside. He breathed a sigh of relief as he rubbed his hands together and glanced around for the others. He spotted them almost immediately in the small confined space. He hurried over to the table. Katie and her boyfriend Sam were already there. They both smiled and greeted him as he sat down.

"Freezing out there," complained Alan, blowing on his fingers.

"Meant to freeze tonight," said Katie.

"Snow as well I heard," added Sam as he handed Alan the menu.

"I don't mind snow at Christmas," explained Katie, "but there's something depressing about snow in January." The three of them nodded in agreement.

"Anyone know if Carol's coming today?" asked Alan. Even as he was speaking the door opened and Carol, dressed in a large coat with fur cuffs, strode into the café. She made her way calmly over to them and sat down in the empty seat beside Alan, greeting them with a beaming smile.

"So we all want to order?" asked Sam when they had all settled. Alan examined the menu. There wasn't really a great selection. There were a couple of different sandwiches, the odd slice of cake and an occasional hot beverage. He bit his lip. Trying to decide between the chocolate cake and the lemon drizzle cake.

A man stopped beside them. Alan glanced up at him. He was dressed in jeans and a t-shirt and was holding a shopping bag. Alan's eye's flickered around the table. Wondering who knew him. But he could see no recognition in his friends' eyes.

The man surveyed them for a long moment. No one said anything. They merely exchanged glances and frowns. After what seemed an age Sam spoke. "Can we help you, sir?" he asked. The man blinked rapidly as though he had been disturbed from a light sleep. He glanced around one more time before putting the shopping bag under the table.

"Now," he said in a calm voice, "I think you're the right crew. Sam, Katie, Alan and Carol. Am I right?"

Alan wrinkled his brow in confusion. How had he known their names? There was something just not right about the man. But he told himself to calm down. The situation was fairly passive currently; they needed to keep it that way.

"Yes," replied Sam, "That'd be us. And what's your name?" Sam stood up, offering his hand.

The man waved it away. His eyes darted around the café before he turned his attention back to them. He stooped over them, his voice almost as low as a whisper. "So here's the offer," he began quickly, "I know a fair bit about you. I know that you're all college students and that at least three of you took a loan out to be here and that you have to budget yourself to the end of the week. That's why I've come to you. In the bag I've placed under your table there are six things: A hat, a mask, a coat, a pair of gloves, five hundred thousand euro and a loaded gun."

Alan's heart started to race. Was this a crazy man talking rubbish or had they just been caught up in some sort of gangland feud. He glanced around at the others. Their eyes were wide open. He glanced back to the man.

"Now," said the man, "what you're about to do next will change your life forever. You can either tell me to go away, which I will, or you can ask me to explain how you're all going to become millionaires overnight."

"Go on," said Katie and Sam together.

The man smiled briefly. "In approximately six minutes a black man wearing a bright red cap and a denim hoodie will walk in to the diner. I don't want him to walk back outside alive. It's up to you how you do it, but you have what you need: a disguise and a gun. When you're done I want you to take all the equipment down to the drycleaners a hundred metres down the road. Go in there and we'll take the weapons and clothes off your hands and give you a further five and a half million euro to split any way you please. You get to walk away rich and forget that this ever happened. If you decide to back down simply take the bag (the five hundred thousand still in it), walk to the dry cleaners, hand it over to them and walk away. No matter what you do, don't try and trick us. Goodbye."

Then in a flourish he was moving swiftly out the door and onto the street. The four friends turned and looked at one another. Alan glanced down at the bag. For a long moment no one spoke.

"We have to make a decision," said Sam suddenly.

"Well, it's fairly obvious," said Carol suddenly, her assertiveness returning to her, "We leave the bag here and walk out of this place as fast as we can."

"Should we not drop it back at the drycleaners?" asked Katie.

"No," Carol assured her, "The moment we walk in there we'll be strangled to death. We've all got caught up in a gang war. We have to get out of here while we still can."

"No," said Alan suddenly, "In fairness to that man he sounded fairly genuine. I think that we will get the money if we go to the drycleaners."

"Based on what assumption?" demanded Sam, "That he sounded like he was telling the truth? That's one of the stupidest things I've ever heard you say. Like seriously. There's no telling what they could do to you there." Alan bit his lip. But he remained unconvinced.

"I'd go to the drycleaners," butted in Katie, "Six million is a lot of money. An awful lot of money."

"She's right," added Alan, "I mean what's the average amount of money you're going to earn in your life time? What, a million? A million and a half? Maybe two? That's with you working your arse off from when you leave here until the government finally decides that you're too exhausted to work anymore. But we've been given the opportunity to more than triple our life's earnings in ten minutes. We wouldn't have to do another day's work in our lives."

Sam shook his head. "Be sensible here Alan," he said calmly, "Think about this realistically. How are you going to explain the fact that you're now a millionaire?"

"There's always a loophole," Katie answered for him, "And even if there isn't I'd be willing to spend ten grand here and ten grand there to keep it all covered up."

"But you're killing a living human being," hissed Sam, glancing at Carol for support.

Carol nodded. "He's right. I mean neither of you are seriously considering the offer? Are you?"

Katie said nothing. Alan chewed his lip. His heart was racing. How long had he wished that he had more money? How many hours had he spent budgeting the coming week and fretting over having to pay back his student loan? And now the opportunity had come. Was he just going to let it slide?

"Maybe," answered Katie, "let's be honest here. The black dude with the red hat and a denim hoodie; he's a bastard. Excuse my language but he is. Nobody gets assassinated for being a nice person and minding their own business."

"That's totally untrue," replied Carol, "There's been loads of assassinations throughout history whose victims have been innocents."

"Name one," challenged Katie

Carol pursed her lips and glanced from side to side. After a long moment she answered.

"Trotsky. The Russian man who was murdered with an ice pick in Mexico City just because he spoke out against a political regime."

Katie sighed and shook her head. "That hardly counts. The Russians did it like seventy years ago. We're not working for a country and I'd be willing to bet three months' worth of rent that this guy's only crime is not liking the government. That sort of shit doesn't happen anymore."

"Fine," said Carol, "what about all the other people that have been killed. Just because they got on the wrong side of the wrong people."

"Like who?" asked Katie.

"Cops," said Sam suddenly. Katie glanced over at him. "Cops," Sam repeated, "What if the guy we've been told to kill is an undercover cop. He got on the wrong side of a big gang and now they want him dead."

"For six million!" said Alan with a smile he didn't feel.

"Okay, okay," muttered Sam.

"He's a high-ranking inspector then," said Carol. "He's efficient and he's eliminating organised crime one step at a time. The gangs are growing desperate. They need to get rid of him so they turn to ordinary people. Try to bribe them into attempting an assassination. We're probably the tenth group that they've offered money to. All the others either failed or had a moral compass and walked away".

"Six million though," said Katie doubtfully, "for an inspector?"

"It's probably not even six million though," argued Sam, "they just said that to get us to do it. Then when we go into the drycleaners, as Carol said, we'll be killed."

"Four murdered college students though," pondered Alan, "I mean if they just give us six million and let us go free then they can't be caught. We don't know a single thing about them. All we know is that a man came into a café, gave us the bag and explained the rules and that the drycleaners down the road is somehow connected to this. That's not enough proof to accuse anyone but us. But if they kill us then that's blood on their hands and from the way these guys have acted so far, they don't seem to want any blood on their hands. They could have got one of their men to just walk right in here with a handgun and shoot their target ten times in the back of the head. Instead they choose us. They're clever. They don't want any connections with this murder what so ever. And if you say that they'll give us counterfeit money, then you're wrong. Fake money would lead to problems for us. And problems for us are problems for them. This is a genuine offer. We could all live off the profits of today for the rest of our lives." Alan stopped out of breath. The others were staring at him. He sucked in his lips. He wasn't the passionate one. He wasn't the one who refused to admit he was wrong. But he wasn't letting it slid this time. This time he was changing his life for the better.

"But I don't think you're getting this," hissed Carol, "You're killing someone. Do you not get that, Alan? You're ending the life of a fellow human being. You're committing an unforgivable sin. You'll be dammed to hell."

"Well at least I'll have a great life first," retorted Alan. "Think of all the things I could do with six million. I could do more than just blow it all. I could set up a business. Invest it wisely. Turn six million into sixty million. I could donate freely to charities and organisations that try and establish good education systems in impoverished areas. Fight crime with education. By committing one crime against someone who is probably an awful person I could prevent the murder and mugging of tens, no hundreds, maybe thousands of people. With the right decisions and enough money I could make even the roughest places of town safe for people to live in without having to fear for their lives and the wellbeing of their children. What happens today could change this country forever. Heck, it could change the world. I could make the world a better place to live in. Just by getting rid of one bad bastard."

"Alan," said Sam with the hint of a smile, "that was some passionate shit right there." Alan didn't respond. He ran his tongue along his teeth waiting for Sam to go on.

But it was Carol who spoke. "I don't think you really understand what's going on. You believe that when you walk into that bathroom with your mask up and your hat pulled low that you'll just be able to gun down that man no questions asked. Imagine what'll be going through your head. You could just chicken out completely and run. And then what happens if the man with the red cap is armed. If he's a gangster I'm sure he is. Then you're dead. You think you'll be able to make the decision to pull the trigger, but when it actually comes down to it…"

"I'll have made my mind up before I even draw the gun," responded Alan through gritted teeth. He couldn't explain why but he was growing more and more annoyed at Carol. Was it because she was being too overprotective? He was twenty-two years old for God's sake he could make his own decisions now.

"You don't even know how to operate a gun, though," pointed out Sam.

"Oh, it's not that hard," replied Katie, "I mean it's already loaded. All you have to do is turn off safety, cock it and pull the trigger."

"But, sweetie you're not actually considering killing anyone are you?" asked Sam. Katie looked at him for a long moment. Alan wriggled in his seat uncomfortably.

"If I'm getting six million to just squeeze a little bit of metal, then yeah, maybe I will kill him," she responded with a cool voice Alan had never heard her use before.

Sam shook his head angrily. "No, Katie. You are not killing anybody. You kill someone and it's over. I'm gone. You can fend for yourself. You hear that. You can't kill anybody." Katie gritted her teeth, her face twisting in to a furious glare but she said nothing.

"I'm going to kill him," said Alan suddenly. They all stared at him. "I'm sick of looking at bills I have no way of paying. I just want to get that money and then I can change for the better. I can do all the things I ever dreamed about and more. Think of all the things I could do with a few million behind me. I'm sick of just being another person in the crowd. I want to be remembered. I want to do something so revolutionary that in years and years to come, our grandchildren's children's children will be learning about me, hearing about my great deeds. I'm just so sick and tired of being a poor fricking pushover my entire life. I can't stand walking into this café every month and warning myself that I can't spend more than a tenner. I want to be able to walk into whatever restaurant I please, order my food and not give a damn about the price. I want to live on as a legend when I die. I know that sounds so bloody selfish now that I'm saying it out loud but it's true. You probably all feel the same. It's just I'm the only one who has enough balls to actually take a risk." He stopped, his eyes flickering from person to person.

"Fine, you know what, you do that," snapped Sam, "but none of us are having anything to do with it. We're leaving."

"No, I'm not," said Katie, "I'm staying here." Sam stared across at her. His shocked expression gradually morphing into one of genuine anger.

"I told you," he hissed angrily, "I said that you can't kill him. I swear to god I will call the Gardaí if you dare even try. I swear I will."

Katie stared back at him, visibly struggling to keep herself in check. Though gritted teeth she spoke. "I'm not killing anybody Sam," she said as calmly as she could manage, "Alan is going to head outside and put on his coat and mask and gloves in an alley or somewhere nearby. And I'm going to stay here. And when the dude with the red cap leaves for the bathroom I'm going to text Alan, who's going to walk in, head to the bathroom and shoot your man. All I want in return is seven-hundred-thousand in cash."

Alan laughed. "Seven-hundred thousand, for sending a text message? Good one."

"No, I'm serious!" argued Katie. "If we're caught then I'll be linked to the crime. I'll be charged with aiding a murder."

"Not if you use code words," responded Alan, "say you text me the word 'honey' if he's gone to the bathroom and 'sugar' if he's going outside."

"Fine," agreed Katie, "Then do we have a deal?" She extended her hand.

"Two-hundred-thousand," responded Alan.

Katie drew her hand back sharply. "No way. How else are you going to do this? You're hardly going to get changed in here and then follow the guy to the bathroom. That looks way to suspicious." Alan bit his lip. She had a point. It would look way too dodgy if he attempted the murder by himself. He needed someone on the inside. But seven-hundred-thousand was just too much.

He looked over at her. "Okay," he said, "you win, you get to send me the text but it's for half a million. No higher, less if you want it to be. What do you say?"

"No," snapped Sam, "she says no. She's not getting mixed up in any of this sort of stuff. I don't care how much money you're getting. This is a man's life. You're turning out to be a selfish little…"

"Don't you dare call me selfish," interrupted Katie, "I'm doing it for us, for the two of us."

"Well, I want no part in this," spat Sam angrily.

"Fine," retorted Katie, "Good, that's half a million that I can spend on myself."

"Well, you can go and spend that blood money all you want," snarled Sam as he stood up and pulled on his coat, "Because I'm leaving." And with a furious glare and a backwards glance he left the café and Alan knew that he was never coming back. He didn't say anything. He'd just managed to ruin his two friends' relationship.

He glanced over at Katie. Her eyes were glistening slightly but she looked determined. "Still up for this?" he asked.

"Sure," she replied in a quiet voice.

Even as she spoke Alan heard the bell above the door ring as another group of customers entered. His heart leapt. He turned around. Dreading what he was going to see. Three men and a woman strode into the café. They were all fairly well built with moderately handsome features, all wearing normal clothes. Nothing out of the ordinary. But in the very middle of the group walked a grinning young black man wearing a red cap and a denim hoodie. Alan felt as though he'd just finished a marathon. He was sweating profusely and his heart was roaring in the back of his throat.

He watched without blinking as the group made their way over to a table in the corner of the café. The man with the red cap was grinning and talking to another man his age who was laughing at some unheard joke. The other two were not smiling though. They wore sunglasses so he couldn't see their eyes, but Alan felt full sure that they were surveying the area. The woman turned and looked straight at him. He glanced away immediately, his heart screaming inside his head. He half expected her to suddenly whip out a handgun and shoot him there and then, but out of the corner of his eye he watched her sit down wearily. He glanced over at Katie.

She nodded at him. "You ready?" she asked.

He nodded. "Exactly as we agreed, half a million for texting either 'sugar' or 'honey'."

She nodded. Alan said no more. He snatched the bag up and left the café as normally as his awkward legs could manage. As soon as he stepped outside into the hustle and bustle of the city he felt the pit in his stomach disappear. His legs carried him down the street. He glanced back at the café. He could see Carol hurrying out of it. He turned away. He could just leave now, no consequences. He wouldn't have to feel the absolute terror of walking into the café again.

But he needed that six million. He needed it so badly. He turned sharply to the right, slipping into a deserted alleyway filled with overflowing bins. He ducked behind one of them. Placing the bag on the ground and pulling out the coat. He put on the clothes and mask as fast as he could, lest he run out of courage. He stuffed the cash into his trouser pocket and rubbed his shoes against the grime covered walls in case anyone recognised them. He took up the gun, flicking it off safety. He cocked it and pointed it at the wall. It was heavier than he had anticipated, the only guns he'd ever held before were pellet guns. He let his finger hover over the trigger for a moment before flicking the safety back on. He shoved the gun into his other pocket just as Carol hurried into the alley.

"Wait, Alan," she cried. Alan glanced up at her. He didn't want her here. He pulled out his phone and glanced down at it. Nothing. His fingers were twitching. He prayed to God that the man in the red cap would hurry up and go to the toilet.

"Don't go, Alan," begged Carol, "please just leave it alone. Don't kill him. No one deserves to be killed for any amount of money. Please don't do it." Alan glared at her. She was shaking his resolve.

"Piss off, Carol," he said more roughly than he intended. She looked at him in shock.

"Alan, if you walk into that café you will regret it for the rest of your life. You will never die content. You'll never be able to forgive yourself."

"No offense, Carol," snapped Alan, "but when have you ever had to worry about money. You've lived your whole life with everything provided for you. You've never had to walk into a shop or a restaurant and have only a limited amount of money to spend. You haven't ever had to worry about paying any bills. So this talk about dirty money coming from you is a bit rich." He glared at her.

She opened her mouth to speak, but Alan's old battered phone beeped. He glanced down at it. It was Katie. She had texted a single word: Sugar. Alan pulled up his mask and slipped his phone into his trousers. Carol tried to stop him. She threatened him at first saying she'd call the Gardaí, but he knew she wouldn't. He just brushed past her. She scampered along beside him as he strode down the street, his hand clenched around the gun. He tried not to think of anything in particular, just let his mind wander. Carol begged him. She started crying. He felt a lump in his throat but he stared at a building over Carol's shoulder, letting her face fade out of focus. Just before he reached the café she gave up and stopped. She faded into the busy crowd but her sobs and pleas still echoed in his ears.

He reached the café, but he didn't stop. He knew that if he did he'd never get going again. He pushed the door open. The bell chimed. People glanced up at him. He saw Katie out of the corner of his eye. She didn't look up. He made for the toilet with his eyes fixed on the floor. He pushed the door open and with a deep breath he entered the bathroom.

The man with the red cap and the denim hoodie was at the urinal. The small bathroom was otherwise empty. Alan kept walking as he drew the gun out of his pocket as he walked. With trembling fingers he flicked it off safety. The man whirled. Alan didn't even hesitate. He opened fire. He winced at the three sharp claps.

The man didn't even cry out he just keeled over onto his bloodied face, three deformed lumps of lead still in his body.

Alan didn't glance down. He just turned and walked for the door. He left the bathroom a multi-millionaire.

I am a tree

By Sanduni Nanayakkara, age 14.

I am a tree

A common thing.

In my branches,

The birds sing.

Under my shade,

Children sit.

At my base,

Dogs shit.

But although I don't move,

I still can see

All the movement and motion

Around me.

I see happy children

Who want to have fun.

Middle-aged joggers

On their daily run.

A homeless man,

Tired and without a home.

A stray dog

Who longs for a bone.

A young girl whose arms bear scars,

A sick man

Who's nearing the stars

I am a tree.

A common thing.

In my branches,

The birds sing.

The world revolves

Without a stop,

Only I remember,

Even when my leaves drop,

How the world was when I was young.

When Light Changes

By Ciara Walsh Subiran, age 14.

Light. A beautiful thing really. It banishes the darkness, keeps you warm, let's you see the world around you. At least that's what I thought of light. That is, before the war...

***

"Jack!!" Papa's exclamation startles me out of my daydream.

"Huh?" I reply, still out of it, then notice that everyone is sitting at the dinner table and make my way over. We chat throughout our meal with a fake cheeriness, pretending not to notice the distant sound of the bombs and shells in London some miles away. I'm the first to finish, though I was the last to arrive, and ask to be excused. Little Ellie still has half of her plate left to go, but the way she looks at me I know she wants more than anything to leave with me, away from the solemn atmosphere around dinner table, and I pity her.

"I'm going down to ready the cows for milking. I'm a bit tired today, is it all right if I bring Ellie to help? Perhaps then we can begin milking them ourselves." I add a good yawn for effect and it seems to fool my parents. Or it could be that they just don't care anymore. No-one has been quite the same since the war began. Especially now, since Papa was just today informed that he had to become a soldier and fight. It was no longer a choice and he would leave tomorrow morning for training. For all we know it'll be the last we see of him. Ellie gets up from the table and follows me out. I can see the relief in her eyes. We head towards the cows in silence with the sounds of war filling our ears, louder now than before. Ellie is just seven years old, but she's always so aware of what goes on around her. She knows exactly where Papa is going, that he probably won't come back. We are losing this war. Germany is so strong. Defeat seems inevitable and now every man in England is being forced to participate. The war started two years ago in 1914 and now we are losing hundreds of men by the hour. I'm so worried for Papa. I think of all that could happen to him and all of a sudden my train of thought is clear.

"I'm going to go fight in the war too."

Ellie makes a choking sound and stares at me in shock.

"No Jack, you can't. You're only sixteen! You're far too young!" she pleads with me, but now that the thought is in my mind I can't seem to let it go. How could I possibly let Papa go alone? If I don't make it Uncle Rick's son, Paddy, can take care of Ma and Ellie.

As I warm up to the idea I respond to Ellie defensively.

"And what exactly do you know about how old a soldier should be, huh?"

"I can read Jack. The posters about recruitment are everywhere. You aren't expected to go until you're eighteen."

I can't help but see now how very smart little Ellie is. What other seven-year-old is this attentive about anything, never mind a war? And I know she's right, but I won't listen. Ma doesn't call me stubborn for nothing. I look into her bright blue eyes, eyes begging me to change my mind, and dread when the time will come to leave her.

"Ellie," I crouch down beside her, "You know I don't want to go. Nobody wants to, but I have to. You must understand. I just can't let Papa go alone, especially with his temper; I'll despise myself for the rest of my days if he doesn't make it back. And you're a very smart girl so you know how to take care of yourself. Promise me you'll be a good girl, Ellie, promise me."

A lone tear slides down her cheek. And she replies, a sound barely audible.

"I promise."

As we round up the cows I curse myself for being so hard on her. It's easy to forget her age when she keeps up so well, but there's only so much she can take. And as the sun begins to set a deep fear of what is to come settles in the pit of my stomach, slowly spreading to the rest of my body. I shiver and begin to milk the first cow with trembling hands.

***

"Absolutely not."

Ma hasn't taken my decision too well, but she knows she can't stop me and I think a part of her, a tiny part, is grateful. Papa has never been a good fighter, but he has such a defensive nature that he often gets himself stuck in the middle of them. The trouble is he never backs down. That's where I come in. I'll protect him. After all he's done for this family I must. Papa doesn't really know what's going on. He's been drinking all morning in an attempt to make things easier for himself. He's never liked goodbyes. Everything that he's worked his life towards he must leave behind, maybe forever. No. I won't let that happen. I'll make sure Papa lives, no matter what. I decide to bring a matchbox and some of Papa's cigars. I don't smoke myself, what I want is the matchbox to bring me the comfort of light while I'm in the trenches, but I don't want any questions being asked. Besides, Papa will probably want a smoke or two when we get there, to bring him some sliver of contentment, so it's a good thing to have either way. Light has always helped me calm down. I used to fear the darkness and even now it unnerves me. Whether it's a candle or a bright moon, I always feel safer when I can see around me. I embrace Ma and she holds me tightly, sobbing into my shoulder, whispering words of reassurance. Then I turn to Ellie and she looks up at me teary eyed.

"Stay strong, El. I love you." I lift her up and swing her around. My heart momentarily soars as I hear a giggle escape her. I can feel tears of my own welling up, but I shan't cry, I won't, not in front of Ellie. This is hard enough for her as it is. Papa drunkenly says his own goodbyes and we head towards town.

***

Training is hard and all the men sneer at me, but I ignore them. I'm not doing this for them, for their entertainment. I'm doing this for Papa. In his sober state, he defends me endlessly, but scolds me daily for coming with him, for having 'abused' him in his drunken state. I always just shrug and apologise. I won't tell him why I really came; he'd torture himself about it. I can sense he's relieved I'm here though. Papa doesn't like to be alone. He's never been too good at making friends, but he's a great guy once you get to know him. He just has a loud persona. This is the last day of training before we head to the trenches. I'm terrified. The tough training

51

has kept my mind off what lies ahead up until today, but now the fear is back, like a bullet in my side. As the sun sets I crawl into my stiff bed stare up at the ceiling, a pain in my stomach like what I used to feel the day before school after summer, when I knew my stubborn nature would surely get me whipped, but in this case it feels ten times worse. I breathe in and out trying to calm my raging heart and slip into a nightmare about what is to come.

***

"The front line?!" I exclaim in shock, caught completely by surprise.

"But we just finished training!"

Commander Hendrox glares at me.

"You will do as I say, Highland, and don't you dare cross me." His voice is ragged and intimidating and he shouts almost all the time, but in his eyes I see sympathy and pain. I realise that he does what he must to keep order in the ranks and return to the line. Hendrox yells for us to march and that we do, stomping down on the dry ground with heavy, unforgiving boots. My khaki uniform is a size too big and sits on my shoulders uncomfortably, but I make do, a rifle slung across one shoulder, my metal helmet jangling on my head with each step. Finally, we make it to the large ship and file in. This is my first time on a ship, never mind the fact that we're heading to another country, Belgium. We head down into the centre of the ship and set sail at first light. We're told that we'll arrive at dawn of the next day. I sigh. The heart of the ship where we're staying is almost pitch black and at this moment I long more than anything for some light. I consider lighting a match, but decide against it. I can't risk setting anything on fire. Everything, everyone is so cramped in here. So, just like I'll surely be doing in the trenches of Belgium, I lie on a measly excuse for a mattress in the darkness. I am not aware that I've drifted into sleep until I see Ellie and Ma and the farm in front of me. I realise immediately that this is a dream even though I've never been aware of such a thing before. Suddenly, before my dream-self's eyes, a huge cloud of darkness consumes everything and I fumble for a match. As the fire lights up a small area around me, my eyes fall upon the mangled corpse of Papa on the battlefield, wire weaving it's way in and out of his camouflage. I gasp and drop the match. As it falls, the scene fades away and I awake from the nightmare to the sound of Hendrox's constant yelling about this and that, and men heading up to the deck. We have arrived. I find Papa and hug him, ignoring the other men around us.

"Good luck," I say, "stay alive so we can make it back home, okay?"

"Of course, Jack. We'll get through this together."

We march off of the ship and down onto the dock. Hendrox yells out his commands and off we go marching again in a whole new country. Papa marches ahead of me and I can see that despite our intensive training he is already getting tired after a few miles. He's never been good at distance and always gets tired quite quickly. And after all, he is getting rather old and the years of hard farm work have taken their toll on him. In the battlefield he'll only be able to manage a few short sprints. Eventually Papa removes his rifle from his shoulder and uses it to help support himself as we continue to march for the whole day, only stopping for short breaks of food and water. I see Hendrox spot Papa, but he says nothing and as our eyes meet silently I thank the commander with a nod. He is a good man. And so we march, days blending into each other and me doing what I do best, daydreaming. I spend my time picturing myself and Papa back home, doing chores around the farm. I picture Ellie and I playing in the fields in the late evening after all my chores are done. It's these thoughts, these illusions of home that keep me going as we march and march and march. And though I hate the marching, how painfully tired my legs become, I continue to hope that it won't end for what is ahead of us is most definitely far, far worse.

***

I don't know how many days have passed before we finally arrive at the trenches. The clenching feeling in my gut threatens to bring me to tears, but I hold them back. I will not cry in front of everybody. I want to keep my dignity at the very least. As we approach, dazed men pass by us, their eyes filled with whatever unimaginable horrors they endured out in the battlefield. No-Man's Land stretches ahead of us and as my ears are filled with the deafening sounds of warfare, a shiver goes down my spine. Men are being carried away on stretchers all around us, and more lie injured within the trenches, groaning in pain. I gag at the sight of dead men and horses tangled in barbed wire in the distance. I come to realise that this ache in my heart for all the lives lost, both for the enemy and ours alike, isn't going to fade or diminish. I lower myself into the trenches and we have another bit of food and water before heading to bed. I find it impossible to sleep, not only from the sounds of shells and gunfire, the screams of dying men, but also from the fear of what I will have to undergo once morning comes. I try to distract myself by reviewing how I would've created this exact trench. This helps, but the dread within doesn't die down, won't ebb away. Instead I get some brief sleep filled with nightmares of war as well as more dreams of home, sometimes even mixed which is the worst. I would never want my world at home to be touched by these hardships, these horrors. And as we are awoken at the crack of dawn I find myself shaking. It is still quite dark and for once I am thankful. I realise now with a deep sorrow that from now on light will be my enemy, not my ally.

***

After marching for a significantly shorter distance than our previous trips, we spot the enemy a distance away advancing towards us. My stomach feels like it's being twisted around and around. The nerves within cause me to throw up what little food I'd eaten and I'm forced now to face the Germans with a burning throat and feeling slightly dizzy with fright. Battle planes fly overhead from both sides and the bombs begin to fall. A shell drops near enough to startle me out of my fearful daze and I dive for cover as I've been taught and a yell escapes me. I grab my rifle and aim at the oncoming army, shooting at nobody in particular, a grim determination to survive powering me on. I watch as men fall all around me and I feel as though a part of me breaks at every sight of the dead on both sides. We're all men, all human. Why are we doing this to each other? But it's not my place to question such a thing, so I drive on, firing round after round. I'm careful to avoid shooting horses even though they're what we should be trying to gun down just as much, if not more, as the men ahead, because those poor creatures really have absolutely no say in this. My aim is quite good so instead I shoot at the limbs of the men riding them, especially those that hold a weapon. I try to avoid killing anything; instead I stop them from killing us. Men drop to the ground howling in pain as my bullets hit home, shattering leg and arm bones. I can't hold back my tears of sorrow and regret so I let them fall freely as I continue to fight. After what seems like eternity, we are forced to retreat, huge numbers of men lost. Relief floods me as I find Papa, but I watch in horror, almost in slow motion, as a bullet glides its way into his leg and he collapses, all from breaking focus to look at me. I sprint over and call for help, dragging him across the ground as he cradles his wound and howls in pain. Medics rush over and lift him away onto a truck filled to the brim with other injured men. Papa and I stare, horrified, into each other's eyes as he is driven away and I'm left standing alone, surrounded by the bodies of comrades and foes alike. I swallow down my emotion and look for Hendrox, finding him as he yells for us to regroup. I run up to him and stand in line as we prepare to march back to the trenches. Though I hate to be alone, I'm happy that Papa won't have to repeat this tomorrow. I pray in this moment to God that he'll be all right. Hopefully the wound will keep him at hospital for a long time, but let him recover healthily. I would hate for him to have to return to this terrible place any time soon. As we gather all the remaining men and march back I notice many familiar faces are gone and my heart threatens to rip itself from my chest.

**

Days go by, weeks, and nothing changes. It's always the same pain, the same hardships, the same darkness. How I long for this to be over so that I can happily and safely stroll through the day, stroll in the light. I miss with a burning passion the days when light flooded me with relief, with a sense of protection against all that is bad, but as the long days drag on I feel empty, like some kind of machine. I see the bodies surrounding me, but now, and though the heartache remains, they don't bother me nearly as much. I step over them as if they were nothing more than the odd pile of dirt. The trenches are so cold. They're getting colder as we head toward winter and I have a bad case of the sniffles, maybe something worse. I see men around me carried away by medics with horrible deformed feet. They call it 'trench foot'. I stay off the damp, murky ground of our trenches as much as possible, trying to avoid that horrible disease. Food and water are getting scarce so now we have to ration them out in tiny portions. As a month of this wretched life passes, new reinforcements come in to replace the fallen and I realise when they peer at me and my comrades that we now have those horror-filled eyes that I noticed when I arrived. This is what war does to us, to all of us. No-one will leave the same. I've been sending letters home, but haven't gotten a reply. I assume they haven't even arrived to England yet. All I have from home is the matchbox. I've already given away the cigars. I keep the matchbox in my pocket, as a kind of comfort. If I'm caught alone in the dark somewhere at least I'll have light. As I think about this simple word, light, I realise how much the meaning has changed for me. Where at one time of my life I would run towards light, I now find myself avoiding it. Light means the enemy can see me and that translates to almost certain death. Papa still hasn't returned. I've tried to speak to him, but to no avail. I don't even know where he is. This war, the fighting, it's all so much harder than I had foreseen. Well, when I think about it, I doubt anyone could ever possibly foresee this kind of pain, this kind of torture. I stop my train of thought as I see that we're preparing to advance once more. Over these past weeks we've managed to drive the Germans back a little. It's given our men a bit of hope, something to hold on to. We march across No-Man's Land and meet the rival army once more. They're extremely strong today and I watch frightfully as shells rain from the sky, sprinting to and fro like a madman. The impact of one sends me flying for a few feet, but I land with no serious injury. As I lift myself up and squint through the smoke I see the silhouette of a lone horse, no rider in sight. I approach it slowly, not wanting to startle it, but it remains calm, obviously well trained. I notice a trail of blood coming from an open wound in its flank and use a ripped piece of my trousers to stop the blood. The horse is a beautiful grey mare with an irregular blaze and lighter spots all over her body. I immediately fall in love and hate that she's been forced into this. We connect on a level of mutual understanding and respect. She's a smart horse and reminds me of Ellie. I call her Storm. It suits her and she responds to the name so I think she likes it too. The battle seems to have diminished as nobody can see anybody anymore so I mount the fine steed and we make our way back to the trenches. I don't know to which army she belongs, but I'd say an extra horse would be good either way. I show her to the commander and Hendrox notices my capability with the mare.

"I want you to ride her into battle. You seem to know how to handle her quite well and we're short on cavalry. You'll scout the perimeter around the men and attack atop her with us."

I'm overjoyed by this decision and agree enthusiastically. For the next few weeks I fight upon Storm and we get along very well. Our understanding of one another lets us take down twice as many foes and we keep each other safe.

***

I head out to the battlefield mounted on Storm. I've now been at war over two months. Storm has helped me greatly. It feels like I have some family here now. I spot the familiar sight of the opposing army and yell out my warning to Hendrox. It's still dark out and, as I have done since the day I arrived, I long for light, for safety. Nevertheless, I prepare myself and charge at the command of the cavalry leader. Storm and I take down many opponents, but suddenly, the mare falls to the ground. I gasp and dismount the fallen steed. She's been shot in the chest, the heart. Whoever had fired the shot had intended to kill. I'm filled with rage, with sorrow, and I cradle Storm's head, tickling her nose as I watch the life slowly drain from her eyes. Then she lies still and stares at me blankly, looking at, but no longer seeing me. All my previous feelings crumble as I am filled with a pain stronger than any I have previously felt here and I weep over the corpse of Storm. I feel my hands covered in her blood and I can't move. I'm paralysed with shock, with anguish. I lie there for what feels like eternity, mourning, crying, pounding the bloodied earth, until I feel a hand on my shoulder and turn to see Hendrox looking down at me in pity. He walks me back to the trenches. I continue to fight for days on end, but this time I'm ruthless. I take no care to avoid killing anymore and don't even glance at the men I shoot down. Deep inside, I am disgusted at myself, but I can't stop. I become as deadly as the bombs that rain down, a machine with no emotion. I can hear my fellow soldiers whisper about me in the trenches, but I ignore them. I finally snap out of this strange and death-inducing daze when I'm handed a letter from home. I'm filled with a renewed energy as I tear open the envelope. I take a long sniff of the letter and I can actually smell the farm air. Well it could just be my imagination I suppose, but it makes me happier than I've been in the weeks since Storm was killed. The letter is in Ma's neat handwriting. I begin to read;

Dear Jack,

Hello dear! We received your letter today, but I don't know when you'll get this one. I want you to know that I'm very proud of you, we all are. Ellie misses you so much, but she's being a very good girl, helping around the farm. Oh Jack, I feel awful about what you're going through. There is some good news and some bad news. I'll start off with the good news. Papa is home now, he's here with us! The bad news is the reason why he's here. His leg suffered irreparable damage. The bone is shattered. The doctor says if he recovers well he'll be able to walk with a cane in a few months. Right now all he can do is lie in bed. He feels awful about leaving you, Jack, and on the first day too. I hope this war will end soon so we can see you again. I love you so much darling. Ellie and Papa send their love too. Stay strong.

Goodbye for now, my handsome boy.

The letter finishes and I read it again and again. So I'm on my own now, for as long as this war lasts. I sigh, longing to be home like Papa. I write my letter home with a fake enthusiasm and send it off.

***

Once again I find myself back fighting for my life in No-Man's Land. This is all so tiring. I never get proper rest or food and drink. Most of my original unit are missing, hurt or dead. I'm all alone, surrounded by a blanket of smoke and darkness. The roar of the rifles and machine-guns mingles with the screams of men to form the most sinister of sounds. I'm so disorientated, I can't see a thing. I have no idea if I'm on enemy territory or my own. I look around just in time to see the German uniform and then comes a searing pain in my stomach. I scream out in agony. The pain blinds me. It's so dark. I hear myself hit the ground, but I can't feel anything anymore. I'm panicking, but I can't get up.

"No!" I shriek, "No, please, I have to get home!"

It's far too late. I'm bleeding so much and I'm sobbing, choking on my own tears and coughing up blood. I'm never going to get home; I won't see Ellie grow up. I'm just going to die a pathetic death with no real purpose. I won't die saving anybody, instead I'm dying alone. I reach into my pocket and try to light a match, but the box tumbles from my shaking hands. I can no longer move. I look up at the sky and close my eyes. And I finally see what I've been yearning all this time for. Light, a brilliant light just ahead. A safe place, a warm place. A figure approaches and as it stops before me I see her. Storm, brighter than ever, welcoming me with her muzzle. I mount my beautiful companion and together we ride towards the light at full gallop. Just before I reach it I think of Ellie. And then the light engulfs me.

A Mother's Instinct

By Ruby Aron, age 15.

The sun was high in the sky, nothing but a wavering hazy blob. I could see the shimmer of the scorching heat on the barren landscape. A fly was buzzing irritably around me and I flicked it away with my strong tail, making sure not to lose focus on my prey. I crouched lower in the long grass.

Slowly and painstakingly, I moved one paw with upmost caution. The breaking of one twig could give me away. I could not afford to let this one escape. I was deeply, ravenously hungry, but despite that it was my cubs I was thinking of. A mother's instinct, I guess. Bit by bit I made my way ever closer to what would hopefully be our next meal. The young ibex grazed peacefully, suspecting nothing of his fate. Funny how one minute all its organs, muscles, nerves were working in perfect cooperation and next – nothing. Not that remorse was something I was even capable of feeling, my hunger was so deep. I stared at the animal, tasting its flesh in my mouth. I was ready.

I crouched even lower, preparing to spring forward. I could feel every muscle in my body tense, anticipating what was to come. My face was a whisker's length from the ground, my shoulder blades hunched above it. Pushing off with all four of my thick muscular legs, I leapt forward and for a brief moment I was flying, my whole body stretched to its limit. The ibex jerked upright, whipping its head to face me. Its ink-black eyes widened, filled with fear and panic. I landed on my prey, the force of my body sending us both crashing to the dry and dusty ground.

My claws were firmly embedded in the ibex's back, but my meal was still alive. I could smell the sweet scent of succulent flesh as I circled my prey, breathing heavily. I felt my own power, in my jaws, my legs, my broad back. Killing this creature was no challenge to me. It only took one fatal bite to the back of the neck. The smell of fresh, warm blood met my nose feeding my hunger and making my stomach contract. I was going to have a feast tonight. I started to drag the bloody carcass back to my family.

Not only was I going to be eating for the first time in several days, but I was guaranteed the survival of my three cubs. They were my first litter, but somehow, I knew what to do. It was as if it was programmed into me, a deep need to protect them, to care for them. An instinct. A pretty amazing one, when you stop and think about it.

"Oh, look, David, isn't that DISGUSTING!" exclaimed the blonde woman shrilly.

"Where?" said David, whipping around, camera at the ready.

"A lion just KILLED that … deer thing!" she continued, pointing her finger accusingly at the crime scene. The lion glanced up and gazed coolly at the jeep.

"The lioness has killed an ibex to feed her young," explained the tour guide, joining the couple at the edge of the vehicle, "Lions, like all big cats, have a strong mothering instinct." The look of horror slowly left the woman's face as she thought of her own son, far away from her now. "Mothering instinct…" she murmured. She leaned forward and observed the lion, her head tilted to one side. The lioness turned and stared back at her. And for a minute they both stood, and looked into each other's eyes. For a minute they both understood.

Helping Hugo

By Ella O'Rourke, age 14.

You dash out onto the beach, pebbles crunching under your feet, the sharp, cold sea wind whipping your hair around your burning face. You stop at the shoreline, the water lapping at the pebbles in front of you, shove your hands into your coat pockets and breathe deeply. The salty, chilly air fills you up and calms you down. Your eyes refocus, the hazy blur of anger and defence fading away – you look at the waves, ebbing, flowing, crashing, reckless, yet somehow relaxing, calming, soothing.

It's cloudy today, dark and foreboding – kind of matches your current situation. You've just had a huge disagreement with, and shouted at, your closest friend, Theodore.

You were hanging out together at the local café, finishing some weekend homework, when Theo mentioned school and the stress of it. He threw in some mental illnesses, which he seemed to think were adjectives; he said that school makes him depressed, and that his parents make him anxious, and that he's fat and wishes he was anorexic. These all came in parts, broken up by more complaints, not in a long, politically incorrect spiel.

You were shocked that your best friend would say those things; you got annoyed. You retaliated; you raised your voice, and said things you would never say otherwise. You rushed out of the café when Theo didn't reply, spilling your cup of tea in the process.

***

Now you're here. Inhale, exhale. Just think about how well you defended Hugo…

Hugo is your older brother, but it often feels as if you're three years older than him, as opposed to the way it really is. Hugo is – mentally – the baby of the family, your mom and dad have to take special care of him; he has OCD, anxiety and depression. They're all linked in some way, which makes it harder for him to do things you find normal.

61

He only comes out of his bedroom for more than a couple of hours on good days. Good days are very rare for him.

An okay day means Hugo goes to school for a few classes, comes home and does online school in his room, and stays in his room.

A bad day means Hugo stays in his room, you hear shouting and crashing and Hugo's frustration, the unbeatable demon that is him, but he can't fight himself... and you can't help him. That's what the doctors say. Medication and regular therapy will. But you have to wait.

***

No. You want to help. Now, standing on this cold, pebbly beach in Killorglin, you decide that you will help your brother, no matter what it takes, how much sleep you lose – you will help him. Defending him and others like him in the café was just the tip of the iceberg.

***

You hear feet pounding on the pebbles a few feet behind you, and you turn around.

The boy's hair is messy and wind-swept, his chest expanding broadly with every deep inhale, his eyes wild with fear and hope.

"Theo?" you breathe.

He steps towards you.

"Elliot, you deserve an apology. I said things I don't have the right to say; I put my foot in my mouth. I know you won't forgive me, hell, I don't forgive myself, but please just hear me out: I'm sorry, I'm so sorry, I regret saying all of it, all of it, I–"

"Theo! Stop!" you exclaim. "What you said was wrong, and quite frankly I don't think you deserve forgiveness, but... I'll think about it. Apologising is a good start, though, so... you have a little bit of a chance."

Theodore smiles.

"A little bit!" you repeat jokingly, a grin slowly creeping onto your face.

"Thank you. Really."

He falls into step beside you as you make your way home. After walking in silence, you stop at your front door and Theo thanks you again.

"I haven't forgiven you yet," you mutter, and he elbows you playfully before strolling to his own house.

You smile and unlock the door.

***

You trot up the stairs and stop outside Hugo's room instead of walking past it to your own. He's the only one home.

You hesitate. Close your eyes. Knock on his door.

You hear a grunt, a shuffling, and a click as he unlocks the door from his side. It creaks open to reveal a moderately physically healthy sixteen-year-old boy. But a very mentally unhealthy one. Appearances can be deceiving.

Hugo looks at you apprehensively. You attempt a smile. His chocolate brown eyes seem to brighten, his face muscles lose some of their tension.

"Good day?" you ask quietly.

"It will be if you talk to me," Hugo mutters.

Your heart almost melts.

***

You talk to Hugo, and listen to him, for nearly three hours. You learn a lot about him and his illnesses.

When you eventually get to your own room, you don't hear the lock click behind you. No crashing or shouting.

***

You glance out of your window. Blue skies, fluffy clouds.

A beautiful day to help someone.

The King of Losers

By Terri Baker, age 15.

The king of losers,

The ruler of fools,

The outcasts and the creeps,

These are the ones I rule.

We have our Kingdom,

Would be as happy as could be,

If the mean ones and the bullies,

Would just leave us be.

We have our customs,

We have our ways,

But the evil king of bullies,

Makes hell for us each day.

The ones they call popular,

They make their lives seem so sweet,

But they only care about what's on the outside,

They don't count what lies beneath.

I may be the king of losers,

But I'm proud of the name;

I love my crazy kingdom,

So here I will remain.

To the mean ones and the bullies,

I have a question for you:

Are you popular ones as happy,

As happy as us fools?

An Uncertain Future

By Adam Behan, age 15.

0

Hybod was quite warm tonight; his fur fleece and boots insulated him and broke the sharp winds of the High Hills that have a tearing bite, especially when the moon is highest in the sky. Hybod went out every Wednesday night, when everyone was asleep. He'd leave his hut, his wife and daughter and would go into the woods that sat at the bottom of the hill on which they settled. He had built a shrine made of simple things, twigs, bones, loose stones, anything he could lay his hands on. He built the shrine alone and out of his clansmens' knowledge. He dedicated it to the Moon, which he believed was responsible for the prey that was abundant in the river valley, especially in the spring. He was alone in this belief. His clan would hunt regularly, often leaving the women and children to look after their settlement, which was far from harm, up on the hill. They would hunt big game like Giant Sloth and Woolly Rhinoceros, making weapons out of their bones, consume their flesh, cooked and uncooked if necessary, and make their durable clothes. The Hunt rarely let them down. But recently, few of their prey have returned to drink at the river. Unusual animals they had never seen before would scare them away, creatures with large fangs, Hybod had watched one take on one Rhino, which was three times its size. It killed the Rhino very quickly, and its companions followed suit, making the Hunt impossible for the clan. Hybod has returned to his shrine tonight, looking for answers. He knew his time would be brief, a storm was soon to come, the clouds would cast the Moon's light into darkness. Hybod kneeled to his shrine, and lay still for a short moment, until he could hear rustling in the bushes behind him. He did not turn; he wanted to dedicate himself to his prayer. The rustling became more aggressive, in that instant, Hybod turned around slowly, as to not alert the beast that was lurking. To his dismay, the beast that arose from the bushes was his older brother Toch, clutching a knife made of Mammoth bone, specially sharpened for this occasion. Toch followed Hybod to his shrine. Toch's face was red with anger, his brother was appointed leader of the clan by his father over him many years ago. Toch still cannot understand. It was his birthright, and his runt brother thieved it from him. Toch plotted against him for a long time, but tonight was his chance to strike. In a fit of rage, Toch lunged for his brother and a struggle ensued. Toch knocked Hybod's shrine to the ground, shattering it into pieces. Hybod shouted in frustration and punched his brother in the gut, winding him for a few moments. He ignored the deep gash that Toch inflicted and slowly limped towards the river. Toch followed in a quicker pace. The noise of their footsteps bounced off the trees and it sounded like an axe against a tree. Toch's steps thundered, but Hybod's were light and quick. They both emerged from the trees at the basin of the river. Its course becoming rapid due to the storm. The bison that rested nearby were startled and they fled in mass, afraid of the strange men that battled ferociously nearby, it was the largest herd seen in seven months, and the chance to hunt was ruined by two men fighting. Hybod glared at his brother and went to tackle him for this misfortune. The heavens rumbled with forks of lightning striking distant places and thunder drowning out any sound, but the two brothers continued to quarrel. It was as if the gods were an audience to their suffering.

The rain pelted the ground, turning it into mud on which the brothers still fought. Toch was able to trip Hybod, who was growing weary, his cuts weighing him down. Toch dropped his body on Hybod and clutched his neck; he felt his breath strain under Tybod's might. Toch dragged Hybod until they were in the middle of the river. Toch groped Hybod and plunged his head into the river. Blood filled the water, Hybod was still putting on a fight, but his power was waning. He threw his hands into the air in the hopes that he could grab on to something, but his vision started to blur as death crept in. Suddenly, a gigantic wave of water washed over Toch and Hybod. Toch succumbed to its force and released Hybod. They were both carried along the river at a terrifying speed. Toch's gurgled roaring could be heard, but Hybod made no noise, he let the course carry him to his destination. Hybod let the river carry him; he was able to catch his breath, which prompted death's retreat. Toch fell out of Hybod's sight, which prompted him to fight the current. He used all of his might to finally break away from the river and he settled on flat gravel, he was now in unknown territory. The storm raged on but it had no influence on Hybod anymore. He rolled onto his back and let the rain hit his face. The tingling sensation soothed him, until he passed into unconsciousness.

1

The year is 6440 B.C.; Civilization is in its infancy. Farming is slowly becoming popular in parts of the Middle East and the Balkans, Çatal Höyük is in use as the first temple for a small cult in modern Turkey, far from the lands that the Ilcah Clan inhabit. This clan has its history rooted in a river valley that will be charted in a few millennia, the Ilcah discovered this valley while they wandered for countless years from place to place. They discovered that the valley would be teeming with wildlife every spring. They found that this place was a suitable hunting ground. They settled on an isolated hill, in the centre of the valley, which was relatively safe from extreme weather and floods. They could watch over the whole valley from there, they knew when their prey came and went, they knew when the river rose and fell, they knew when the forests would advance and retreat. Remarkably, they cannot speak or write, they didn't have written language like the Sumerians or the Ancient Chinese. They communicated with simple vocal sounds and gestures. That was the height of their sophistication, apart from their masterful hunting techniques. Hybod was chosen to lead the clan of 44 for this reason. He has a record 30 Woolly Rhinoceros kill count under his belt. He uses a sling made from a rare material, and his ammunition is of a material that's even rarer. His father Poj was very fond of his son, Toch on the other hand was rarely acknowledged for his hunting. Poj chose the best forager in the clan, Uilki, to be Hybod's wife. She bore him a daughter, Telfa, who will grow up to be a forager like her mother. The women foraged wild berries and fruits and cooked them when they returned. Everyone, young and old, had a role to fulfil. Recently however, the clan has been short on food stocks. The game they hunted has not returned on time and in fewer numbers. Packs of Smilodons have infiltrated the valley, keeping the clan on their hill, afraid of death. The clan's shaman, who has no name, blames the unfaithful wives of some hunters for this predicament. Hybod is always spotted on Wednesday night descending the hill into the woods, but none would dare follow him. Many believe he is consulting spirits of their ancestors for help; the clan is desperate for it. It is feared that the next generation of men will not know how to hunt, for there will be nothing to kill.

Hybod watched as his kin lumbered around the camp. Bored, starving, the clan was dying from the inside. Hybod stroked his long blonde beard, he usually would when he was deep in thought. He wondered how he could save his brothers and sisters, he would give anything to see his clan be normal again. Last month, the population dropped to 39, this month, 34. The elderly died first. No one had the time nor the muscle to bury them, so they were either burned or tossed off the hill. It was hard, but some of the members resorted to cannibalism, it was horrible for those who ate their dead, they needed to, but they were ashamed to. Hybod awoke from his daydream, he jumped off his wicker chair and went around the camp. Toch was sharpening his personal stabbing tool, Hybod witnessed this, but paid no thought to it. He found Uilki washing Telfa in a straw basket, the water spilled out through the gaps on the side of it, but it didn't matter. Hybod knelt down to his daughter. Telfa seemed to be the only person in the clan not stricken with fear by the problems they faced. She loved every moment of her bath, splashing and kicking about, which made it hard for Uilki to wash her. Hybod caught Telfa's attention, he pinched her cheek in a playful gesture and he grinned. She grinned back and began to laugh. It made Hybod so happy to see her like this. He had to leave, he relished in the time he spent with his daughter. He didn't lift his gaze off her until he strode around the corner into their hut. As he entered, he saw the shaman sitting in the middle of the floor. In front of him laid a bowl of water, with stone pebbles floating at the top. The pebbles were of significance as they foretold the future, one pebble meant good fortune for the clan, two meant misfortune for the clan, three meant fortune for the one the shaman visited, four meaning misfortune for the one he visited. Four pebbles lay in the bowl. This confused Hybod, he knew of no one that would want to bring him misfortune. The shaman rose to his feet and left the hut, leaving the bowl behind to let Hybod ponder about its meaning. Leaving Hybod's hut, the shaman looked at the far side of the camp, he saw Toch sitting in Hybod's direction. His knife stuck in the ground. Toch gave a stern look to the shaman, but the shaman kept his eyes to the dirt and he went back to his own hut which sat at the highest point of the hill. Before he made his way inside, he noticed, in the distance, a small group of tapir were drinking at the river, 5 or more. He fulfilled his duty, went inside and blew into a horn which signalled the clan's hunters that game was nearby.

A great cheering and the clattering of spears could be heard. They spotted a small group of tapir whom they would slaughter and take home. The hunting party would not leave until Hybod would join them. The group were given no indication of his preparation. They watched for any movement in the area of his hut. Suddenly Hybod burst out with his spear in hand and he gave the go ahead. They sprinted down the hill in a pace never reached before. They were ravenous with hunger, but their spirits were unbroken. They gave out a cry so tremendous, those left at the camp were proud to have them as their own. The tapir were too late to notice the 20 or so men with sharpened spears charging towards them, the men were quick to surround them and they jabbed their spears into the centre. The tapirs squealed and wailed in pain, the hunters blocked their hearts from their cries. Hybod raised his fist into the air and the men stopped at that instant. They pulled back, and they marvelled at their biggest haul in a long time. Seven tapir, torn to pieces, their blood trickling down the damp grass into the river. The men gave a heartened cheer and they clambered the carcasses together and started to bring them home. They managed to make it halfway up the hill, when a Smilodon attacked the rear of the group. The screams of the men who were unfortunate to be ambushed caused the men at the front and the middle to drop their prizes and help their comrades. Two more Smilodons appeared and joined in with the first one. The struggle was distressing to watch. The noise of the men's shouting was drowned out by the growls and roars of the sabre-toothed felines. The women and children at the top of the hill were too afraid to come down and see what the commotion was. The Smilodon pulled out and fled leaving one behind, killed by the men. So the tally grew even larger. 7 men lost their lives. The Smilodon stole two of the tapirs. Those remaining were devastated to see their brothers' mutilated corpses strewn across the hillside. Their blood did not flow down the hill. It created puddles; the blood loss was severe. The remaining men broke out of their grief and hurried back up the hill with what was left of the hunt. As the men stumbled to the summit, Uilki rushed to Hybod's aid. Hybod bore a slash across his chest, deep, but not fatal. The wound bled little, but he looked as if he was in great pain. Telfa stood behind Uilki, afraid to see her father's distress. The wives of the remaining men tended to their husbands. The tapir carcasses were delivered, but it brought the camp no comfort, their numbers were dwindling too quickly. The tapir would feed them for a week or two, but it would not soothe their hunger. Many questioned Hybod's ability to lead the clan any further. Or if there even was a clan to lead anymore. The day passed quickly. The moon revealed itself, with it a sky full of stars. Hybod sat on his stool, munching on a chunk of grilled tapir. He took his gaze to the sky, he watched the curtains of the Aurora Borealis flutter back and forth. The smooth feeling of the breeze slid over his face. This would be the only night Hybod felt at peace. He knew his father watched from above, and his fathers watched with him. He remembered the shaman's warning, which interrupted his peace, he thought the shaman was wrong however, the bowl contained four pebbles, but his whole clan suffers as much as he does. This thought disturbed him. He looked back to the sky, the green and purple aurora was gone, far to the horizon, he watches as the red sky rose, entailing blood would continue to be spilt.

4

Hybod's sleep was restless, he feared for the life of his clan, and for the lives of his family. The two weeks had passed. They had run out of food, again. They were lucky to catch an idle rabbit or an unsuspecting weasel now and again, each of the 22 remaining clan members got a ration of the meat that was caught. They kept no record of the recently deceased, but their deaths were engraved in the memories of the living. Hybod had grown distant from his wife and daughter in this time. He decided to go down the hill one evening. Toch saw him leave, and spat at the ground in resentment. Hybod went down to the river, not a single life form could be seen for many miles. The clan was isolated from anything that was truly alive. Hybod cupped his hands and scooped some water. He threw the water at his mouth, the excess trickled down his chin into his beard, nourishing it. Hybod came down for one purpose. He scaled the length of the river for a time until he found the resting place of his ancestors. A small cave-in on the edge of a forest he dared not to explore alone. He entered the cave. The chamber was adorned with the possessions of the dead. Necklaces, hides, bones of Mammoth, and the weapons of the dead. Hybod hunched down, above the resting place of his father Poj. The skeleton of his father made Hybod feel disheartened. He knew he would join his father in the spirit realm soon. He released the sling that he placed in his father's hands many years ago as a token. And he scanned it. He had fond memories of the days of old when the Wild was plenty with creatures of all sizes. He remembered his largest kill, he remembered his hunting party, he remembered the competitions with Toch. He smiled in his recollection, but he deeply missed those times. He did not stay long; he was quick to disembark on his return journey. On the journey, he spotted a beautiful Elk slurping from the river, not far from home. He brought his ammunition with him. He loaded his sling and swung it in a figure 8. The Elk raised his head and twisted it towards Hybod. The Elk's eyes pierced his soul, Hybod's swinging motion started to slow down until he stopped swinging entirely. The Elk marched away; Hybod did not let his eyes follow it. He stared at his sling, and at the rounded stone on the pouch. He cast them aside, fell to his knees and began to weep. He clenched his fists in torment and looked up to the sky. He let out a cry that echoed through the hills, through the mountains, through the skies, and beyond.

5

The clan's shaman's death was a shock to all. He was found within his hut in a pool of his own blood. His staff was broken, his bowels spewed across the floor. His heart lay in his left hand, and in his right a cutting tool. The manner of his death was uncertain, did he perform a sacrifice upon himself to please the gods, or was he murdered in cold blood. Hybod initiated his cremation, he carried the body of the wizard to his resting place, a wooden monument at the centre of the camp. All the men remaining at the camp received a torch, they lit the fire, and watched as the flames charred the shaman's skin, then his flesh, then his bones, until his body was nothing but ashes. The smoke emitted smelled foul. The two children that were the last of their age alive, Telfa and a warrior's son, held their noses in disgust. They didn't understand the importance of this event. The Ilcah Clan was no more. There were not enough members left to call it such. 12 remained this day, 3 warriors, Hybod, his family, Toch and the women were the only ones left. Hybod had never felt so low in his brief existence. He was only 27, his muscles were deflated, his bones brittle. Hybod seldom left his house after the shaman's death. He was paranoid of his wife, his daughter, his brother most of all. He kept an axe near in case of an assassination attempt. Telfa no longer smiled, her happiness had faded. She was on the brink of death, she was too weak to live on. Uilki never left her side, her hope would die with Telfa. Outside, Toch wandered the grounds of the camp. He had never married, he slept with a few women, but it brought him no pleasure. His glory days ended long ago. He kept a close eye on Hybod's hut. Even with the threat of annihilation, Toch never had a desire to reconcile with his brother. His knife always remained at his side. The winds were picking up and Toch felt the knife tatter against his thigh, it reminded him that he will strike against his brother soon. Two days, in two days Toch planned to vanquish his runt of a brother. The 3 remaining warriors did not pose as much of a threat to Toch, he trained himself in secret, he knew their weaknesses, he would soon exploit them. Hybod never moved the bowl that the shaman lay on his hut floor. He watched the four pebbles bob along in the water, he'd watch as they would slide against each other. Uilki and Telfa entered the hut, they stared in confusion at Hybod, he sat in front of the bowl, not even lifting his head to look at his family. They knew what the four pebbles meant, but they dismissed it, they loved Hybod, and Hybod loved them, but Hybod has been lacking in expressing any sort of emotions in the past two weeks. The end was coming, Hybod constantly told himself this. He embraced this idea as truth. If he wanted to badly enough, he would kill the remnants of the former clan, to truly end it. He'd even kill his own wife and child, out of love. His thoughts would cause great exasperation among his clan, if only he had voice to express them. Hybod finally looked up, and only discovered that his wife and child had left. A great sorrow filled his heart. He looked back at the bowl. Disgusted with himself, his face contorted into rage and he flipped the bowl, the stones scattered across the floor. Hybod paid no attention to them as he left his hut.

6

Two days had passed. Toch had been waiting for this day for many years. Although he did not expect the clan to disintegrate, it aided his plan greatly. Toch slid his finger up and down the blade of his knife, it cut his finger open, and drops of blood fell onto the knife, staining it. Toch chuckled, it was sharp indeed. He paced his hut numerous times, he was prepared to accept defeat as he longed for the death of either his brother or himself. He did not care for his dilapidated old hut, it would crumble against the slightest gust of wind. He left the hut and did not plan to return to it ever again. He wanted to be unseen for a few hours. He was aware that Wednesday night was the time when Hybod disappeared, he would look out for his departure and he would follow him. It wasn't long now, only a few minutes. Everyone was asleep, but himself and Hybod. Somehow, Hybod knew Toch was awake, but he did not think it was unusual, Toch was already mysterious. Hybod believes Toch has been dead for many years. The shell of his former self is the only thing that keeps his memory alive. None will remember Toch after this day. Hybod was careful, as he always was, not to wake his family. Hybod felt like his old self for a brief moment when he looked at Telfa, for the first time in a while, she was smiling, she did not move however. She clutched a small toy in her hands, she looked pale. Hybod placed his hard and scarred hand on her soft cheek, she was cold. He then knew. She passed away shortly before Hybod awoke. Hybod did not mourn her death, she was at peace. He looked at his wife, she faced away from him, so she fazed out of his thoughts. Hybod put his boots and fleece on. He hesitated before leaving the hut. He didn't dare look back to his family. His breath held for a moment, he then left his hut. Toch sat out of his sight, in the dark. Toch had killed the remaining clan members, while they slept. Toch would not be satisfied until his brother was face down in the dirt. Hybod, unaware that his clan was officially wiped from history, held on to the idea that the clan may be great again. His prayer was the only answer. He took no weapons, but he was swift in his movement. Toch began to slowly follow him. He would soon know what he was up to every Wednesday night.

7

Hybod gasped and fought for air when he awoke from his unconsciousness. He raised his hand, but quickly retreated when he felt his wounds. He lost a lot of blood. Thoughts rushed through his head, it was the first time he had woken up without his family, Toch was washed away by the river, but his mission was complete. Hybod winced in pain as he struggled to lift himself. He held his hand under his cuts to stop blood dropping to the ground. He limped into the forest that was beside the river that deposited him there. The forest was full of life, but was very dark. Trees stood like watchtowers above Hybod, he felt very uneasy, he stumbled many times and his will to live was slowly fading. He had to do one last thing before he died. Hybod used the trees that were held tightly together to keep himself upright, if he fell, he wouldn't get up. The sounds of whispers began to enter his ears, the whispers were indecipherable, but he knew who the voices belonged to. Clan members that died during the time of sorrow slowed him down, the guilt of their deaths made Hybod grow angry, he blamed himself for everything that happened to them. His hopes were lifted by the sight of light. A small raised chunk of land resided in the centre of the forest Hybod wandered, he made his way there. A pack of Smilodons picked up his scent and followed closely, the smell of blood fuelled their appetites. Hybod wouldn't fight them. He crawled up the small hill, he lay on his belly and slithered like a snake, his arms were useless at this point. He was able to reach the top. He used all of his power left to stand, he scanned the countryside, until he could see his home. He gazed at the now deserted village, the huts were like dots of brown and black from this distance, but Hybod could tell each of them apart. The hill on which they settled was like a beacon of hope to Hybod, a ray of light in the darkness. Hybod finally fell to his knees, accepting his encroaching demise, he raised his arms to the sky, he would meet his brothers and sisters again. He burst out with laughter. The Smilodons were behind him as he performed his final battle. They lunged on his body and tore him into pieces. No noise was heard but the crunching of bones and the chewing of meat.

Make it Last

By Ivan Budanov, age 15.

'Mr. Sutton... one of our dearest terminally ill patients... emm, we have to say we're so proud of you for hanging on. But we predict today will be your final day here on Earth.'

The word 'last' punctured his heart more than the myocarditis ever would.

'Live every day like it's your last'.

The words rolled around Benjamin Sutton's tongue like a fine whiskey in a tumbler, as he imagined all of the crazy, ludicrous things that phrase stood for.

Bungee jumping off a cliff, crossing the country on a motorbike, climbing the world's tallest tree... all that he would never do.

Was this day his last? Definitely.

Would he really live it like it was? Definitely not.

The ECG continued beeping like it had something to say, and on the other side stood Dr. Peska, his contained grin lingering as he pumped more Vasotec in the IV.

'Alright, Mr. Sutton, I'll leave you to yourself. After all... we wouldn't want anything rash happening on your last day...'

He walked out, slowly turning the door handle and snapping the door shut.

Was this really the end? Twenty-four hours alone on a cold, hard cot?

No. He wanted more.

The anger flowing through his alcohol-hardened veins, the Vasotec bubbling, he swung his frail body around and got up on his feet.

He stumbled over to the window, swiping aside the curtains, the rays of light hitting him like he'd never seen them, and he looked out at the world.

All of that beauty, and Benjamin never had time to see it…

His gaze fell upon the nearby grounds.

Suddenly the stench of dirt attacked his nostrils and the cold air turned colder. He saw it.

Squinting to make out the small tombstone, he read, 'Benjamin Sutton, 87. Loved by all', and two men in overalls digging his grave, the tombstone covered in crow droppings.

No. He wasn't ready for that just yet.

Nine o'clock on a stormy Irish Tuesday, Benjamin Sutton walked out of St John's Hospital with only one thought in his head – to live the day like it was his last.

And so he did, leaving the Spar as fast as he came in, a scrunched up bag of crisps concealed in his pocket, a childish smile stuck on his face.

For a moment he stood on the street, chewing, thinking… would the tartness of the salt and vinegar be his last taste of this world? No. He needed more; he needed speed.

And just then did his eyes fall on a bright pink Volkswagen Beetle.

He spied on it for a moment, as a young, tall woman climbed out.

'Miss O'Reilly!' a voice called out, and for a moment the woman sidetracked to greet the voice. The Beetle was wide open.

And so he ran. He ran as fast as he could before his knees broke down, sliding in the front seat, as the woman turned to face him. He locked the doors, getting ready for her scream, her bellow, her cry. But, instead…

'Mr Sutton, looking great! Why aren't you at the hospital?'

He felt that white hot pain in his knees turn to anger, clenching his jaw, and pressed the pedal as hard as he could.

Driving out on the main road, all he could hear were her screams, bellows and cries. But that was all in the past.

Forty kilometres over the speed limit and with no sign of slowing down, the pink Beetle flew down the road.

Where was he going? The thought crossed Benjamin's mind for a split-second... and then he heard the sirens.

Two sets of asynchronous din grew louder and louder, until he was sure they were right on his Beetle's tale. But he wasn't going to stop. Not now.

The Gardaí on his left and right, Mr. Sutton's only choice to look straight ahead, he himself did not know where to go.

Was this enough for a last day? Had he really lived? His contemplations interrupted by the sirens sandwiching his car, Benjamin knew he had one thing left to do.

One hand fumbling through the glove compartment, one on the steering wheel... both eyes on the destination coming closer and closer, Benjamin knew this was it.

He pulled out a sticky tube of pink paint, blistered around the edges, and held it at the ready.

SCREECH! Four sloping, deep tracks in the mud, he ran out, looking directly in front of him, same childish smile.

Benjamin fell on his knees, the burning raging through his body, and struggled to squeeze out three long tubes of pink paint on the stone slab.

The din was behind him. The Gardaí were right there. But this was it.

The paint fell from his grasp, as he lay on the marshy ground, eyes lit up, looking at his creation.

'Sir! You are under arrest!' A voice boomed from behind him.

'Look. Look!' Benjamin screamed, bony finger pointed at his tombstone.

It read: 'Benjamin Sutton, 87. Loved by all', and at the bottom in bold pink: 'MAKE IT LAST'.

'Look!' he kept screaming, as the Gardaí lifted him up and propped him up on a stool.

'Cuff him, James. You... Benjamin Sutton, are being arrested for vandalism, car highjacking, and... stealing a bag of crisps. Is that right?'

But Benjamin kept pointing at the pink letters, a happiness like he'd never felt before...

***

Seven years later, the lonely tombstone still stands. The words 'Benjamin Sutton, 87, Loved by all' have long since disappeared behind a thick barrier of crow droppings, but three visible, pink words hang on to the tombstone, saying everything that needs to be said, and immortalizing Mr. Sutton as The Man Who Made It Last.

Life is Unpredictable

By Wiktoria Dzialak, age 14.

Today, I was woken up by the deep snoring of my best friend, Max. For most people he isn't the prettiest but, to me, he is the handsomest companion in the whole world. He doesn't want to change me in any way; he loves me just the way I am. You can never be sure which direction he looks in, but he always says that he thinks he is looking at the nicest thing in the world. Normally, I would feel very depressed this time of the year as it is the last day of the summer holidays, but not today as I have many reasons to be excited.

Tomorrow is the first day of my last year in the secondary school, the first day of the year of big decisions for my future adult life. I only have one more year to choose my college, but I already know that I want to be a vet and work in Warsaw. My best friend helped me make this decision. Tomorrow, as it is Friday, we will go to the cinema after school – our weekly ritual.

I hop out of bed and put my chewed slippers on and throw the curtains open wide. Warsaw looks so gorgeous and so mighty in the morning sunshine. Suddenly, Max flipped his ears along with all his skin folds and jumped out of the bed to join me on our morning walk. Max is a full breed pug. The streets look so quiet this morning with various shades of red, yellow and brown surrounding us in the park. Max loves to play with the first leaves that have fallen at this time of year. He learned a tough lesson today not to bite the green chestnuts with spikes.

We got back home for breakfast. Max never skips this important daily routine. He loves his food, my slippers and Dad's best pair of shoes; the ones for the special occasions only, of course. On our return I found my dad sitting in our dining room. He was enjoying the last drop of his strong morning coffee before he has to go to work. I love to watch him reading the newspaper above the clouds of smoke rising upwards from his pipe. He looks so serious and dignified. The mixture of tobacco, the scent of my dad's aftershave and the aroma of strong black coffee in the mornings always make me think of Dad's love and protection towards us all. I am daddy's girl, but not his only one. My little sister Weronika is extremely excited; tomorrow is her first day of school. At least she will finally stop counting the number of nights left before the first of September. My mum just finished ironing my sister's first school uniform and her new books, copies and colourful crayons are already and packed in to her new school bag. My sister loves to smell new books and I have to admit that I always smell new books as well since I was her age.

Our mum looks so cheerful and relaxed this morning. She is so pretty, even without make-up and with messy hair. However, I've noticed that Daddy seems to be more pre-occupied this morning. He switched off the radio and when he looked up at me I saw something very strange in his eyes – fear. It is something that I have never seen before. Even Max sensed something unusual about my dad as he lost his interest in chasing his tail and started looking for some cuddles when Daddy looked at him and patted his head. Daddy hugged all three of us today for longer than usual and left the house to head to his office.

Later this afternoon I am going to meet up with my friend from school in our favourite coffee shop in Warsaw. It has become somewhat of a ritual for us on the last day of the summer holidays. Anna goes to her grandparents in Krakow for the whole summer each year so I can't wait to tell her all about my summer activities. Nowadays, the coffee shops seem to be more than just a meeting place for gossip and consumption; it has a whole social and cultural life. In a more local and less anonymous world, people go to coffee shops to read the latest newspapers and books, to celebrate anniversaries, discuss politics and literature, not just with their friends, but with anyone who is interested. However, today we will just order our favourite creamy cakes and while savouring them we will share our secrets from our summer holidays.

As usual I'm late and, as I enter the coffee shop, I see Anna sitting at our usual table-for-two near the window. Anna is sitting there patiently, having already ordered our treats and looking as glamorous as always; she has her blonde hair down and lovely blue eyes. With my red hair, green eyes and freckles all over my skinny body, I am far away from being pretty. However, this time I have amazing news for Anna and I am sure that this time her news cannot be as exciting as mine.

I was so eager to tell her all about my family trip to the Mazury Lakes in July and who was there as well, most importantly the tall, handsome brunette from our neighbourhood. The one who is starting veterinary studies and loves animals as passionately as I do. The one who has the most charming smile with two small dimples in his cheeks. The one who never so much as looked at me during the last school year and the one who is now saying that my copper hair is so soft and gorgeously shiny in the sunset light. The one who held my hand tenderly during our walks at the lakeshore each balmy summer evening. Adam understands me, makes me laugh and always protects me. Even Max loves him. I absolutely cannot wait for our tomorrow's date.

I came back home just in time for dinner. I was very disappointed as my dad didn't come back on time, which was highly unusual. My daddy and Max always insist on regular dinner times to make sure that everybody is home and we can sit around the table together. We tell each other about how our day went, chat about our good times and about our worries. We have always been a close family, but something was different tonight because this time I couldn't even trust my mum when she said that everything was fine. I could see, through her glazed eyes, that something simply didn't sound right when she said that Dad would just be a little late home. As I didn't want to upset my mum any more than she already appeared, I went to my bed a little earlier than usual. Max always gets excited about the thought of going to bed early because, as much as he likes his food, he also likes his naps.

In an ideal world, Max would choose to be either eating or sleeping with short breaks for cuddles. He licked my face a few times to say 'goodnight' before he spun around a few times to find his most comfortable sleeping position. Shortly afterwards, he fell in the 'land of nod'. I was anxiously waiting to hear Daddy come home from work, but I was getting really worried with every long minute that passed. I could only imagine my poor mum's anxiety. I reminded myself about my dad's unusual behaviour this morning and that fear I witnessed in his eyes. I put my arms around my best friend's chubby body for comfort and I was waiting for the Sandman to pop by to fall asleep.

Suddenly, the door of my bedroom burst open with a loud bang and my dad's frame appeared in the opening. Since morning, he seemed to have aged about twenty years. My mum was following close behind with my sleeping sister in her arms. My dad ordered me to get up, pack the necessary things only and run with them.

What was going on? I didn't understand. What has happened? My mum was in floods of tears. My innocent sister was covered with only her blanket and she was holding her bunny tightly as always. Her bare feet were sticking out under Mummy's arm. What should I bring with me? What should you take in an emergency situation? What was the emergency? I was looking for any explanation. Daddy said that there is absolutely no time to go into detail. My little sister woke up crying and mum tried to calm her down. She didn't want to leave without her new fully packed schoolbag. I grabbed Max and we ran downstairs and dashed straight to the street where Daddy's car was parked.

'Daddy, what is going on?', I asked while clambering into our car.

'We need to go to the school. It's nearly the morning time', he replied. 'German planes bombarded our cities this morning. Germany declared war!', he declared.

There was absolutely nothing I could say to this. I was simply horrified. Cities including Katowice, Krakow, Tczew had been attacked with incendiary bombs. Air raids on Warsaw began at 9am on 1st September 1939; a date that is forever etched in the history as the day the world went to war. The world would never be the same again.

'So we're not going to the cinema today, as we are in a war now.' Who knows what the future holds…our cinema trip, my college life, my career as a vet. Life can never be the same again – for anyone.

An Ode to the Blind Man

By Sineaid Whelan, age 15.

All the praises you whisper in her ear

Dress her in smooth, satin robes;

Every disparage hissed my way

Stripped me bare.

Every promise you made to her

Lifted her higher on her pedestal;

Every threat and sneer aimed at me

Sent me flying back to the ground.

The compliments and reassurances,

They sculpted her throne,

And every tear you wept for her

She wears as a crown.

She needs people like you

To elevate her,

But she doesn't need you

She does not even want you.

You are expendable;

I suppose that every queen

Needs a pawn or two.

I hope you know that I was drowning,

That I was thrown overboard

With my hands tied behind my back

And lead weights on a chain around my neck.

I hope you know

That every time I almost got a breath

You'd add another weight

With your

Words.

Words never screamed,

Words whispered or murmured,

Or worst

You said nothing at all.

That was the heaviest weight of all.

I hope you know that as I was gasping for her

Each breath grew further apart,

And while my lungs burned like fire

I saw you.

You were on the surface, with her,

With everyone else who floats

And you looked at me

As though it was my fault

That I couldn't swim.

I know that these words I speak

Fall on deaf ears.

I know these wounds I expose

Are nothing to blind eyes.

And I know these bitter memories

Are spat out by unforgiving forked tongues.

But that's okay

Because I untied my own hands,

I lifted off my own weights

And I let them sink to the bottom

Where they belong.

I did this on my own.

And now I have people by my side

Who look at me with love in their eyes,

Not pity and loathing.

And I do not step on these people

Or use their skulls as stepping stones,

Their spines as stairs,

Break their bones and use them as rungs for my ladder,

Rip out their eyes so they follow blindly,

Cut off their feet so they cannot climb themselves.

I build these people up

I explore the galaxies in their eyes

I write love stories on their skin with my fingers

I paint pictures of their beauty with my words

I build these people up,

As they do me.

I hope you know that I am better. Almost.

I hope you know you are nothing to me. Almost.

I hope you know I forgive you.

Almost.

Come, Join the Carnival

By Kitty Wallace, age 14.

By any stretch of the imagination Bob Sullivan was a perfectly normal man. He had his middle-class job, a perfectly normal family, even a cat by the name of Humphrey. His day started at 7 am and ended at the time at which grown-up people tended to go to sleep. This continued until one day when his normal, to some people 'bland', lifestyle changed. And nothing would ever be the same again.

The day started as it usually did, Bob got up, had a low-fat breakfast (much to his disgruntlement), brushed his teeth and drove to meet his perfectly bland day. Arriving at his workplace he was struck with the notion that for 8 am on a working day the office was strangely silent. Where was Henry? Or Sylvia? Never was there a day that Sylvia didn't peer at him reproachfully from behind her spectacles. He felt a cold feeling sweep through him, a sudden notion of dread. Had he taken his pills? Yes… Had he perhaps come in on a bank holiday? No, Alex had been babbling to him about a school project that was due today. And that was when Bob saw the man in the suit.

He'd never come closer to breaking 'The No Swearing Rule', a rule he had implemented himself in his household. His obvious discomfort did not appear to affect the man however. He merely walked no glided over to Bob bringing the shadows and the doubts of the cramped grey office with him. "Bob Sullivan" he rasped.

It wasn't a question, but Bob felt the need to check that his vocal chords were still in working order "That's me, sir". The silence lingered, hovering like an uninvited guest in the empty space. The man clearly felt its presence as he cleared his throat and tried to sew some normality into this cloth of a conversation.

"My name is Mr. Smith and I'm afraid that I have to deliver some news that will affect your entire life. I'd be best starting with some moderately good news first; Mr. Sullivan, you have won a draw."

At this Bob's ears pricked up. He never won draws, in fact he'd stopped entering those years ago. Was this Alex's doing? "What would this draw entail, Mr. Smith?" The man seemed uncomfortable now, more uncomfortable than even Bob himself felt. It almost seemed silly to call him a man, he was more a boy than anything else. Just a boy delivering a message.

"Sir, your daughter is going to die on her 12th birthday. After contracting leukaemia, she will be in care for 6 months before her demise. The purpose of this visit is to ensure that you can say your goodbyes and perhaps be prepared…" The boy was clearly new to this, it was probably his first job and what a first job, proclaiming that an eleven-year-old girl will die.

An important thing to know about Bob is that he wasn't the kind to get angry easily. Well, unless he has a reason to. And in Bob's mind this was as good a time to get angry as any. "So, you're telling me, that you came to my workplace to tell me about how my daughter's going to die? And you're making it look like you're doing me a grand favour. What a sickening thought that people like you exist, when there are individuals who give up their life to ensure that others are safe! You're a damn waste of space, now get outta of here boy!" Bob was breathing heavily, not used to this sudden sensation of pure rage. The youth didn't even flinch at this tubby man's anger but simply drew out a piece of paper and handed it over to Bob.

Whatever was on that piece of paper is still unknown to this day, but it had the desired effect on Bob. As they sat down together, Smith told him a vital piece of information formerly left out of the previous conversation.

"Every year our…company draws out a name. That name will be told when a close friend or family member will depart this world. They are also given the chance to prevent their loved one's death." At this Smith looked expectantly at Bob. Bob didn't even appear to have noticed the significance of these words. Smith sighed: these types of people were difficult to handle. Too young to possess the wisdom of elders, too old to possess the belief of youngsters. What Smith wouldn't give to be free of this musty, grey place with its cold aura and cynical people. It had been a battle of six nations to get this damn job and in retrospect it hadn't been worth the trouble.

"Sir, you can prevent your daughter's death" he repeated in order to get it through those thick layers of ear wax.

Bob's head shot up, he had heard that. "I can prevent her death?"

"Well not prevent as such as... rather delay the inevitable..."

"How long? How long can I ...delay?"

"Ten years at most"

Bob considered this. "So, do I need to die in her place?"

Smith could detect a quiver in Bob's usually boisterous voice. Nothing scared a human more than the possibility of losing their life. Except, of course, the possibility of losing their loved ones. "You'd need to take up residence in the Carnival." Taking Bobs' expression as a clue on the trail of ignorance, he continued quickly with, "The Carnival is a place that's not quite in the living not quite in the dead, a place where humans can take a journey through their life and their accomplishments. A place that offers solace before the journey of the third level. It's like life is the main course, nice and meaty and the Carnival is the taster course to prepare you for the desert, the reason why anyone goes to the restaurant. Anyway, you'd work there for as long as you can because the longer you work the longer your daughter's lifespan will be. When you've finally done as much as humanely or not so humanely possible, you get your ticket and boom you're reunited once more."

Smith stopped to get his breath back and saw Bob staring at him with a hint of disgust on his face. "You speak so mindlessly of living people, it's not like you'd know the emotions we have, being a grim reaper or whatever you are!"

Smith had to resist a snort. Grim reaper my arse! He thought but simply responded with a passive, "I'm only a normal worker sir, if you want to talk to a grim reaper go to a crime scene. They all go for drinks after those."

"Well you're still not human" Bob responded defensively. Why was he wasting time talking to this insolent boy? He'd just been told his daughter was going to die.

Meanwhile Smith was quietly simmering and replied in a low voice "I was human. Well until someone stabbed me thirteen times in the chest." Silence, the unwanted guest had returned with a suitcase this time.

"I'm sor-"

"Quiet, enough time has been wasted. Make your choice! Live, go home and spend your limited time with your daughter and let her know you love her or come with me and give her years of life, the product of your labour. What will it be?"

Bob scrunched his eyes up, whether it was to prevent the tears or attempt to contain his over-brimming thoughts he didn't know. And quietly he whispered under his breath the prayers he hadn't let pass his lips in over a decade. Ever since Sarah had died and left him behind in this grey world full of people who let harsh words fall off their tongue in perfect synchronisation. A grey world where the only source of light was Alex. Was he prepared to turn away from the safety of this night light, to walk forward into the dark unknown where monsters could leap out? He didn't know but sometimes it is the absence of knowledge that fuels our life decisions. He whispered to Smith who was waiting respectfully for his decision. He spoke the only words he could think of, "take care of my little angel", words to which Smith replied with "with all my heart" as he tapped him three times with a cane Bob hadn't noticed before. And that would be the last thing he noticed. In this world.

**

He was soaring through the atmosphere now. He couldn't distinguish anything that flew by him. It all just seemed like bright lights, lights that intended to blind him. He instead focused on closing his eyes and remembering. Remembering sunny days walking with Alex in the park, eating ice-cream and observing the clouds chasing each other out of the sky. Playing games that Alex probably shouldn't be allowed to play on the ever-whirring Xbox. Watching silly films about ridiculously good-looking people, Alex chastising him about his salt intake while greedily gobbling down crisps herself. And lastly, he remembered this morning; getting up in a bad mood and just saying a simple, "See you at three" as opposed to goodbye. At this Bob winced, wishing to be taken back to those early hours to say something else. But maybe things were better this way, after all what could he have possibly have said that would condense years of love into a journey to school?

When the lights had faded, Bob found himself in…he didn't quite know where. It appeared to be a sitting room, adorned with red brocade and filled with elaborate armchairs twinned with poufs. Quite luxurious really, yet Bob couldn't help but feel a wave of unease swirling in his gut. He then realised someone was talking to him; "Mr Sullivan, correct?" someone asked, voice as silky as a dog's ears. He turned to the direction of the voice to see a curious looking person staring at him. Curious was the only word in Bob's inner-city high-school vocabulary to sum up this person. For starters they were wearing a ridiculous waistcoat and top hat and secondly Bob could not fathom what gender they were. "Mr Sullivan, correct?" they repeated, seemingly oblivious to Bobs' confusion.

"Ah, yes that's me!" The person gave a crooked smile suddenly, lips reaching the sides of their face,

"Pleasure to meet you Bob, the name's Eli and I'll be your…manager from now on! Now my role in this place is to bargain with lives. Basically, I control people's lifespan. If someone passes the interview with me then they are granted however many years I deem them worthy, to return to live on earth on the condition that when they, once again, die they will work in my office or at the Carnival. But of course, you have no interest in that. You're not here for yourself, you are a good man." There was a strange, greedy smile tugging at Eli's mouth as he uttered the words as though they were a grievous insult. "Anyway, shall we have some tea?" Bob was once again reminded of the fact that these people ran out of breath easily. "Katrina! Go boil up some tea and fetch the cakes! You know the ones with the jam-"

"There'll be no need to do that…I'll just be on my way…I have to get to work and all-". Before Bob could finish his sentence, a large cloaked figure stalked into the room. "Ah, Mr. Sullivan, please meet my very close associate, Cain! He's just a carrier…oh and here's Sybil with him!"

Sybil, a tall redheaded lady paused only to scowl at Eli and drawl out "Pleasure is all mine, beware of this ninny though" Although Bob had only just met Eli he had gathered that no one talked down to any of them, except each other. As Sybil walked on she called over her shoulder, "Don't eat the cakes; they're bloody rancid."

And so, Bob started his work. The Carnival was full of tents with eerily lit entrances illuminating Bob's pathway, casting shadows against the large merry-go-round. According to Eli, each person could choose which attraction to start with and made their way to different ones over time. The merry-go-round took you straight into your childhood with all its tumbles and jumps. The fortune teller's tent tells exactly what happened in your life, your true loves, your true enemies. The puppet show showed you your influences in life. The cotton candy stand showed the sweet aspects of life while various 'freaks' represented those closest to you. And the final show tent showed the entirety of your life in a condensed way.

Bob's job was to handle the merry-go-round and ensure people were shown certain parts of their life while other less pleasant aspects were left out. He was to pull the lever over and over again all the while sorting out the person's childhood memories into categories A, B and D. A being acceptable, B Being Bad and D being Depressing. Fortunately, each memory had the person's perception tinted in green, red or orange. The real trial was the lever. As Bob was not really dead, as the guests of the Carnival were, he could see the Carnival as it actually was. Its glamour and the sweet smells that other people took such pleasure in were a torment to him, their sickliness pervading his entire vision. And still he pulled the lever keeping in mind the fact that the longer he worked, the more years Alex had to live.

Time passed, and eventually Eli, as the proprietor of the place, took a walk around to see how things were going for the quiet little worker, who had the eyes of a determined man. Perhaps they could get him to eat the cake? For only Eli knew that once you've eaten the cake, consumed it in its entirety you were forced to stay in Eli's office for eternity. Quite a lot of time for a cake no matter how tasty it was. That was how Katrina had fallen, being a confectioner in her last life. Eli had heard the reason why Bob was working here and was sorely tempted to feed the man some cake. Just to cheer him up. However, once they approached Bob's workplace, they came to the realisation that the man was beyond the help of cake itself. Sweat was pouring profusely down his face and veins were bulging in his wide forehead. The standard office shirt he wore was stained with the juice of his labour.

"How're you doing there, man? Like the view?" Bob allowed himself a minute of indulgence to glance at the sunset which was a permanent fixture in the fairground. It truly was stunning, the iridescent blues and pinks washing together to mask the otherwise bland atmosphere. "Can I get you anything? Cake? Tea?" Bob laughed bitterly, a guttural sound that threw itself up into his oesophagus.

"Glass of water might be nice. Maybe slice of pound cake an' all. No one made pound cake better than my ma. Spent most her life making the damn thing, only to die of diabetes. The irony, eh? What I'd do to have her here with me now. Da never really was around; he preferred to spend his time in the pub. Want to know how he died? Got knocked down by a yeast truck. Seems fitting." Bob laughed humourlessly. Eli didn't really know how to respond, which was strange of itself.

Eli walked to the nearest pump and poured water into a tin cup. Walking back Eli wondered why it seemed so important that Bob receive this glass of water. The man had signed up to this, after all. Eli discarded this thought into the space where we usually toss unwanted common sense and fed the water to Bob, feeling a thrill of fulfilment that they hadn't felt in so long. That moment faded, and Eli wiped damp hands against an ornate jacket. "Anyway, enough reminiscing man, back to work!"

The time dragged on, pulling its chains of loneliness behind it for Bob. Considering he had no one to talk to, not even the people who entered the merry-go-round, he was left to think about memories. Not of Alex, but of Sarah and his best friend Tim. At school the three of them had thought themselves invincible, invincible against the teachers who taught them, the peers who barely knew them, the police even. They had spent their childhood in an eager attempt to grow up, to have freedom, to be able to run across the train tracks unaided. Yet, once the last wisp of childhood had flown away they were left empty and grey, still hungrily grasping for the chance to run unaided. They were unable to. Whether it was bills, work or simply the thought of judgement of those they didn't even know, they were trapped in a box, never to emerge again.

Then Bob and Sarah had gotten married, Tim being his best man, and for once in all the years of their lives they were free. And they gladly indulged in the freedom, travelling to places and doing things they hadn't even dreamed of. When they had returned, bright cheeked and merry, to the grey life they were accustomed to they had brought with them the wisp that had flown away before. And this time it was going to stay.

When Sarah had died the wisp had tried to escape and Bob had nearly let it. Until Alex grabbed it in her chubby baby fist. And that was when Bob knew; he had to be there for Alex now. And forever.

***

He barely recognised the touch, years without it had resulted in avoidance of the memory. He barely dared to look up, for fear of disappointment, for fear this was some glorious mirage. However, once he did he was rewarded with the honour of looking into his wife Sarah's beautiful face. A quick look to the left told him Alex was there as well. The joy leaped up into his throat and the only words he could utter was a simple "oh baby".

His time was up. That meant Alex's time was up as well. Almost as if she had read his mind she told him "Twelve years, daddy. You gave me twelve years of life. Twelve years that I spent in pure fulfilment. You don't know how hard it was daddy to realise you were gone, to get over the pure shock of not having you there. Once I knew that you were looking out for me, I knew I couldn't let your sacrifices go to waste. And, so I dedicated my life to following the train tracks, unaided. Well until Aidan decided to accompany me" for a moment her face was sad, but then she whispered as if to comfort herself, "but he'll be okay."

When they offered to take him on his last tour, Bob burst out laughing "I've had enough of that for a while I think!" And so, with their hands in his, his ticket handed to him by Smith with a, "Didn't think you could do it, breaking the record like that! Can I take a picture?"

"Oh, me too!" Eli piped in. Bob stood in a daze while they fussed over the lighting. Was this real?

When the office had paid their respects the three set off into the sunset, custom balloons in hand. They did as they were supposed to; they followed the wisp.

96

Conclusions

By Siobhán Brosnan, age 15.

The sunlight rippled across the lake, bright and clear. The lapping of the water made a gentle chorus with the rustling of the leaves. It was the sort of day the poets wrote about, Mary thought wistfully. Sunshine warmed her arms and made the afternoon hazy. The rocks beneath her rattled as she shifted on the low stone wall. She felt a little drowsy, but she couldn't shake the feeling of finality, the end of something glorious. Mary took a final gaze across the water, then turned to her companion, and began to speak.

"Do you remember," she said quietly, for the day required gentle tones, "the very first day we met? Right here, on this crumbling wall?"

She did, for sure. He'd been here with a crowd of friends, and they were splashing around by the lakeshore. She'd come down to the shore to search for water roots – it was before the war, but food still wasn't plentiful – and had been distracted by this boy's disarming smile.

"Bet I'll beat you at cards," he sneered. Mary could never resist an opportunity to prove someone wrong.

James beat Mary, three games to two.

Mary emerged from her nostalgia. "I wouldn't have guessed that we'd become friends," she grinned.

Not in a thousand years. But somehow, something about James' messy dark hair and charming brown eyes drew her in. They were only fourteen, and life seemed eternal. Mary met James day after day by the lakeshore for cards. As their friendship blossomed, they expanded their repertoire: soon they attempted draughts, and riddles, and even worked their way up to chess, despite neither knowing the rules. Conversation was so easy with her James. He didn't require a façade or pretence.

The memories pulled at Mary, but she forced herself back to the present. "I'm pretty sure that becoming friends with you was the best thing to ever happen to me."

James finally moved; a few quick blinks. Mary's heart skipped. It always did.

"I love you, too." She kissed him gently on the forehead.

Their first kiss was the first time she'd ever seen James truly ruffled. He was so charming, so put together, that seeing him blushing and flustered astonished her. Mary liked being able to do that to him. They were sixteen, and she knew they wouldn't be young for much longer. They had time, though. She knew they had time.

The war was announced the next day.

Mary sighed, and looked across the present day lake. The sun was beginning its descent, now, and she knew they didn't have much time. She wondered how James was feeling, knowing what was ahead. With that thought, she carefully wrapped an arm around James. His wheelchair was cold against her sun-warmed skin. She rested her arm on his shoulder and allowed herself to pretend that they were seventeen again.

At first, they took no notice of the war. The newspaper proclaimed each day's events, but it didn't feel real. The war was far away, unimportant, a problem for the London boys. No business in their corner of Wales.

The first bomber planes flew overhead on a balmy September night. They'd gathered outside and stared, transfixed, as these ugly monsters passed overhead to another forsaken town. The war was real, Mary realised. But it wasn't their battle yet.

As Mary sat, wrapped around James and wrapped in her thoughts, a bee flew over her nose and James' brow. Mary watched it. So much life around this lakeshore.

It was the freezing middle of February, and Britain was losing the war, and in a peal of bomb alarms everything that wasn't real was. The war had finally arrived on their doorstep. Mary was terrified beyond compare, as she huddled in the tiny hut of corrugated steel. Flames burst outside, punctuated by screams and the sickening smell of sizzling flesh. They emerged the next day to a broken town. James, her James, had survived, and she held him tightly for what felt like hours when she found him by the lakeshore.

"I'm joining the Army."

Mary could feel his heartbeat, now, slow and steady. She wriggled around until she found his hand. Smooth fingers, calluses at the tips. Her James. She knew his every inch.

Mary begged him not to join up, but James was sure he knew his duty. He was seventeen and a half, too young, but the Army would take anyone if you said you were eighteen, James told her. His tone was matter-of-fact, but his fingers trembled. Mary gripped his hand and knew he'd never change his mind.

James wrote Mary a letter, every single week.

Thinking about James' letters sent a little shiver down her spine, even now, forty years later. He'd come so close to death so many times. Yet now…

The past was almost more bearable than the present, so Mary let herself slip into nostalgia.

They'd played games, like noughts and crosses, painfully slowly by letter. Mary was awake at six in the morning every Thursday, waiting for the postman at the front gate. He wrote each week without fail. Mary thought she'd never survive those two excruciating years of waiting. She was on tenterhooks, desperately dreading the telegram 'sending most grievous condolences'.

It never came. Her James arrived home on a warm May morning.

The sun was now sinking steadily towards the horizon, and Mary felt her heart drop with it. Grief threatened to rise within her about what was to come, but she quelled her despairing thoughts, and lightly brushed James' wrist. No mourning. Not yet.

When Mary married James, a year after he came home, she knew she was the luckiest woman in the world. They lived twenty years in sheer bliss. They'd watched the post-war world transform, through astonished eyes, and travelled on the new-fangled passenger planes. They went to London, and further, marvelling at the Statue of Liberty in New York City and the Eiffel Tower of Paris. Mary couldn't imagine happier days. Life with James was paradise, every minute of it. They had no children yet. After all, they had more time, she was certain.

James had his first fall on his fortieth birthday. He was sure it was a momentary blip. He had another two days later.

Mary listened to James' laboured breath and steady heartbeat as the lake rippled gently in the background. They were both watching the sun's downward progress.

Motor neuron disease was almost unheard of, back in those days. Mary still remembered the white colour James' face had turned as the doctors warned them of what was to come.

Mary nestled her face in the crook of James' neck, as a cool breeze washed in from the water. She could hear the bee's quiet buzz. Her heart was bursting with love for him. How could she ever go through with what had to be done at sundown?

His legs had been paralysed, first. It worked its cursed way up his body, slowly. He wryly quipped that after all the battles he'd faced in the war; it was his own body that had betrayed him. The last thing left was his eyes. He'd learned Morse code, and blinked to communicate.

Only the tiniest sliver of sunlight was glimmering on the lake now. Mary turned and stared at her James. Even blinking pained him by this stage.

Once his eyes were paralysed, he'd be a living statue, heart beating and brain whirring, but unable to move. Then, there would be only one thing that could be done, the doctors said. Sympathy ached in their voices when they told her, at least you'll be able to do it yourself, wherever he wants. James had requested that it be done at sunset at the lake. Mary had blinked back tears and nodded. They'd survived the war. She always thought they would have more time.

Now, James stared right back at her, and blinked three times. I love you.

"I love you, too," she whispered. The last time.

The injection was fast-acting and painless, they'd said. It was done with a syringe to the shoulder. It was the newest technology, euthanasia.

Darkness had fallen, and James closed his eyes. Mary closed hers, too, and listened to his soft heartbeat.

She plunged the needle into his shoulder, and waited, until there was no sound at all except the low lapping of the lake.

Shattered Glass

By Philippa Brennan, age 14.

Mr. Conn Reilly's house was in a state of absolute disrepair, and so was he. Sprawled on his bed, his features contorted into an expression of terror and a knife wound at his chest, it was apparent that he had been dead for several hours.

"What happened?" I asked the Inspector.

Detective Inspector Smith was a broad-shouldered man with silver hair that perfectly matched his uniform. He hesitated before answering, the result of asking a fifteen year-old amateur sleuth to help solve a case.

"Were you at the psychic fair last month?"

"No, why?"

The psychic fair had been the most exciting event held in our village in years. It began when a local witch approached the council with the idea and, snatching up any money-making opportunity like a magpie with a ring; they were eager to comply. I decided not to go, avoiding crowds at any given chance; I spent my afternoon buried in the pages of Crooked House.

"You're lucky you didn't waste your time; there weren't half as many tents as we expected. Anyone who got their fortune told said it was a farce. I was on duty, obviously." He adjusted his polished police badge. "Anyway, MacDermot was walking around, saying how happy he was to benefit the community."

I inhaled the scent of mould and alcohol. Damp patches were visible on the walls behind peeling beige wallpaper, the carpet a faded brown coated in grime. Sunlight burst through the window, reflecting off the wine bottles on the nightstand.

"Alastrine was having a ball until Conn showed up. He didn't believe in magic, like most of us, but he couldn't help making a scene."

"What did he do?"

"He started shouting that MacDermot had wasted the town's money on Alastrine's idea; how we hadn't enough to begin with and that Alastrine was a fraud. Everyone was watching when she cursed him."

"Cursed him?"

"I know, it sounds ridiculous. May your blood spill upon shattered glass. Everyone laughed then, and she left pretty quickly. I had to remove Conn from the square."

"I'm sorry, but what has any of this got to do with the murder?" With cases like these, it was never the dramatic events that provided vital information. It was the needle-in-haystack clues; miniscule and almost impossible to find that, if discovered, could complete the intricate tapestry of a mystery.

He gestured to the corpse. "See for yourself."

Conn's face had a greenish tint with eyes wide and dull. He wore old trousers and a grey t-shirt, ripped where he had been stabbed.

"There isn't as much blood as I had expected."

He shot me a disapproving look, crossing his arms.

"This isn't the place for jokes, Beatrice."

"I'm serious."

There was something in the dead man's white knuckled fist. Taking it from between his fingers, I held it up to the light. It was a torn fragment of paper; magenta edged with silver foil.

"It looks like a five hundred euro note."

He nodded and dropped it into a plastic bag marked evidence. "The most interesting part." He pointed to the foot of the bed. A glass had been smashed on the floor, jagged pieces gleaming like ice. Its presence sent a shiver crawling down my spine; the killer was playing a dangerous game.

"Just like the curse."

"Exactly."

"Which means that the murderer was either at the fair or heard about it from someone else, which doesn't simplify matters in the slightest."

He opened his mouth to say something but closed it again.

"Why would Alastrine kill anyone in such a distinct way? Everyone knew about the curse, so why break the glass?"

"Nobody took her seriously after the fair; she lost most of her business. Maybe she got tired of it and went after revenge."

I started at the sound of three sharp taps on the door. Whoever was on the other side did not wait for an answer, opening it to reveal what I thought at first to be a huge glittering insect. Realizing it was a woman, the first I saw of her was a patterned silk dress that blew clouds of dust into the air as it skimmed the carpet. Her silver hair was piled onto her head in an elaborate knot. She seemed to shimmer from her masses of jewellery; crystal bracelets, rings on every finger and an opal hanging on a chain around her neck.

"Miss Scott." Said Smith, shaking her hand.

"Good morning, Inspector. I came as quickly as I could."

"Thank you. If you'll come into the next room, I have a few questions that I must ask. Routine practice, you understand."

This room was less dusty, but just as neglected; a wooden floor lay beneath two squashy armchairs that looked like they had been thrown out of a window several times. Hoping to remain unnoticed, I perched on a crooked stool at the back. However, Alastrine scrutinized my pixie-cut hair and woollen jumper as she sat down, straight-backed and still as a cat.

"I'm sorry, but is it necessary that she sits here?"

"Beatrice has done great work for us in the past, so whatever you say to me can be said to her as well."

"But I am under no obligation to speak to a teenage girl."

"If you would prefer, we could continue this interview in the police station."

She let out a sigh. "What do want to know?"

He took a notebook and pen from the mahogany desk beside his chair. "So you live—"

"Around the corner."

"Could you tell me where you were last night between 10pm and 2am?"

"Certainly. I was at home all evening. I read from 10 to 11 and went to bed after that." She spoke confidently; either a true or rehearsed answer.

The Inspector's eyes sparkled. "And do you recognize this?" Producing another evidence bag from his pocket, he held out a knife that appeared to have been taken from a Victorian novel. It had a deadly sharp blade and was small enough to be carried around unnoticed. Celtic spirals were engraved on the handle with two opals set into the end, glittering like the eyes of a snake.

She sprang up from her seat. "I definitely do not! I understand your implication, but an affinity with opals does not make me a murderer."

"I did not intend on implying anything. I simply find it curious that Mr. Reilly was murdered according to the curse that you put on him one month ago."

"And that gives you the right to accuse me of killing him? I would never do such a thing, but that scoundrel deserved to die! How dare he humiliate me when he never had anything against me?"

Her face turned a deep purple as she stalked out, her jewellery jingling like Christmas bells. I watched her march away through the window. Alastrine was the ideal criminal; a brilliant actress with a short temper.

"The knife looks like something she would have." said Smith.

"Where would anyone get that?"

He dropped his gaze. "They were sold at the fair."

"You sold these at the fair?"

"As ornaments – we didn't think anyone would be killed with them."

I rolled my eyes. Wondering how safe we were with a police force sporting this brand of stupidity.

"Were they all like this?"

"Some had different crystals in them."

The roar of an engine drew my gaze to the window. An arrogantly orange car pulled into the drive, gravel crunching under the tyres. Its removable fabric hood was down and the 2018 license plate demanded appreciation. A man got out and sauntered towards the door.

"I'll get it." I started down the stairs where I noticed something I had missed earlier; four scratches were cut into the wood at the foot of the staircase. Deep and raw, obviously new.

I opened the front door to a tall man with a wide grin, flashing brilliant white teeth. "Cecil MacDermot." he said. "You must be that young lady who helped with some of our little problems." I led him upstairs, his booming footsteps reverberating through the hallway.

"Good morning, Mr. MacDermot." Smith said.

"Smith, how are you? I'm just sticking my head in to see that everything is running smoothly."

"We haven't run into any huge problems so far."

"I've done my best to keep the journalists out for now, but they'll be back." His eyes darted around the room. He seemed out of place in this derelict house with his designer sunglasses and gelled hair; an actor on a set.

"It's nasty business, but it has to be done."

"Unfortunately. I'm going to the bathroom and then I'll be off. I've a meeting."

"I'll show you—"

"No, no, it's fine." He charged downstairs and into the bathroom without hesitation. Barely a moment had passed before he returned, waving his car keys. "I'd better go, unless there's anything else you need help with?"

"No, we'll get back to work."

He closed the door, his engine revving to life as he hurtled down the lane.

"Alastrine did have a point." I said. "Why would Conn try to humiliate her when he hardly knew her?"

"He was that type, I suppose. Liked gossip and being the centre of drama."

"There is no sign of forced entry?"

"No, Conn would have to have let the killer in."

"But again, that could have been anyone."

He fell silent, listening to the squawk of a raven outside.

"There are scratches on the stairs."

His brow furrowed. "That could be from anything."

"They were new, I'll show you."

I led him into the hall where he knelt down, frowning.

"What do you think?" he said, brushing the dust from his uniform.

"I think this case isn't half as simple as it pretends to be."

The front door was opened by a woman I knew had to be related to Conn. Short and thin, she wore a black suit and tie with her platinum blonde hair falling to her shoulders. Her nails were perfectly shaped, painted scarlet. She had eyes like her brother's, but hers were wide and bloodshot; emeralds on her dangerously pale face.

"I'm Aine Reilly, Conn's sister."

"Miss Reilly." Smith said. "I'm so sorry for your loss. Perhaps you'd like to come upstairs and sit down?"

She followed him, taking a tissue from her bag to wipe a tear from her cheek. She settled in the chair and turned to me. "You're Beatrice. I've heard about you, solving cases for the police."

"I'm sorry about this."

"I don't mean to upset you, but I have a few questions." It was Inspector Smith's business-like manner that made him a competent policeman. He was unaffected by feelings, but did not forget them.

"Do you know if your brother had any enemies?"

"No, not real enemies anyway. He was loud and sometimes – insensitive, but I didn't think anyone would murder him."

"Could you tell me where you were last night between ten and two?"

I saw a slight flicker in her eyes, a change so miniscule I almost hadn't seen. "I was at home, finishing some paperwork I had from my office. I went to bed at ten thirty."

His hand moved towards the dagger on the table. "Did your brother own this?"

She flinched at the sight of the weapon. "I never saw it." She sniffed, her hands trembling.

Smith turned to me. "Have you anything to add?"

I shifted in my seat. Despite needing the information I knew she had, I hated myself for asking for it.

"What about Conn's drinking problem?"

She whirled around and stared at me with frightened eyes, like a bird's on seeing an approaching car. Burying her head in her hands, she started sobbing violently.

"How did you know?"

"It was obvious, look at the amount of wine everywhere. He spent all his money on drink, judging by the state of this house. You are grieving his death, but trembling hands are a sign of nerves."

My gaze stuck to the floor, my cheeks burned. Taking uneven breaths, she collected herself.

"There's no point in lying – I came here at ten last night and fought with Conn about his drinking. He kicked me out at half ten and told me to never visit him again."

"But you gave him money?"

"No, he wanted some but I've never given him any." I looked up sharply. Her eyes were bulging, her face pale grey. "I understand this makes me seem very suspicious." She sniffed. "But I can assure you that I would never dream of – of murdering my brother."

"I'm sorry." I repeated.

"Do you have anything else to ask me, Inspector?"

"No, you're fine."

I twitched on the stool as she shut the door. My brain was a tangle of loose threads, fractured information occupying every thought.

Inspector Smith glanced at his watch. "That's all the interviews done. I think it's time for a lunch break."

"I'm going to get coffee. I'll be back by half eleven."

I squinted in the sunlight when I left the house, ducking under the yellow crime scene tape. I shuddered when I passed Alastrine's cottage; the building itself almost completely hidden by her garden. Trees cast shadows on the façade roses climbed, blood-red and prickly. The ground was a vibrant carpet of flowers with a hedge that spilled over the wall and into the lane.

The bell chimed above the door as I entered Mildred's, a coffee shop on the corner. I approached the counter and, ordering a cappuccino, breathed in the aroma of caffeine and sugar. Finding a table, I sat down and closed my eyes to think.

It became an endless cycle of frustration; no sooner had I supposedly uncovered the killer than another clue sprung to memory to smash the illusion to pieces. There was ample evidence against Alastrine, but other clues didn't fit. This case was the broken glass, and I had to put the pieces together. Of all the fragmented facts, however, the sharpest point was how Conn had died of a stab wound and not bled out.

It hit me like a brick being thrown at my face, my eyes flew open and I leapt up. "Cappuccino?" someone asked.

"Yes." I flung my change onto the table and took the coffee, sprinting out of the shop and back towards the house. My heart raced and my fingers burned from the spilling drink, but in moments like these; moments of perfect clarity when everything fit like a jigsaw puzzle, the only thought in my head was how I could have been so stupid.

I approached an officer outside, gasping for breath. "Could you get Inspector Smith to come here as soon as possible? I know he's on his break, but it's urgent. I also need you to call everyone who was here back, thank you."

Inside, I found the living room. The windows were framed with cerulean curtains, the light passing through illuminating the dust in the air. The scent of wine wafting from an open beer can of the oak coffee table. I sank into the cloth sofa and that stood on the rug, moss-like underfoot.

"Seriously, a five-minute break?" It was Smith's voice in the hallway.

"I'm sorry, but it's important. One of your officers is calling the suspects-"

Aine stumbled into the room. "Did you solve it?"

"Yes, we're waiting on the others now."

Relief spread over her face. Silence fell over us like a thick veil; Smith knew better than to ask me anything now, he had to wait for my reveal. "There's Cecil." he said.

Cecil strolled in and leaned against the mantelpiece.

"Well?"

"We're still waiting on Alastrine."

The noise of her bracelets announced her arrival long before anyone saw her. "I can't spend all my time here! I need to find new work since no one will have tarot readings anymore."

"This won't take long Alastrine." I offered her my chair and moved to the centre of the room.

"Although this case appeared at first to be one of the usual newspaper crimes, it developed into something more complex. I arrived at ten o'clock this morning as requested by Detective Inspector Smith. He told me about the psychic fair, an event closely linked to the murder. A broken glass lies at the dead man's feet, a parallel to Alastrine's curse. I found a ripped scrap of five hundred euro note in his hand. Conn was stabbed with an opal-encrusted dagger, a crystal that you are particularly fond of, Miss Scott." She said nothing, avoiding my gaze. "Of all the clues found, the one on my mind most was the lack of blood where he was stabbed."

"A pretty gruesome clue to remember." Smith muttered.

"Gruesome, but helpful. When you were interviewed, Alastrine, you argued over the knife. You will forgive me for saying you were the immediate suspect. You fit the role of murderer perfectly, but several loose ends were left behind, like the scratches on the stairs I noticed after your departure.

"But I didn't kill him – you must believe me!"

"You could have lost your temper and stabbed him, taking the money you had given to him. Suddenly, you were at the top of the suspects. I was in Mildred's when I discovered the truth." I paused, my heart beating faster than it had when I was running. "I see you got a new car, Cecil."

He looked up from the mantelpiece, his eyes wide. "What?"

"A brand-new, 2018 car."

"What has that got to do with anything?"

"It's strange that you could afford that when everyone was disappointed by the fair due to lack of money. Alastrine said Conn had no reason to say those things about her. Maybe his words had a double meaning; when he said we hadn't enough money to waste on the fair, he meant that he knew what you were doing.

"Conn has been blackmailing you for almost as long as you've embezzled the town's money. You bought the opal knife and, using his drinking problem, a bottle of wine. When you visited him last night and sat down to discuss the money, you slipped poison into his glass. After he died, you dragged him upstairs, scratching the foot of the staircase. You took the knife and stabbed him, the fact that he was already dead resulting in the absence of blood. Destroying the evidence in the most arrogant way possible, you smashed his glass, fulfilling Alastrine's curse. You took the money and left without a second thought."

The colour drained from his face as he laughed, harsh and cold. Reality sank in quickly and he bolted for the door. He knew as well as I did that he was the strongest in the room; what he didn't know was that Smith was the fastest. He locked the door and whipped out a pair of handcuffs before he could make an escape.

"You haven't any real proof!"

"Have you got someone to test the glass upstairs?"

"Wilson can check it." He opened the door and shouted to the officer I had spoken to earlier, a wide grin displaying his crooked teeth. "Could you test the glass upstairs for poison?"

He shrugged. "Sure, but it'll take a few minutes."

"Thank you."

I paced the room, my footsteps keeping time with the ticking clock. The silence hummed with anticipation, like being backstage before the beginning of a play. Cecil's shoulders were slumped in defeat, his empty eyes gazing at nothing.

"How did you know?"

"You knew exactly where the bathroom was, suggesting you visit here regularly."

Wilson entered the room, his smile replaced by a grave expression.

"Traces of arsenic poison have been found on the glass in question"

Aine shook my hand. "Thank you."

"You really are a clever young girl." Alastrine said, and for the first time I saw something like kindness in her eyes.

Inspector Smith stood up. "Mr. MacDermot, you are under arrest for the murder of Conn Reilly."

Keep Calm and Carry on

By Joe Reidy, age 14.

"I can make good quiche!" he shouted, his throat cracked from the argument he was having.

"Great, let's see you, then!" his wife said, with more than a trace of sarcasm. She was leaning on the kitchen worktop. "When I first met you, you respected me," she muttered. "Now, I make you quiche and it's not good enough for you? It's a bit too 'rubbery', eh? Let me tell you Fred—"

Fred began slicing tomatoes unevenly with a knife, managing to cut himself in the process. "Where do we keep the plasters?" he asked innocently.

"Third shelf on the right," his wife spat angrily, then turned on her heel and left. She closed the door forcefully, almost, but not quite, a slam.

Fred applied the plaster and looked up to see his dog, Rover the Second, snuffle in. (The less said about Rover the First the better.) Fred cracked eggs into a bowl and beat them. A little unsure what to do next he looked towards his dog, who was making a brave attempt to lick his privates, for advice.

"Must be easy being a dog." Fred muttered. "No worries, not a care in the world."

Rover the Second cocked his head to the side as if contemplating this statement. He woofed happily and got back to his altogether more important task of licking, in an almost smug manner.

"I wonder would she like an omelette?" Fred asked to no one in particular. Rover looked at him critically. "No one asked for your opinion," said Fred.

The dog's withering look of disdain persisted. Fred went to the fridge and bent over to find some cheese. His hand groped around, in the unnatural white light, until he found a worn block of Kilmeaden. He heard

114

a crashing sound behind him. He swivelled around quickly, aghast to see Rover the Second licking the beaten egg from his muzzle, his tail wagging.

Fred let out a string of language that would cause even the coarsest sailor to blush. This lasted for approximately one minute. Following his outburst, Fred surveyed the damage. One broken bowl, his wife's best ceramic. Interestingly, the Coco Pops bowl that they had got for free by buying three boxes of Coco Pops was untouched by canine paws. The beaten egg had spilt all over the floor, and in the middle of it an ecstatic dog was barking excitedly. Said dog was swiftly relegated to the back garden, where a deft kick was aimed at him. (Thankfully for all dog lovers, it missed).

Upon closer inspection, there were no more eggs left in the fridge. At this point a lot of people would give up, but not Fred. He scoured cupboards, the freezer, under the sink, anywhere and everywhere to find eggs. His quest was unsuccessful, but he did find a packet of wine gums, dated 1998 (it was tempting, but he threw them away), two and three-quarter boxes of Coco Pops, never eaten, (the definition of false economy) and a carry bag with the words "Keep Calm and Carry On" on it.

He poured himself a bowl of Coco Pops. Other people at this moment would be chugging some stiff whiskey, but Fred was and always will be Fred. He wondered would his wife accept a bowl of cereal instead of the quiche. He dismissed the idea. He watched the milk turn a light shade of brown. He watched the Coco Pops go soggy and unappetising.

His wife opened the door. "Love," she said, "I was thinking about the argument we just had and well, maybe, I was a little quick to take offence."

Fred said nothing. "Are they Coco Pops?" asked his wife awkwardly.

"Sheila, I'm useless," murmured Fred, "I can't even make a quiche."

He sighed and held his head in his hands. "Useless." He repeated.

"No, you're not, you just don't know how." Sheila said. "I'll teach you."

Fred stood up. They embraced. The carry bag was right. They would just keep calm and……

"Wait," Sheila said, "what happened to Auntie Ethel's bowl? Fred gulped.

"Oh, em … Well, about that …' he faltered.

Soldier Diary

By Anne McSherry, age 15.

23th September 1914

We had a wake-up call at noon, followed by a stale lunch of sauerkraut and tea made from ground raspberry leaves, and then a brief period of time to clean our rifles before daily inspection. Ersatz doesn't stave off the voracious hunger for long, and I can tell, by the ubiquitous frowns on my fellow soldiers' faces, that this is a unanimous opinion. Being a landser means we miss out on the majority of the action behind the scenes, some of the more cynical of us even suggest we refer to ourselves as cannon-fodder, as the terms can be mostly interchangeable.

I'm not quite so jaded yet, but I have to agree that the dull monotony of cleaning the muzzle of my rifle, muttering quiet prayers to myself, and chatting tentatively with some of my more talkative trench mates is growing tedious as the days blend together like coffee. The real kind, not the shitty acorn or bean amalgam that's replaced it nowadays.

Our trench is wide and deep, with strong parapets, embrasures and loop-holed steel plates to cover our riflemen. They're only useful during the day, providing a safe view across the terrain in front of the ditch, but are devoid of their purpose at night, so we have to use sandbags as makeshift steps to look over the top of the trench. My stahlhelm helmet is uncomfortable at the best of times, and restricts my eyesight at the worst. Unfortunately, the fact that it could potentially save my life outweighs its numerous minor faults.

It's bad enough that we have to fight against our fellow man, but another enemy of ours invades our personal territory each night, with little we can do to dissuade them. Lice; the majority of them pale fawn in colour, seemingly having a personal mission to leave blotchy red bite marks over every soldier in our squadron. To combat the lice, bloody troopers of the night who use our bodies as battlefields, each soldier gets a neck pouch full of foul smelling stuff to hopefully deter them.

They lie in the thrummy seams of trousers, in the deep furrows of long thick woolly pants, and almost seem impregnable in their deep entrenchments. Some men have resorted to using a lit candle to burn the monsters off with a satisfying crackle, and I often see splotches of blood staining the clothes of my companions, a triumphant expression donning their features.

One of my troop mates, Jochen Balke, sent a note over to the other side, addressing one of the Tommys in a degrading manner. Language barrier excused, and aside from the fact they clearly only understood 'train station', the intent of his message was clear by the tone of his voice. I say he's tempting fate, riling them up for no good reason. Jochen is one of my least favourite trench mates. He's a sweet-talker for sure, always asking for an extra sausage from the sergeant, but his inane palaver gets on everybody's nerves, especially when sleep has become a rare commodity that few can afford.

With the enemy so close by, we have to have at least four men on watch all the time. Guards are relieved every 2 or 3 hours, but I often get insomnia so sometimes I offer to take an extra hour of watch. The strangely soporific quietude of the night helps to placate my anxious mind and still my jittery hands which can't afford to shake with a rifle in their midst. After rainfall, the particularly sweet and musky smell of petrichor emanates from the soil surrounding us, giving some soldiers a heady fever akin to the effect of drugs. It's actually quite relieving when this happens; the potent aroma covers up the unpalatable stench of smoke, diesel fuel and general organic decay.

Otto

***

19th November 1916

It's one thing to hear tales of war - subjective anecdotes full of vainglory, didactic propaganda and patriotism - and it's another thing to actually experience the Kafkaesque nightmare yourself. Your life outside becomes a blur, because your entire reality is confined to these dingy trenches, your state of being is reduced to knowing that you can die at any given moment. War turns every soldier into a philosopher or an aeolist depending on how you look at it. Everything becomes so much more real, and your memories turn vivid with the life you wish you could go back to.

I wish I could take back all of the time I spent staring out of my window at home, or at my ceiling in my cosy bed, just wondering about the universe in general, and how exactly I could make an impact. The only impact I can think about nowadays is the noise of my body being flung to the ground by the force of a stray bomb or enemy pellet, piercing through my skin in a race against light.

A bullet doesn't discriminate. A gun is neither our ally nor our foe. All land between the trenches is neutral, but even neutrality merely veils the patent peril waiting to catch us unaware; a melancholy desert of restless spirits that stretches out into a vast nothingness between us. How many of them are thinking the exact same thoughts as me? How many of them could have been my friends if we had only been born at a different time, in a different place? I'll never know, and that's one of the things that saddens me the most.

I think one of my main fears is being forgotten. All of my reflections and speculations, the tens of thousands of thoughts I have had every day since I could first elucidate my opinions will be gone in a moment. The vacant feeling of surrender that rumination stirs inside me is ineffable in its compulsion. Even if I escape this abysmal tribulation, my memories made here will make up a significant epoch of my life until the eventual denouement of my narrative. We tend to avoid chthonic talk here in the trenches, for obvious reasons, but my mind can't help but stray even further into the abyss at the darkest times. I've turned into a rather yonderly character, and I'm afraid not even my parents could be able to recognise me now.

I would kill for a hot meal and a decent night's rest. It scares me how much that sentence rings true, and how little weight my conscience holds over my actions, lately. That tiny voice preaching the immorality of my actions has grown as faint and dim as my memories of home. As soon as my family's faces have been renewed inside my mind; the dubiety of my mental state can be put on hold until then. Despite my acceptance of the inevitable estrangement from clemency that all soldiers are forced to go through, the guilt festers in my stomach each night as I go to sleep.

So many nameless faces flash before my eyes, an unholy chorus of a thousand voices chime together and call me a murderer. I try to rationalise my thoughts, they would have killed me too if I hadn't been faster. For every mother, father, brother, sister, wife or girlfriend they have left behind, I am truly sorry for your loss, but I can't regret my actions. I, too, have a family to return to; I have no time for self-doubt. Every second I waste, is just another second that I can die. It's only a matter of what place, what day, what second, and what bullet.

I have a feeling that sleep will evade me once again tonight.

Otto

***

3rd February 1917

Liberty is a lie; an illusion of hope and peace merely constructed to harbour our fears, and bolster our spirits so we can be of use to venture our lives in the name of martyrdom. Three years ago, this would have been a reasonable interior monologue for my quixotic, younger self, but my cynicism has merely increased with every hero lost. I was a braver man, but also reckless and wanting of true exposure. War has fulfilled my need, but left my want longing.

I'm currently on leave, for the first time in over a year, in the middle of a small, sequestered town called Salzberg, near Galizien, where the main bulk of my compatriots are fighting for their lives. Only two of them are with me, but neither are appropriate conversational partners. I had hoped, like the rest of my company, to be able to head back to the Fatherland, but I knew that such an excursion would be unlikely, even for the most decorated of officers. Of course, that didn't stop me from hoping, as is human nature.

Unfortunately, like I had predicted, home was too far a prospect to consider; the expedition itself would have used up half of my days already. And so here I bide, awkwardly sitting by my lonesome, with only a half-drunken Kyselitsa to entertain me. It is of a propitious light for sobriety's sake that my cognizance is still hinged, but this seemly tiding is ironically lamentable at the same time; I hoped to drown in my own asinity, but now

I can do everything but forget. Oh, well, as the saying goes – make haste with leisure. There is no standing on one leg. Hoch die Tassen.

It's two hours later, and I'm still sitting here, but the most unusual thing has just happened. One of my fellow soldiers, the two on leave with me, just came up to me, and addressing me by name, asked me to be best man at his wedding tomorrow. Naturally, I inquired as to why, and he told me that since he doesn't know anyone here, and none of the locals were Galiziendeutsche, he wanted a German-speaking best man. I may not be the maudlin fool I could have been described as in my youth anymore, but I do have a heart. I think he'll excuse my lack of a Smoking.

The wedding was an intimate affair, evidently simple, but the ceremony was so poignantly moving that not an eye was dry the entire evening. Not even mine. And although I truly felt happy for the couple, I had to suppress the unjustified sting of anger I felt at the two of them for being so joyful while so many of our friends were still out there, grappling with guns while he danced with an angel. The groom was clearly head over ears in love, and the bride, decked in an unvarnished, white garment – looking quite ethereal overall – said her vows with such emotion that I had to look away, as I almost felt that I was intruding on a private confession.

As they waltzed, I stewed in the corner, a frown etched onto my face. The bride noticed, and offered me her hand, which I took with some reluctance. She paused for a moment, and then held out her veil. It took me an embarrassing few seconds to understand, and I dropped a few pfennig coins into it. We spun around the room, and I returned to my chair breathless, my pulse racing. I had almost forgotten it was still beating. She gave me a ribbon from her bouquet, as is customary, but since I didn't have a car, I tied it around my wrist instead. I had some drinks with the groom, and then we went our separate ways.

It's later in the night now, and I've been staring at the ribbon she gave me for the past hour. I finally realised the reason for my anger. I was jealous. Jealous that a man who has experienced the exact same things as me, who has gone through the very trials and difficulties I have had to face these past few years, has something so wonderful to come back to. Whereas I have nothing. I have no one. Who am I kidding? I'm not even sure if I'm capable of loving myself, let alone expect anyone else to be willing to love my broken shell of a self. Then again…If such a kind soul existed, maybe my faith in humanity could be restored.

Otto

***

October 18th 1919

I went to the store this morning, and bought some groceries. The shop assistant enquired as to whether I needed any help but I refused, and it felt good. It felt nice to finally be out by myself, free and independent of the constant stream of thoughts and worries that barraged me at home. I saw some kids playing in the park, and they smiled at me tentatively, trying to avoid staring. It gave me a warm feeling in my chest, knowing that it all had been worth it, even for just a single smile.

The feeling dissipated as I arrived back home, and my mother started berating me for going out at all. 'You should have asked one of us to take you,' she told me. I just hid my eyes, as she propelled me towards my room.

Sometimes I hate them. The people who did not experience the war like I did, and even the soldiers who were 'injured' and sent home early. I know it's unwarranted to be piqued at their blind innocence, or ignorance upon asking certain questions. 'What was it like?' with wide eyes. 'How did it feel?' when the bullet ripped through my spinal cord, severing all feeling in both my legs. I couldn't tell them, even if I wanted to. Couldn't describe the hellish pain that jolted my every nerve for a split second – an impossible perpetuity of affliction – or the gravity pounded into my mind after I grasped the true wretchedness of my actuality was yet to come. If I could, they would regret even asking.

My doctors say it's practically a medical miracle in and of itself that I survived at all, let alone can move around to my extent. They couldn't perform a debridement so there were many anxious months after my initial remedy, anticipating any intimation of infection. Of course, I wasn't conscious for this disquiet period, but their shock when I woke up was almost as palatable as my own.

122

No one ever doubts me when I inform them of my service, for most perceivable reasons. They thank me, the same old, diplomatic drivel, and then go merrily on their way, nothing to have been gained by either party from our brief, inoffensive interaction. They have their own worries, mostly financial, if their handsewn flour bag dresses and mended shirts said anything.

The government hasn't been very helpful, and public opinion of them has decreased dramatically ever since they signed Germany's fate in the Hall of Mirrors. Ebert hasn't been able to restrain the apt fury of the people, and has forsaken Berlin in exchange for Weimar, like the feigling he is. Some of my past companions are patrolling the streets with Parabellums and Knarrs, causing chaos and pandemonium wherever they go. I don't particularly want to go around spilling more blood, but the vindictive part of me is satisfied, knowing the officials are having a troublesome time trying to keep them contained.

I was in Haidhausen, Munich two days ago, visiting one of my friends who served with me in the List, when I passed a restaurant called Hofbräukeller in the Wiener Platz. My inceptive impression of it was that of an institution; not particularly aesthetically enthralling with its pale walls and pallid exterior, but I was pleasantly surprised by the inside.

A beer garden, with a generally homey and comfortable ambiance. The place was packed with maybe a little over 100 people, all staring in veneration at a single man, standing alone, and giving a speech. Some of his assemblage glared at me, for making so much noise upon my entrance, but his eyes flickered towards me for a split second, and I froze in place. As soon as they caught sight of the Iron Cross pinned to my left (as a reminder), his mouth twitched up into a half-grin, before he continued on with his oration.

It sounds so strange, now that I think about it, but I thought I recognised those dark, impassioned eyes from somewhere else. Filing that thought away, I occupied the corner of the room, and started listening in. That speaker – he was something else entirely. Voicing each and every one of my concerns, leaving no rock unturned. While not the most articulate, he made his point very clear and I just couldn't help but agree with his ardour and fervency. I felt myself getting inspired for the first time in years.

As I left Munich, I remember looking back on his words and thinking, 'that man is going to make something of himself'. Regretfully, I couldn't manage to learn his name as nobody else in the hall knew either, but I did learn that he was part of a party called the DAP. I've never heard of them before, but maybe I'll check them out, one of these days. If every one of their members is as zealous as the man I saw – I might even think about joining.

Otto

Sources for descriptions of trench warfare: *Diary of a German soldier. Courcy, France 1915*, translated by Robin Schäfer (www.gottmituns.net) and from the first word war diaries of British soldiers George Coppard and Harry Patch (www.spartacus-educational.com/FWWlice.htm).

Openings

By Olivia Lawton, age 15.

Open your mouth wide

And shout out what you believe,

For you have a voice.

Open your mind

Wonder what life could be like

If you love again.

Milk Teeth

By Emma Harris, age 16.

I know what I am, like. The fishwives, they tell fortunes in their husbands' scraps, runtling mackerel grasped in selkie-brown hands, glassy eyes all bulging as it squirms and jerks till a fat, calloused finger digs a nail in and unzips its belly like a coin purse. Out slaps your lot in life, ruby and glistening like a bab, but always that stench of sea water and newly dead things. There's me, lost now to the stale prattle of future lovers and lucky numbers 'cause of what's twined round the innards and half digested crab larvae. Myself incarnate, blunted head and iodine eyes. All stretched out and flat, dull olive with slits of iridescent underbelly, sequins a-yammering until my own ruddy hands and puppy fat start to feel like the imitation. I must've hollered, after they scooped me in a jam jar and shucked my elver skin. Ma's teeth still frosty with the film of it, one flem-wet gulp dooming me to a life of sucking in air.

I know what I am, and what I am is eel-folk.

In the playgrounds, I keep my eyes a lighthouse. Flashing cinemas across faces, wanting for girls like me: snared changelings stuffed in skin that's not their own.

Aislinn. Doubtless.

Aislinn has sea-foam hair. She pulls out her eyebrows and picks at her skin like she wants to unstitch herself. Every day her body builds an altar to our lost lives; her collar bones hold rock pools and she dilutes, puffy cheeks all pale and see through, her body, water thin.

Aislinn's room is deep-sea frizling, windows gawping at the moon. In the middle of her nightstand sit two baby teeth, unhooked and glinting like the upsides of shells. Pearly dead. I suck the air out my mouth and push them in until they cling to my gums like limpets. In the black I spit whispers in her ear, but her teeth slosh the words till I'm speaking in bubbles.

"Theetsch meh…

Theetsch meh…

Theetsch meh…"

Come morning we stand with eyes on each other, her mamo's patio slick beneath our feet, blistering cold. Her arms brim with lace curtains and yellowed doilies. She lets them slump to the ground, where they huddle like ghosts with the spirits sucked out.

"C'mere," she says, "I've to show you something." She clasps my wrist, a wedge of frilled trimming beneath her palm. Her fingerprints press the underside of my arm, sandpaper and prunes, like she forgot herself in a bath. It leaves a red indent, imprinted lace like flowery scales.

"Y'see," she nods, "You've got ghosts on your skin," and chucks me a tablecloth.

We waste no time, primed for it we are, blotching with cold. My night dress tangles round my ankles so as I'm half in myself, half out. Aislinn's body is glassy and long, not like mine with its round belly and little tufts of hair, coarse and yellow as gorse. Wrapping frills tight round each other, merlasses the two of us, with fading scales.

In the fresh air we play at drowning, lungs blue burning, spinning, small mouths gasping, blood purple and round. We slop into her Disney paddling pool. The water is goose pimples against our thighs; we let it settle in our burning chests. Lower your lashes and our skin is the colour of veins.

Where There Are Witches

By Niamh McCann, age 16.

There is a witch in the woods where I live.

Sitting cramped in the back seat of a battered Ford Fiesta, I twiddle my pen and read over the long list of worries I have written on the page in front of me. I'd never had therapy before today, and I'm starting to think my lack of tact at Mya's birthday party has cost me more than a few sympathetic aunts and a box of floral tissues. Maybe if I'd locked the door sooner I might have quenched the flood of fussing relatives and saved myself the anxious enquiries and a slice of cake so big I made myself sick trying to eat it all.

"You 'right back there?" Trish asks, grinning at me in the rear-view mirror.

I manage a shaky smile, which crumbles the minute she looks away. I don't like smiling. It's confusing when people smile. I'm never quite sure what they mean by it. I'm told people smile when they're happy, but I've seen people who smile when there are tears in their eyes, or when they want to tell you a secret without using words, or when they're trying to win the favour of a cute boy. Sally Kinine smiles when I answer a question correctly in class, but she's not happy, because when the teacher turns her back she puts the sharp point of a pencil between my shoulder blades and tells me to stop being such a suck-up.

Trish pulls in just off the main road at a set of wrought iron gates mounted with triangular spikes. She kills the engine and snaps on one broken fog light.

"Right, out, I'll see you next week."

I breathe hot air on the window. As I rub at the grime with my sleeve I notice my fist peeping through the thin wool, criss-crossed with the scars of knife tips, swollen around the knuckles that connected with my bedroom mirror.

"But it's getting dark out."

"As does it every even'."

"And the sun is setting."

"Well noticed, now come on, out."

Her tone leaves no room for discussion, so I gather my belongings, notebook, schoolbag, elastic band, conker shell…

If only she knew, I think, but how could she know, how could anyone know? There is a witch in the woods where I live.

***

The tiny muscles in my forearms strain against the cold metal as I pull myself up and over the gate. Gravel crunches under my feet. The sun, a pale and watery yellow, gleams through tatters of white mist. I reckon I have ten minutes before it sets.

Behind me the Fiesta's engine splutters to life with the biting grate of gears. The light on my back dims as Trish fires the ignition and trundles away.

"Bye, Trish," I mumble, slinging my schoolbag onto my back.

I turn to face the woods.

Silence presses down, and moving through it is like dragging my whole body through tar. Branches sag under the weight of their own foliage and the atmosphere is close and heavy with the smell of decomposing leaves. The twilight nurtures a sense of claustrophobia inside me, even though I know the woods stretch unbroken for many miles.

I become vaguely aware of a throbbing ache down the side of my arm, and of the growing dark splodge staining my cardigan, crimson on white, like the skin and flesh of a ripe apple. I grit my teeth and loosen the strap over that shoulder. One of my scabs must have split open when I climbed the gate. I had hoped that one would heal over and wouldn't scar. At least it's discreetly placed, I think. Then again, they all are.

An icy breeze hisses through the grass and the cold nibbles at my toes. Here the trees are tightly knit, a single strand in an intricate web. Wet soil squelches under my feet releasing a heady fog, sickly white, with the milky texture of a blind man's eye. I knew a blind man, once. He could see everything, except the witch. She blinded him. That man was my father.

I stop.

On the branch beside me is the raven. Bristling with talons like razors and eyes like hot coals, his gaze is steady, burning into me, stripping away the layers of skin and sinew right down to my core.

His head tilts. Impatience.

Then he jumps. His claws sink into me, straight into my bleeding shoulder.

Shock forces a cry from me. The pain is strange, like acid, spreading down my arm until I am numb. A cold sweat breaks across my temple. I can't move my arm.

Fear clenches like a fist around my neck, choking me of breath.

Then he bites me. Blood gushes from my brow, dribbling thick and sticky into my eye. His beak is in my ear. I turn my head, mouth open, desperate. There is a loud crunch.

His guttural cry is like a dentist's drill. The taste of sour, inky feathers is on my tongue as I scramble up the dirt track, spitting and trembling, my bag banging against my back, trying not to vomit. Branches materialise out of the grey haze, slashing my face even more.

My body shudders and my stomach lurches. I swallow a mouthful of sick with difficulty, sinking to my knees. I cannot hear the bird. I hope his wing is damaged. I hate that I hope that, but the metallic taste of blood on my lips reminds me of what I hate even more.

Scars that show.

Crouched in the muddy undergrowth, I string my fingers through my hair and inhale deeply the rich earthiness of the woods. There is something comforting about being this close to the ground, it steadies me. The sudden relief is nearly as painful as the raven's claws and I'm consumed by the desire to curl up and lie here in the darkness, in the safety of mother earth's embrace, forever.

I walk this path every day. Why do I walk this same path every, single, day?

In the quiet recesses of my mind I begin to understand.

Under the black shroud of night, I lose myself to dreams, living nightmares that gorge on my energy and fester on the border between reality and make-believe. Why must I wait for the raven to come? To hurt me? Do I enjoy being hurt? No, I don't. But pain is subjective. A paper cut on the thumb can be just as distracting as a twisted ankle. This is my paper cut. This is my distraction. This is not my problem.

Slowly I peel my fingers away from my face. My clothes are plastered to my sides, the contents of my bag are spilled and my shoulder is releasing a steady trickle of blood. But my forehead is not bleeding. My hands are relatively clean. The taste of raven feathers is gone.

The dream is gone.

But there is still a witch in the woods where I live.

My scars are real, my pain is real. She is real.

And now I'm going to face her.

***

Her home is an old white-washed cabin, rounded at the edges and cut into segments like a large pumpkin.

My heart flutters against my ribcage as I knock on the door. I was never given a key. She doesn't trust me to carry one around. It also means that I'm totally reliant on her goodwill to let me in.

I can see her shadow flit around the kitchen, the dark outline of her hand that selects a knife from the rack, hacks the heads off vegetables and tosses them into a steaming cauldron of soup.

The distance between us smells of fire and thunder.

I knock again.

I see her pause, considering, tightening the string on her apron and adjusting her grip on the knife. A shudder runs through me and hot blood races to the scars on my shoulder, my back.

But it falls from her hand onto the table with a dull metallic clatter. Her shadow leaves the kitchen.

I arrange my feet into a wider stance and force my spine to straighten.

The lock snicks, the handle bends, the door squeals on its hinges.

And then she stands before me, all six foot of her.

The witch in the woods where I live.

"Yes?" my stepmother says.

"The raven is dead." The words tumble out of me so fast I barely hear them.

She sighs, softly, delicately, leaning against the doorframe with her arms folded across her chest. If I didn't know her better I'd think she was bored. But her eyes are hungry; she looks ready to devour me.

"You're mumbling."

The sight of her almost breaks me. Almost.

Instead, I smile. The biggest, sweetest, sickliest smile I can manage. If the wing I had bitten was real, I might even have blood on my teeth.

"The raven is dead." I say, and push past her into my house.

There was a witch in the woods where I lived.

Rusty Doors

By Sam Enright, age 16.

Oft does the flow of life spawn many doors;

many lives we could have lived but ignored,

of songs that could have their melodies sung

or lovers who could have their hearts' won.

God's hand brought to life the arrow of time,

damning these doors to wither as clocks chime.

Their edges will degrade and frames will rust

while through panes fate shall taunt with lust

When entry through these doors becomes barred,

upon the hour that broken dreams' embers char,

when waves' ebb and flow land us on life's shores,

we ought live at peace, alongside our rusty doors.

The Wishing Well

By Helena Brady, age 16.

Mummy says the Wishing Well is magic. That it makes all your wishes come true, no matter what they are. I believe her. The Wishing Well is magic. She says the fairies that live there hear your wish, and when you throw money in they collect it and grant you your wish. I've never seen the fairies that live there, but the Wishing Well is so deep and dark that I can't even see the bottom. They must live really far down.

Last time I was here, I wished that Barney would come home. And he did! An old lady from down the road found him in a bush. His collar had gotten caught on the bush, and he was stuck. Then she found him, and brought him home! Mummy had hugged the old lady, and Barney wagged his tail so fast I thought it might come off!

Another time, I wished for some money so I could buy another doll to play with. Then, on the way home I found five euro in the grass. Daddy had laughed, and taken me home to get the rest of my money. He brought me to the toy shop and I was able to buy another doll.

And another time, I wished for it to snow. It was the start of the summer holidays, and I was too hot so I wanted it to snow so I could cool down. And it started snowing! Barney loved the snow, and I did too. It was nice and cold, but it stopped after a while. Mummy says it was magic. Daddy did too.

Whenever we go to the Wishing Well, Mummy brings a picnic. We have sandwiches and cakes and drinks and some fruit. I can't have some cake unless I eat one piece of fruit and all my sandwiches. It's fun at the Wishing Well, Barney comes with us and he brings his favourite yellow ball, and I throw it for him. Daddy comes when he isn't working. I like it when Daddy comes, because he gives me money to throw into the Wishing Well. Mummy never gives me any.

I'm not supposed to be at the Wishing Well by myself. Mummy says it's too dangerous, that I might fall into the well. But I'm not on my own.

Barney is with me, and my doll, Susie. I'm not on my own, and I will be careful. I won't fall in.

It's cold, and the wind is really strong. The clouds are dark, so I think it might rain soon. It's not bright, but it's nearly two o'clock. The dark clouds are covering the sun, so everywhere is cold and dim. That's how Daddy says it. It doesn't feel... right. But I need to make my wish, so I have to stay. But I should have brought a coat. I thought about taking my bright red coat when I was leaving, but it was up really high on the coat hanger and I couldn't reach it. I only have my scarf and my pink rain boots. It is really cold. But I have to stay and make my wish.

Barney is walking around, smelling the ground. He starts digging into the ground, and I laugh. His tail is wagging really fast again, like when the old lady brought him home. Susie is cold too, and I hug her tighter to try to keep her warm. I should have put her coat on too. But the coat is really ugly and feels weird, and I like her in her pink dress.

The money is in my hand. I took it out of Mummy's purse. I know I shouldn't have, but I need to make a wish. And Daddy wouldn't give me money, or take me here. So when they were downstairs, I took the money and put Mummy's purse back where I found it. It wasn't much. It is only a small brown coin, five cent I think.

I walk up to the edge of the well, and Barney starts barking. I look at him and he runs off into the bushes, probably chasing rabbits. He always does that. But he never catches them. I wish he would, so then I could have a pet rabbit. Jessica from school has two rabbits, and they are really soft and fluffy. Next time I come here I'll wish for a pet rabbit!

I look down into the well, and the water is dark and disgusting. I can't see the bottom. I take Susie and sit her on the grey bricks that go around the well. The bricks are really dusty and dirty, so I hope Susie doesn't mind. I can get Mummy to wash her dress when I get home.

My hands are cold and hard to move. I hold the coin tighter and hold my hand out over the black hole of the well. I close my eyes, and think about my wish.

I wish Mummy and Daddy would stop fighting. I wish they would stop shouting at each other. I wish they would be friends again. I wish we could all be happy again.

"I wish it would all stop." I whisper, and I open my fingers and the coin drops into the well. I open my eyes when I hear the plop as the coin hits the water, and I lean over the wall to look at the little waves in the water. I just watch the water for a while, until the waves have disappeared. Barney still hasn't come back, but I can hear him barking and running through the bushes, so I know he is okay.

When I get home, will Mummy and Daddy be friends again? I hope so. I hope they stop fighting and shouting at each other. Because they used to be friends, so I hope they can be friends again. And I know the Wishing Well is magic, so my wish will come true.

I hope.

Time to go home now and see if my wish came true. I try to turn around, but I am stuck. I can't move. Maybe I am frozen here. It is so cold, and my fingers are nearly blue. What if I freeze and become a snowman? There is a bubble stuck in my throat. I don't want to freeze here. It's too cold, I want to go home. I want to go home!

"Barney!" I shout, but it hurts to talk. My lips are cold. I still can't move. Please, please, let me move! I want to go home! There are tears in my eyes, and I try to shout for Barney again. He doesn't come.

I want to go home! I want to go home! Please!

The wall starts to shake, and I can't get off it. I start to cry. Please, I don't want to be frozen! I just want to go home!

Susie falls off the wall and onto the ground beside my feet. Her dress is dirty. She looks all fuzzy. My eyes are blurry, and I can't see properly.

Please...

I want to go home!

I shouldn't have come here.

I'm sorry.

Then the wall breaks, and I start falling into the black hole. I scream, and try to grab onto something. But the wall fell in with me and there is nothing to grab onto.

I make a loud splash as I hit the dark and dirty water. Everything goes much colder, and I freeze again. I try to breathe but the water fills my mouth and it hurts. I can't move. Everything is so cold that I can't even feel it anymore.

No. No, I have to get out! I have to get out!

I try to move my arms, but it's hard because I can't feel them anymore. All I can feel is the pain in my chest. I have to swim up. I have to swim up and get out! Swim like Daddy showed me. I try to kick my legs, but I don't know how to move them anymore. I can't do anything anymore.

Everything is dark here. I can't see. I can't look up. I start to cry again, but the water keeps coming in my mouth, and I can't breathe. I can't breathe! It feels like fire in my chest and my neck. I have to get out! Please, please, let me out!

There are little lights in the water, floating around me. They are blurry. There is water in my eyes. They float around me, almost like they are dancing. Are these the fairies that live in the Wishing Well? Why are they here? Why won't they help me? I open my mouth to ask for help, but I swallow a lot of water, and the fire gets worse in my chest. It's really sore! I don't know what to do! Help, please!

"This is what you wished for, is it not?" I hear a whisper in my ears. I can't look around to see who it is. The lights are getting brighter, and swimming faster around me. I can't do anything. I think something bad is happening... I think I'm dying.

I don't want to die! I don't want to die like Nanny did!

"You wanted it all to stop, did you not?" The voice whispers again. What is going on? I can't feel the pain anymore. I just feel really tired. But I don't want to go to sleep. I want to get out, and go home, and hug

Mummy and Daddy! I want to see Barney wag his tail really fast again, and get Susie a new pink dress!

"Help." I try to say to the voice, but I can't. I am full of water, but it doesn't hurt anymore. Everything is going fuzzy. No, I don't want this to happen! Please! Help!

Help me!

The lights slowly get darker, until they are gone completely. Only one is left, and it swims up to my face. It's hard to keep my eyes open.

"We'll take care of you, don't worry little one." The voice whispers to me again, but it is hard to hear it. The whisper is really quiet. Everything is really quiet. I am too tired to try and get out anymore.

The light is going darker.

No...

Please...

Help...

And everything goes black.

And I am nothing.

Ethel Creek

By Megan Maguire Bruce, age 17.

Home was a rickety thatched cottage perched atop a decrepit farm, which lay on the outskirts of a small town called Ethel. Willow and red oak surrounded our few acres, and a pond played host to the frogs that stayed loyal to the south field year after year. Everything wooden shrank and swelled in the rain and the house seemed to groan whenever the wind decided to dance through the cracking outer walls. Despite all the building's shortcomings, I loved it dearly. I loved the seemingly permanent scent of cinnamon and nutmeg in the pantry and the way golden light filtered through the window shutters every morning. I loved the animals and their noisy chorus of 'hello' any time I entered the barn. But out of everything from my childhood, I recall loving my older brother Jem the most.

One of the most vivid memories from my youth occurred during my fifth summer. I awoke to gentle June air tickling my nose and the sounds of Jem polishing his boots out in the hallway. Sunlight trickled in through the open window accompanied by sweet birdsong. I stumbled from my bed to the hallway barefoot and yawning and met Jem, still vigorously scrubbing his boots. Black polish discoloured his hands which were covered in hard earned scars. In the three years since my father's passing, I hadn't seen him in any other footwear. I'm still not entirely sure if it was through necessity or love.

After deciding the boots were adequate, he followed me into the kitchen. Mother was busy with breakfast and the eggs for the market. She counted them, quickly turned to the stove and stirred two steaming pots at the same time, then returned to counting; her faded blue apron barely keeping up with her. Noticing my presence she handed me a bowl of porridge with a smile, knowing it to be my favourite. Our mother was strange. Her personality was like a slap followed by a hug. To this day I have still not cracked this changeable force of nature. In those years I was often swept up in the irrational and fanatical then suddenly gentle ways of our mother. Jem loved her as much as she would allow, but her love for him nearly always seemed to manifest itself in criticism and demands. In hindsight, maybe she became that way only after my father died, but I was too young to remember or notice a difference.

"Jem, you ready to milk them cows yet?" Her voice quick, unable to disguise how her words were a demand not a question. With an obedient nod he was out the door and into the slowly building heat of the day, eyes crinkled against the sun. As I sat, savouring the sweet porridge, quiet tunes filled the kitchen. Perched in the corner was a dusty wireless which was turning out tune after tune. It had been a present from my father's brother, Floyd. He had stepped in after my mother's bitter realisation that a single mother and a fifteen-year-old weren't fit to keep our farm going.

When I had finished breakfast, I strolled to the cattle shed counting the steps. Twenty-three, same as always. I leaned against the rusting gate waiting for Jem under the watchful gaze of the midmorning sun. Lying on a hay bale by the barn door was a worn notebook. I could not yet read, but I eagerly scrambled up onto the bale and grabbed my brother's notebook and began flipping through the pages.

Quickly scrawled text covered every page with the most exquisite drawings my five-year-old eyes had ever seen. I was in total awe of his marvellous sketches, mostly of people, and although I did not possess the skills to understand it, I was also in awe of his writing. I only understood the full extent of his talent through the reaction his writing had gotten from Ms Dale, the local school teacher. She had tried, in vain, to stop Jem from dropping out of school when he was twelve. I don't think he wanted to leave at all, but there wasn't much choice when the farm had needed the extra pair of hands. He'd told her resolutely his family had to come first. She wasn't the only one to notice that he didn't belong on the farm. Even as a naïve five-year-old I could see that he was meant to work with words, not crops. His ideas needed an outlet, but the farm, and my mother, only served to suffocate him. She just didn't understand, and my dear sweet brother was too loyal to her to ever break free of the chains she had unknowingly tightened around him.

"Hey, Daisy, what you got there?" I gave a small squeal and dropped the book, but he just gave me a knowing look. Fortunately he turned his attention to the glistening bottle of lemonade Mother had sent me with.

"For the walk." I told him, "You ready?"

He popped into the shed for a second and reappeared with a bundle of keys.

"Ready."

With that we began down the dusty path towards Ethel Creek.

The sun beat down as we made our way through the fields. The smell of cut grass mingled with the air. Jem was always good to me; he treated me like an equal, not the over-eager little sister I'm sure I must have been. That boy must have had the patience of a saint. We crossed a fence and the nearby sheep scattered in all directions, sending loose earth flying into the air. By the time we reached the end of the field we could see the creek just beyond Fletcher's land. Fletcher was a strange, heavyset man and I can scarcely recall much more about him than his constant sour mood. His dog shared the same unfortunate temperament and the yappy beast terrified me well into my teen years.

When we reached the creek after what felt like hours, we sat under the forgiving shade of a towering oak. With sweat clinging to us we quickly drained the lemonade bottle and reclined against the cool trunk. A gentle breeze played with our hair and sunlight found its way between the tree's foliage as it swayed slightly in the wind. The day was lazy and content.

I quickly became restless, as young children tend to, and left Jem behind and wandered over to the creek's edge. A rusty tangle of wire that apparently passed for a fence surrounded the banks. That water was higher and faster than normal, still aided by the previous months surprise downpours. Cardinal flowers had sprung up just on the other side of the fence and I was mesmerized by the way the red petals danced with the wind. I decided mother must have one for the kitchen table and determinedly I squirmed my way through a gap in the fence and happily began picking only the very prettiest of the wildflowers. Jem, who had been resting against the oak, opened his eyes and was horrified to see me on the bank.

His yells to get off the bank fell on deaf ears as I continued harvesting the precious plants. He scrambled over the river edge and began pleading with me.

"Daisy, it's not safe! Please come back here, you have enough flo-"

"Jem, I'm fine!" I exclaimed, "I'm just picking some for Mother—", but before I could finish, the earth beneath me suddenly gave way and I was sent tumbling towards the river. I landed just short of the currents in a mess of mud and roots. Shocked, I looked to Jem and found the same terror painted on his face.

"Oh, Jesus, just stay right there. I'm gonna get you out, okay?" He scrambled for something I could grab onto. "Just … Just don't move".

He found a sturdy branch and lowered it down to me, but it didn't quite reach the full six feet I had fallen. Shaking I tried to get a better footing, but I just kept sinking further and further down the bank, up to my ankles in muck. He frantically tried to navigate the edge of the bank, being careful not to fall in himself. He realised it would never reach down far enough if he didn't jump the tangled fence, and desperately leaped over it. He let out a small grunt when his leg caught on a rusted nail protruding through the rotting wood, but wasn't distracted from lowering down the branch. I could just about reach the bottom of the branch and clung on for dear life. He grunted again as he heaved and there was an audible 'squelch' as my feet left the grip of the mud. With one final pull he dragged me up onto the crumbling bank and wasted no time in picking me up and throwing me over the fence to safety.

But just as I began to let myself breathe once more the bank groaned; it was not letting us go that easily. The ground began to crumble beneath Jem's feet this time. Before he could jump the fence he was thrown down onto the very edge of the rushing river, clusters of fence falling with him. Then a deafening crack. I ran as close to the formidable edge as I dared and my stomach churned when I spotted him. Crumpled in between wire and wood he was panting for breath. Tears flooded my eyes as I called out for him. He shakily tried to rise to his knees, but his arm had gotten tangled in the fence.

"D-Daisy, across the road there's a house. The Andrews. Get help!"

His words were shaky and breathy. I responded with a frantic nod as my lip started to tremble. Just as I turned there was another sickening crack. I looked back at Jem. He had jerked his hand out and was cradling his mangled wrist in front of him. I only saw the beginning of the blood before I was bolting across the field. Jem's wails of agony cut through the air like a knife.

I don't remember much of the rest of that day I was in such a daze. I do remember the Andrews boys pulling Jem out as their father got the pickup ready, and how astounded the physician was by the extent of the break. Not in his thirty years of experience had he seen a wrist so thoroughly broken. Most importantly I remember how for the first time my mother returned the love my brother had shown her for years. Well, she showed it in her own way; through worry and holding onto his other hand with an iron grip. The doctor told us it would take at least four months to heal. It felt like an eternity.

But we didn't have to look far for the silver lining; Jem had broken his left wrist. So for the first time my brother was able to write as much as he liked while he recuperated. He would joke with me that it was all an elaborate scheme so he could do just that. I don't think the pen left his hand for that entire four months. Eventually even my infamously stubborn mother couldn't deny how talented he was. She had reluctantly hired a farmhand to replace him and to her surprise found the farm actually doing better. The chains around Jem were slowly releasing and eventually I was standing by the kitchen door, warmly waving him goodbye, tears lining my cheeks, as he left for more schooling. And miraculously, my mother was standing with me.

Black Mirror

By Aoife Dudgeon, age 17.

Like, subscribe and comment down below,

All the ways in which life has changed.

Next time you're taking a selfie to post on Snapchat,

Take a moment to look at the reflection of the person in the blank screen.

A black mirror into our souls.

The person struggling with depression doesn't care about views,

Struggling to view their own future as anything but darkness.

The person fighting an eating disorder doesn't care about likes,

Fighting to like themselves.

The person dealing with anxiety doesn't care about followers,

Dealing with being followed constantly by stress and fear.

The person trying to cope with bipolar disorder doesn't care about figuring out what's trending,

Trying to figure out what emotion is trending inside their own mind.

The person battling schizophrenia doesn't care about comments,

Battling to turn off the constant commentary in their head.

Turn off your screens and look beyond the surface,

But that's not going to happen.

Is it?

Let's choose to like meaningless posts rather than like each other.

Let's choose to tweet about anything, something irrelevant, rather than talking about how we feel.

Let's choose to leave a comment on someone's Instagram rather than asking them how they're doing.

Let's choose to focus on how many friends we have on Facebook rather than the ones right in front of us.

Let's choose to live trapped in a black mirror rather than live the life right behind it.

Right?

The Necklace

By Cian Mcgrath, age 17.

"I'm leaving," she said, and she meant it this time. She stood by the door, suitcase in hand, a bag on her back. She wasn't threatening anything; this was the end, simple as that.

He knew what she'd do if he said anything. She'd say that she'd said all this before, that he should have known it was coming. And she was right; he saw that now. She'd tell him that he was a bad husband, a bad person, maybe. No, maybe not that far. She'd say that he neglected her, that he hadn't paid any attention to her needs. She'd say that there was once a chance, so many times when he could have made things work if he had just tried. But he hadn't, and now here they both were.

He didn't want to argue with her. She was only waiting for him to say something, was adding the final touches to the monologue she'd been preparing for weeks, maybe months. But he couldn't be sure. All these years, and he felt like he would never understand how her mind worked. Maybe she thought the same thing when she looked at him, but he didn't think so. He would say something in a few seconds, but for now he stayed silent. Time was playing out slowly. He felt a rush of blood go to his head and overwhelm his senses. He wanted to lie down, to do anything but try and convince her to stay.

His eyes darted around the room, zigzagging frantically from pieces to furniture to the paintings on the walls to the colour of the blinds to her face, until his eyes landed on the necklace, and everything really did go silent, in that moment; that's what it felt like, anyway.

He bought it for her nearly five years ago. It was night time, and they'd been walking through the city centre when he said they should stop. They'd gone out for an expensive dinner earlier that evening – a rarity in those days – and he felt good about himself for taking her out. Expensive meals were a sacrifice back then. He usually thought of them as a waste of money, but tonight was different. Maybe he was living in the afterglow of that moment, or maybe it was something else, but before he could even see that it was a jewellery store he felt like telling her to stop walking, and it was that same inner voice that told him to go inside and buy something, anything, for her.

They both stopped and went inside. They'd both been looking around for a few minutes, without any intention of buying anything – their income wouldn't allow it – when he saw that she'd stopped walking around, and that she was looking at a particular row of jewellery. When he came up to her he saw her eyes were fixed on the necklace.

"You want it?" he asked.

"It's beautiful," she said.

It really was. He could see why it held her eye; there was something about it, a glow, a touch of beauty that seemed to resonate within him. He normally looked at these things with indifference – to him they were all indistinguishable from one another – but this was different. It was almost magnetic; when he let his eyes glance over everything else he was drawn back to it every time.

It probably would've been better if he'd bought it a few weeks after that, when she'd forgotten about it. He remembered being so scared when he bought it – it was the first large expense he'd ever gone through with. He still thought the price was ridiculous, and at the time it had been a financial pitfall. That was when they were both poor and in love and nothing else seemed to matter. He could put up with a lot more then, and so could she.

He could remember the expression on her face like it was yesterday. It reassured him about a lot of things, more than she could have known. She didn't wear it on the subway home – she said she wanted to put it on with just him there. They went back to their tiny, cramped apartment, where the water and electricity usually went off, without warning. They moved the small table they had their meals on, and he put the two chairs in the bedroom. He helped her put on the necklace, and then, since they didn't have a mirror anymore, she looked at it through the distorted lens of an empty jam jar.

"You sure you like it?" he asked.

"It's beautiful," she said. "It looks a little strange."

He saw himself through the jar, and almost smiled at how distorted he looked.

"I look insane," he remembered saying, and she smiled, but she didn't say anything back. She just kept on looking at the necklace and touching it lightly, brushing it with the tips of her fingers, like she was afraid it would break. She didn't notice it, she was somewhere else, but after a while a slow smile crept onto her face.

They had a mirror, but he'd broken it the night before. It'd been after a pretty bad argument, in which they both said they didn't ever want to see each other again and that their relationship was doomed to fail from the very beginning. She told him to start packing and was grabbing his things and throwing them on the floor when he said he never loved her. He didn't think she'd react the way she did; he didn't know what he'd been thinking, he'd just said it, that's all. She let his shirts and boxers drop from her hands and looked like all the life had been drained from her.

"I'm sorry," he said, but she was silent. Her eyes were glassy as she looked off somewhere else, but he knew she heard him.

Then he went into the bathroom. He put the seat cover down and sat on the toilet seat and listened out for anything, but she made no noise. She hadn't left; that was something. He sat very still for such a long time that he thought it was too late to solve things; that he might as well live here forever than go back out there. He thought if he left this room then she would leave before he even got close to her. So he just looked up at the ceiling and counted all the tiles and pretended he wasn't listening out for any noise she might make.

There was still no noise from outside the bathroom. Nothing that he could hear, anyway. He looked at himself in the mirror and hated what he saw; that was why he broke it. He didn't stop to think, he just did it, and then his hand was cut and bleeding and the mirror had shattered. Shards of glass were sitting in the sink, and he saw his face in them as he washed his hands. But he was too tired to be angry.

"Are you okay?" she asked after a while. He was leaning against the wall opposite the sink, holding up his cut hand so it wouldn't touch off anything. The tap was still on, but he didn't have the effort to turn it off. He felt useless. He wanted to go to sleep and forget they'd ever argued.

He realised too late he never locked the door. She came in and switched off the tap, and only then did she notice his hand.

"Oh god," she said.

"It's fine," he said.

"No, it's not," she said. "Let me look at it, at least."

He showed her. She touched it gently, turned it over.

"Don't grab it," he said.

"I won't," she said. "Where are the tweezers?"

"Below the sink."

He stood back and she bent down to look for them. He looked on as she searched through the cabinet. When she came over to him with the tweezers he held out his hand.

"I'm sorry," he said."

"I'm sorry too," she said.

He hardly slept that night. He kept turning it over in his head; everything they'd said, everything they hadn't. He didn't have to look at her to know she was awake. He could feel her warmth from the other side of the bed, and he moved closer to her. The lights were off. Neither of them moved. His mouth was dry, and he told himself any minute now he'd get up and get something to drink. But he just lay there.

"Hey," he said.

She moved closer to him, but she didn't open her eyes. He put his arm around her and she let him, manoeuvring her body so they could both sleep like that.

"I love you," he said.

"I love you too," she said.

He wanted to say so much more. He wanted to tell her what she meant to him. But he was tired; he could hardly keep his eyes open. He'd make it up to her tomorrow, he told himself. There was still time, they were okay. He'd take her for a meal out, somewhere nice. Somewhere he knew she liked.

He was thinking about what restaurant they could go to when he fell asleep.

"Are you going to say anything?"

"What do you want me to say?"

She looked at the ground, and sighed.

"I don't know," she said. She sounded tired.

She looked back up at him, and this time it was his turn to look at the ground, at her feet.

"I love you," he said.

But the words were so hollow and hopeless it was like he wasn't even saying them. She didn't respond, only looked at him and then around the room.

"Do you love me back?"

"I don't know," she said.

He just wanted to sleep. He just wanted to bury his head in the sand and pretend it never happened. He couldn't even look her in the eyes; he only got as far as the necklace, he couldn't go any further.

"The necklace," he said. "Do you remember?"

"Yeah, I do," she said.

"The look on your face when you tried it on."

"I loved it."

"You started dancing. You started dancing in the apartment, and then the neighbours from downstairs came up to our door and said they'd have us kicked out. Then we opened that champagne bottle your parents bought us, the one we'd been saving, and we both started dancing. What was the name of the song?"

"I can't remember," she said.

"I can't either. It was beautiful, though, whatever it was."

"Look at me," she said. He did, but he already knew she'd have tears in her eyes.

"You were so excited, it's like you were a kid again. You had that red dress on, the one you only wore on special occasions. God, you were so beautiful." He stopped looking at her. He was looking way off, into the distance, and he could still picture that red dress and her face as she looked at him so tenderly.

"Frank," she said.

"And the way you looked at me. The love in your eyes. The love in both our eyes. Do you remember that?"

"Yes," she said, but she was so quiet he barely heard her. "Yes, I remember."

He'd just gotten inside when he saw the note. He was a little drunk, but he understood it well enough. It was short, simple; she'd come back for her clothes, the ones she hadn't had enough room to pack the first time around. He nodded, like she was there, talking to him. He realised he needed a drink, and he looked in the fridge, but there wasn't anything left. His feet swayed, and he fell back against the door. He stood up, and was about to go out again when he saw it, sitting on the kitchen counter.

The necklace, sparkling and bright, like an old memory long forgotten.

Giving and Receiving

By Annie O'Neill, age 17.

she handed him

her heart,

took the key

from the chain

around her neck

and simply

gave it to him.

she put her soul

in a pretty box,

tied it in a bow,

and watched as

he wrapped it,

smiling.

she handed him

her secrets

on a silver platter,

served with hot stew

she cooked herself.

she polished the cutlery

for him

to dive in to.

she tied her hopes

and dreams

to the string of a

balloon, floated it

to him.

and he untied

all her wishes

with careful fingers.

she gave

all she is

to him.

and he

cherished her,

loved her,

kept his promises

and minded her heart.

he tended to her

soul, her heart, her being,

like it was

the most beautiful

of flower gardens,

the softest

of melodies,

the most precious

of gems.

and to him,

she was.

Easter Gone Egg Shaped

By Stephanie Keane, age 16.

"I found another one!" I called back to my egg-hunting team with glee evident in my voice as I had the blue, shiny, foil-wrapped egg in my hands. It was a bright Easter Sunday morning with the sun shining down as we searched for eggs hidden around the fields making the nearby seawater glisten. I skipped happily along, my eyes peeled for eggs; ready to narrow in on the first glimpse of the trademark shiny foil that was hidden in the long grass and in the many hedges and trees that dotted the fields. I felt myself trip as my body fell downwards. I tumbled head-first into a hole. My hands flew around me, searching the walls for a grip to halt my descent. Failing to find anything that I could use to steady myself, I had no choice but to let my body fall, for what felt like forever.

I hit the ground with a heavy thud. I looked around and saw a large, dull cavern. The cavern had nothing to make the brown muddy walls look interesting, or different to each other. The entire situation was incredibly bizarre, and reminded me of the classic tale of my childhood Alice's Adventures in Wonderland by Lewis Carroll. It took all of my self-control to stop myself from calling out to the Mad Hatter and the Cheshire Cat. I spotted a small corridor leading off of the cavern and decided to follow it, my curiosity getting the better of me.

I stopped dead in my tracks. I blinked. I pinched my arm. I tried to trick myself into believing that I was having a nightmare. I was, eventually, forced to accept reality – my childhood hero, Egbert, the Easter Bunny, was dead. I ran over. The body was limp, lifeless and already cold. His blood was gathered in a pool around his body, with a gash in his neck still pumping blood out of his jugular vein.

Egbert was holding what appeared to have been an Easter egg, ready to be put into the world above for the local neighbourhood children to find during their hunts, just like my own team's collection of eggs. There were several slashes in the bunny's clothing, as a result of what appeared to be knife wounds. I felt my hand go up to my mouth as I muffled what would have otherwise been a blood-curdling scream. My body started to shake. A tear escaped my eye, as my childhood innocence was instantly lost, and my memories of Easter destroyed.

Out of the corner of my eye, I saw another one of my childhood favourites, Jack Frost, walk up to me in a detective's uniform. He wore a charcoal grey suit, with a gold, star-shaped badge pinned to his chest-pocket. He introduced himself as the lead detective in the town of Spring Valley and proceeded to ask me questions about the tragic scene that lay in front of us. I gave a detailed account of the day's events, and when he heard of my tumble, he rushed over to a hidden lever on the side of a wall and used it to pull a hatch across the hole I fell through. Based on my statement, Detective Frost informed me that Egbert was likely killed as he was on his way to deliver the egg to the children above, as I had suspected. He told me that the other detective of the town was out sick and as an eye-witness he would appreciate my assistance on the case. I happily accepted his offer and asked about any friends and family of Egbert's around the town.

Once the crime scene clean-up crew arrived, Detective Frost and I set off toward the main streets of Spring Valley. The town's residents gave me curious looks as the Detective lead me through the streets towards Egbert's house. As we walked, I soaked in all the wonders the town held. After leaving the cavern, it was no longer obvious I was underground, as the sophisticated structures and vibrant colours were not what one would expect of an underground civilisation. Spring Valley was full of life, people rushing to get where they needed to go, with an urgency that would rival central London during rush hour.

As we approached the residential area that Egbert lived in, Detective Frost pointed out Egbert's house to me. It was painted a bright blue colour, with flowers on the window ledges and an Easter-themed garden, with a basket of colourful mini eggs sitting by the door. I refocused on the case at hand and started examining the door for signs of a break-in. Once it became clear that Egbert's attacker had not broken into his house in an attempt to find him, we entered the house to look for information on any possible enemies he had. Egbert had framed pictures of him with various family members that I made a mental note to speak with, and one photo of him with a young woman. Both of them had smiles wide as could be and Egbert had an arm wrapped around the woman. I called the Detective over and asked who it was. He told me that that the young woman was

Holly Claus, daughter of Mr and Mrs Claus. She was Egbert's girlfriend of three years and they were known to be the sweetest couple in all of Spring Valley. Detective Frost recommended that we go find her if we wanted to know more about Egbert's life.

We set off an hour later, after we had finished examining Egbert's house for any other information. We went to Holly's house to break the news of Egbert's death. She broke down into tears as Frost consoled her before gently leading her into questions that he needed to ask her. He asked if she knew of anyone that held a grudge against Egbert. She was convinced that he didn't have any enemies, but to go speak to his best friend, Sandman. She told us that if there were any unsettled disputes, he would be the one to know, as his gentle presence often calmed Egbert. Sandman often acted as the town's judge and mediator due to his reputation of a being a calm and serene influence. Holly also recommended that we question Hopper, Egbert's younger brother. She told us that Hopper had always been left in the shadow of his big brother and that she always felt a strong rivalry between the two brothers when they were in the same room for too long. As part of the process, we also asked if she had an alibi for the morning. Holly told us that she was in her house all morning, and that her parents, who had left in order to give the three of us some privacy, could confirm this statement.

With our new information, Detective Frost and I headed off towards Sandman's house, ready to pose our questions once again. As I knock on Sandman's front door, I turn around to see Frost shifting from one foot to another, looking extremely uncomfortable all of a sudden. As the door opened to reveal Sandman, I could see why. Sandman greeted Frost as a brother would, complete with a fist-bump. We questioned Sandman, and once he got over his shock at the death of Egbert, he provided us with information about their childhood years, saying that he couldn't think of anyone that would want to kill his friend. When I mentioned Hopper, Sandman grew ever so slightly stiff before conceding that he may have motive, but couldn't picture him brutally murdering his own brother out of spite. I asked for an alibi, but before Sandman could answer, Detective Frost cut in saying that they had been together until Frost had received the call about the discovery of Egbert's body.

As Frost finalised the statement, I looked around Sandman's living room and spotted a picture sitting on top of a cupboard. In the picture,

Sandman was pictured with a pretty brunette that looked vaguely familiar. When Frost called my name, I was brought back to reality. I caught up to him as he was walking out of the door. Frost told me that the girl in the picture that I was looking at was the Tooth Fairy, Sparkle. She was Sandman's wife.

Frost turned to me and said that we only had to go interview one more suspect – Hopper. He walked up the garden path and walked to the house just next door to Sandman. Frost knocked on the door his knock suddenly sounding a lot louder and harsher than the previous times. The door swung open to reveal a younger looking version of Egbert. He seemed on edge when he saw Detective Frost, his eyes bloodshot. Hopper invited us inside, knowing we would have questions to ask him. We asked the standard questions, and Hopper failed to produce an alibi, saying he was at home, alone all night long. Hopper was defensive when we asked him about his jealousy of Egbert, but claims that he loved his brother and didn't want any bad to come to him. The lack of an alibi combined with the possible motive given to us by Holly led to Frost arresting Hopper on suspicion of first degree murder. We brought him up to the local police station, locking him into the single holding cell in the building.

I had a bad feeling about convicting Hopper. He had seemed too upset at the news of his brother's death, and I didn't believe that anyone could fake those tears. I decided to go back to Egbert's house and re-examine the scene. Detective Frost dismissed the idea, so I went back alone. The house was quiet. If a pin were to drop, it would have been clearly audible from a different room. I went up to Egbert's room, wanting to see if there was anything that we had missed. I looked at the obvious things first – his dresser; desk; the pictures on his walls; and then I moved to the more discrete hiding places such as under his bed and in his wardrobe.

I was just about to give up, tired of sifting through all of Egbert's clothing, when I noticed a slight discrepancy in the colour of the wall on the side of the wardrobe. I pushed on the wall gently, getting excited when it moved ever so slightly. It slid open, what I had taken as a wall was actually a divider. There was only one thing behind the divider – a small, brown cardboard box. My curiosity got the better of me and I opened the box, wondering what other secrets this town held. I opened the box and my hand flew up to my mouth as I gasped. I was shocked at the box's contents. Inside the box was a very recent picture of Egbert and the Tooth

Fairy. The picture showed the happy couple, laughing as if they had no other cares in the world. I was confused. I thought back to Holly, and Sandman. I thought back to what I had been told about Holly and Egbert's relationship, about how happy everyone thought they were. I looked into the box again, to see another picture Egbert and Sparkle. In this picture they were sitting on a park bench, making silly faces as their eyes sparkled.

Since Holly's parents had already confirmed her statement, and they had time-stamped pictures to back up her up, I decided her alibi was solid. I went to the bar that Sandman and Frost said they were at together and checked the CCTV footage. There was no sight of either man during the night. I double-checked that they hadn't been in the bar at the time of the murder with the barman, who said he hadn't seen them all night. I felt sick to the stomach, suspicions creeping into my mind.

I brought Sandman in for questioning, and sat across from him. I told him that his alibi had fallen through, and that it was in his best interest to tell the truth now as a 'guilty' pleading would get him a lower sentence than a 'not-guilty' plead if the jury found him guilty. He admitted to the murder, and that Frost had stepped in knowing that Sandman didn't have a solid alibi and tried to provide one for him. I wrote down his statement and officially put him under arrest for suspicion of murder. I tracked down Detective Frost and arrested him for aiding and abetting a criminal, as well as obstruction of justice.

Three weeks later, the trial for the two partners-in-crime was held. The townspeople were shocked when they heard of the perpetrators of Egbert's murder. Nearly every person in the town went to the trial, supporting Egbert's friends and family. No one was surprised when both men pleaded guilty to their crimes. Sandman was imprisoned for twelve years, while Detective Frost received a seven-year sentence and his detective licence was revoked.

After the court hearing, Mrs Claus walked me to the exit from Spring Valley into my own town. She thanked me for my assistance on the case, happy that it had been solved. When I arrived back into the world above, I found that only three hours had passed rather than the three weeks in Spring Valley. I re-joined my team on the search for our shiny Easter eggs. I had a few in my pockets from Hopper, who had taken over the Easter egg production business. There was a small smile hidden on my face as I searched for eggs to help my team win the competition. From that day on, I kept the rabbit hole a secret from my friends, knowing they wouldn't believe me if I told them. The secret was kept until now, as I pass my story along to you.

The Horizon Stared Back

By Áine Winters, age 16.

They stared out towards the horizon

and found the horizon staring back.

It glowed, golden and glimmering, a soft, sweet sunset,

Filled them with wonder, warmth and well-being.

In their ears it whispered sweet

nothings of their future.

It clad the world in radiant light,

setting it aglow.

The last rays of sun reached out,

Offering up their warmth.

Crowned them with a halo of hope.

Shrouded them in a cloud of promise.

But

Darkness soon swept in.

Dimmed their golden light.

Dispelled all their hope.

Dulled their joyous warmth.

Dark dominated.

Doom bent them to its

Desires. Broke through their

Determination.

Delighted in their

Distress and despair.

Dragged them into a

Downward spiral of

Depressed dejection.

And yet.

They pushed on, would not cave in entirely.

For they knew,

That the dark feared the light.

And soon, the dawn would break through.

That first ray of light speared for them in the dark.

Cleaving the gloom in two.

Forging a path in its wake from the horizon,

In which others were soon to follow.

As the streak of light neared,

They smiled, shoved the darkness back.

And that brave first beam of light did not let go

While it pulled them from the shadows.

And back to the vivacity of day.

Paradisiac

By Finghín Little, age 17.

"Tıraş" is the Turkish word for shave, and that's what I read, twice reversed, in brilliant vermilion on the back of the door, through the mirror to my front. I sat up straight in my tall red seat, glancing over to the reflection of the man who ran the business, a musky Turk himself, cleanly bearded and of stocky build. I got ready to relax, and told him to do it like he means it.

The place was empty save us two; it was about nine on a weekday, and most of the folks that came to this place were the working-class immigrants that were getting to the building sites around now. I was an immigrant, too—but a pasty Irish kid that speaks French with a British accent can't help but feel out of place when surrounded by old Turkish men betting on the card games their grandfathers played. It would have been quaint, if they didn't reek of those awful (counterfeit) menthol Marlboros that they would bet with. Me, I went to enjoy the shave and cut I would get, and I found the banter of their maternal slander tiring while I was trying to enjoy having my hair scorched by a big guy.

Gob lathered and skinned, I breezed out the glass door, heaving the fumes of tobacco and exhaust pipes. As I stepped out, I snuck my bruised knuckles into my pockets, pushing my finger through a hole in the silky lining of my trousers. Reaching with my left hand, sighing, for my coat pocket, I unbuttoned the brass fastener awkwardly and slid out the little white box, delicately fingering the red racing stripe. I shunted the last fag into my mouth. After lighting up, I continued to walk down the street onto the quays towards the river in front of me. An old Megane passed by me to my left, window rolled down, blaring some bassy grime. I kept going until I met the crossing, waiting to find a gap in the traffic. A blue lorry trundled past, making way for me and the hurried woman at the other side. She reached quite a speed in her spotted blue heels, before nearly tripping in her stride, and dropping her leather briefcase. After swiping down to grab her case, she looked up at me as I hid a smirk, with a confused face, turned her head, and loudly paced the way I came with a clearly feigned confidence and a heavy step.

After crossing, I poked around a painter's stall along the path for a little
while. She had a large canvas filled with these fantastical flowers, in strokes
too broad to tell one from another. The smell of fresh flowers burned a
hole in my nose, filling my chest with their sharp perfume. I flared my
nostrils and looked around for a stall selling roses like there sometimes is
on the less windy days on the quays, but this woman was the only one
around. It must have been a daydream. I smiled a faint but honest smile at
her; she was around sixty, with her drab grey fell tied back, leaving her
eyes, true and blue, open to mine.

—Where are the flowers from? I chanced, expecting her to tell me she
just dreamed them out of nowhere.

—My father's grave, she curtly responded. She mirrored my former
smile to my drained face, humbling me. Not wishing to bother her any
more, I stared at her other paintings, hardly taking them in. I stepped out
of the stall and brushed my way through the final lunge to the next bridge.

The bridge was long and built from stone. Bridges are supposed to be
watersheds, or picturesque or something. It's a symbol. You're supposed
to cross a bridge and think you've gone far, or that things have changed.
This menacing bridge stepped over what was basically sewer water, and
crossing it I only got to see these idle middle-aged trophy wives in
designer sneakers and a couple sleeping beggars waiting for change. I
looked down at this lady sleeping on the ground below me, with her head
on a puffy coat and a stained covering over her still body. Her skin was
somewhere between jaundiced and actually grey. She looked about forty,
but still really old, older than my parents. I think it was the creases all over
her face, which also bore a couple of stains, or marks or bug bites or
something, in this constellation pattern that stretched down the side of her
neck. Something snapped me out of my rambling gaze. She sort of
stopped me in my tired vulnerability, even though she wasn't moving. I
felt a tear coming, with that choking mist you feel in your throat, and I
guess in that moment just didn't know what to say. I looked over the rail
and tossed the end of the fag in the water and sniffed, pretending I just
had a cold. I looked back at the woman, who stretched prostrate as I
turned back, and almost seemed to groan silently, if that's even possible.
As she pulled her arm up over her head I saw the bites trace down her
underarm, the trail dotted with these shrivelled black spots, into more
marks on her palm. At this point I shut my eyes fast and threw up over the
rail. My skull was pounding with a white-hot sweat that was itching my

brain like the bile in the back of my throat. I slowly widened my raw, stinging eyelids, and turning back to the direction I was headed, she stared me down from behind with a look that made it hurt even worse.

It felt like forever to get over the bridge, and once I did I poked my nose into the nearest express chain supermarket to pick up another pack. They were cheap here, and although I'd had a habit before, I was now bored enough and furnished with the purchasing power to smoke about a dozen or more a day. I definitely wasn't counting.

It was a shabby ditch of a store, with electric blue fluorescence beating down from the long tube lights, practically inviting me to explore. I bathed in the light for a while, like an actor, playing the antihero I thought I was. I danced quietly in the frosty glow towards the fridges' buzz, feeling the chill of the frozen lasagne scrape the heat from my sweating skin. I had the eyes to match the light, and the icy sapphire was shining just right to sharpen out the outline of my maxilla. I was dying for a mirror so I could see myself; it was fucking perfect.

Returning to the till empty-handed and slowly losing my swagger in the must of the dingy front of the store, I swiped the Economist from the shelf and stuffed the rolled mag in the back of my trouser, hiding it with the back of my jacket. Now, I really felt like that guy in Taxi Driver does, in that scene where he shoots a burglar dead in a grocers. This store looked a lot like that, actually. I struck up a conversation with the bloke at the counter about cigarettes, visibly alarming him with a brash exaggeration of my voice. He asked me where I was from, so I barked back that I was a citizen of the world, smirking sharply and fake. I let him know that I had all the faith in the world in stealing from the rich to serve the poor of the earth. I bought another pack and got out of the store, back into the glazed daylight of the bright morning.

I tore the film wrapper off with my stained canines and stuck another fag between them. I lit up and walked on, crossing the dozy street to meet another longer avenue, about a half-mile long and facing southbound towards the place I'd been meaning to visit. The street slanted uphill a little, so I could see the town's palace at its head, partly obscured and disfigured by the mirage over the hot asphalt. This was the first really busy thoroughfare I'd been on this morning. I guess by then it was probably getting to the point where the people who worked during the day would go for a lunch break. There was a frightfully bleak travel agents' with a scummy blue-and-yellow front, and I was surprised to see that travel agents still existed, but I guess it's more power to them, even if all they do is scam people by selling them photographs of idyllic retreats to numb them from their lives. The TV in the window showed a sunny day on the Bahamas or someplace exotic, with block capital captions telling me how cheap their resort was. I looked up at the gaudy gold sign naming their shop. 'Paradisiac,' it was called. As much as I can say I hate everything the marketing industry stands for, sometimes a good name or brand sticks out to me. It's about as poetic as capitalism tends to get for me. Paradisiac… well, other than having some kind of foreign mystique about it, I guess that just about sums me up as a person. I guess it sounds like a sufferance—amnesiac, insomniac—so it's kind of like a syndrome where you let yourself fool yourself into believing in utopia. You keep going back to this ideal you've got in your head. It's a memory, or a place that you might only have heard about. I kept walking by, with a dejected gaze on the pavement. I was still falling in love with a different distant paradise every day, and I think I was getting to the point where it didn't matter that the dreams I was chasing weren't real anyways.

I tried to look a little more satisfied, chin up, imbuing some kind of limp spring into my step. There were a couple of cracks in the slabs that got dangerously big at points, so I kept an eye on my slow stride, but it's worth it to watch people squinting at whatever distractions they've got going on trip themselves up and spill their iced refreshments all over the floor. Even more so when they look up at my calm and collected figure, all flustered and gobsmacked that the municipal pavement has failed them so gravely. I stepped aside to let a man in a wheelchair cross me without having to plough his way through my bandy legs, and that, I've will concede, made me feel like a proper hero. The guy looked like my little brother somehow, but he was far too old to really be him. He was dead five years now. Five years the other day. I spat out the fag-end and stamped on it.

I passed the town courthouse, to my left, a hyper-modern glass-faced gaff with a steel girder for some kind of hanging cover for the smokers that usually hung out outside. Now there were no smokers, but about five black cars sitting out the roadside right outside and a crowd of journalists, flashing cameras at a suited, bearded man. I kept moving, speeding up, making effort not to pay too much attention, trying to get myself ahead and out of the way, until I pushed into the guy who was trying to get out of the court. I knocked him back, but his open mouth said nothing. He only looked up and stared at me, with this look of complete bewilderment, eyes all but crossed in confusion. His hair was rufous but dull, and his nose was thick and rounded. His eyes changed to a softer tone, and he turned again at me with this awful look of pity, of remorse, like I was some form of redemption to him. He looked at me like my dad would, when he brought me out to the lakes to walk, years back, and we'd all but finished, sat at the top of the hill. I guess it was just for an instant though, because he really quickly stepped past me again, into the open door of a Mercedes, and promptly sped away.

There were only brick-fronted coffee shops and bland clothes stores for a while. The road was bare. A mirage danced on the tar, and the town hall's glass cupola coruscated, blinding me if I looked at it right. A waft of hot, dusty air mixed with dry smoke breezed into my face. I shut my dry eyes. I was getting exhausted and a little flustered, so I stepped into one of the cleaner-looking cafés to take a rest.

As I quietly closed the little hardwood door behind me, I found myself in a rather different establishment to what I thought I had come upon. The air was thick and dark, the lights were low, and although at the counter the menu read the usual coffee, the seats were low, made of dark leather, with tasselled coverings embroidered with Arabic calligraphy and fascinating geometry. It was kind of psychedelic, until I recognised about half of the population (so, about two people) from my favourite Turkish barber, breathing in the smoke from the shishas that sat on most of the little benches.

I got a coffee from the strong-armed woman. She smiled at me. She wore a black shirt and jeans, her hijab a light silky lilac. She served me a cute Turkish biscuit with my espresso. I sat down in the far corner of the room, glancing at the Lebanese newspaper on my stout table's cloth. I understood nothing, but I could see others reading it attentively, keeping up with things back home, like I should have. One of the last things I remember is the song changing to "Only Love Can Break Your Heart" just as I sat down. The Saint Etienne version, not the Neil Young one. That really pushed my button, bringing me back one of those awkward pangs of childhood. I felt myself crying in the passenger seat of my dad's ugly silver Megane, November rain at the window, my throat raw from adolescent rage. I chuckled inside, remembering how when he bought it they thought they were sporty, exotic French automobiles, and not the dull banger it eventually turned out to be. The windows eventually jammed in all four, so the car turned itself into a boiler room (only uglier) toasting me and my dad and sometimes my brother too.

The thought of crying in my saintly dad's Megane—after an ugly shouting match over whether Portishead or Massive Attack were better—suddenly appealed to me more than ever. I picked up the perfumed biscuit and washed it down with the coffee, served in a little copper saucepan. I can't even fucking stand coffee. Acerbic as it was, it could not erase the sting of remembering, which may have forced me to leak a few tears in my lonely corner, away from the sweaty geezers reading their homelands' newspapers, getting in touch with the old country from a safe distance. The memories, the car rides, my brother—it wasn't real, and I knew it. When you remember the things that happened a long time ago, you think you've remembered all the details so perfectly; everything's so vivid, like a new TV, like the back of your hand, but the truth is it's all lost. If I fooled myself into thinking I can really remember what I felt so long ago, I might as well admit the postcards and the shop window is the same as the paradise itself. While I was recoiled in the loneliest corner of the loneliest hookah bar in the world, the thing that hurt the most was that. I can be as close or as far on a map, but time is constantly cutting me loose from my memories. Things are spinning, and as I get older, it gets so fast I can't even see the blur that made me feel so sick when we were kids.

***

I don't think that I slept for that long. I get this sleepy haze when I cry, a lot like a baby does, and I usually don't remember much of falling asleep. I wasn't gone long enough for the girl at the counter to change, at least. I picked myself up and smiled at her as I made my way, and mentally bookmarked the little bar.

Closing the door behind me, I saw that the park was just opposite the café, which didn't make any sense. I was on my way to the park before, so I didn't see why I would have stopped if I was already almost there. The road was busier now, but I managed to get across the road with just one car beeping at me. The gate to the park was a tunnel, two wide stone arches linked by a copper net that let the light through in a pretty grid. I stomped ungracefully through it, the beige gravel crackling under my feet. There were families here, mothers and sons and daughters, scrambling with their dogs' leashes, shouting and screaming, throwing frisbees and flying kites, and I watched them while I moved into the lush park.

Making my way towards the pond at the other side, I passed by a pair of curly-haired kids scuffing each other, yelling high and frenziedly. Their tall mother stood over them, pulling the two apart. Her sunglasses fell off as she stooped to disarm their conflict, and were shortly stepped all over, serving only to heighten tension between the parties, with the mother further raising her tired voice. She should have just let them fight. When you're an adult, all you care about is how much trouble your kids cause. You can't step into their shoes, you can't see why they pick the fights they pick, or why they care about the most nonsensical things. When you're a kid, everyone thinks you're just an adult, but small, and stupid, in immature oblivion, where things don't make sense. But the truth is that they just can't remember the things that you felt, that they felt, too, once. They can't even remember that they can't remember. Things do make sense, but it's a different sense.

She shouted again at the reckless kids, but this time it sort of soothed me. It reminded me of my brother's voice. He would have been 23 the other day. I turned away, feeling the choking frustration get to me again, biting at my knees, and I paced faster now, away from them, but I could still hear his voice in my head, trying to convince me again that, not only did Massive Attack make better music, they also released more albums. It should have made me laugh, but it only made me feel the strings in my chest, already taut, start to break apart.

When I got to the bench by the pond, I did not sit down straight away. I fumbled for another cigarette, but my fingers began to shake too much. I could not look down, for some reason. I felt something take my eyes and make me look over the water at a pair of teenagers lying back on the shining grass. I needed to sit or I would fall over, so I crouched down on the green and breathed heavily, steadily. The force was comforting me, oddly. I reached over to put my head down and sob, but as I put my head in my hands, I sensed a soft touch on my back.

I didn't need to think about who it was. I just smiled through the tears, and looked back up at the kids, lying together, finding shapes in the clouds.

The End of Summer

By Viola Pioli, age 17.

And I left

At the end of summer

A hot hot summer

And I left

A beautiful day

On the beach with my friends

The fire burned

As the sun burned down

Into the sea…

Leaping firelight, the colour of sunset

A colour palette

Colours mixed

And I left

When the sun was gone

There was only us

Water and sand all around

Voices in the darkness

Voices without a face

Prey

By Victoria Keating, age 16.

She hadn't eaten in six days.

She danced along the silver trail as if she weighed nothing. She flicked her forked tongue over her fangs as she took another silent step on the canal. She lazily watched her breath form in front of her, each breath having a half-minute break in between another frosty exhale. There was a chill, yes, but not enough to affect the natural subworld around her.

Her feet tread atop of water, not ice.

The inky night sky was reflected in the ripples of the canal: a bright half moon framed by a blanket of stars. They whispered to her in their subtle twinkles. Bad, naughty suggestions.

The moon merely smirked.

She felt her long lily-white hair tickle the milky scales on her back. From the neck down her entire body was covered in these, and they shimmered in the moonlight. Talons replaced fingernails on her petite, slender hands. She glanced down at the water to gaze upon her reflection. She was greeted by amber spheres, both lacking pupil and iris. She was tall, yes. In fact, she stretched over six and a half feet in height. Her stomach was sallow and practically non-existent, lacking nearly a week's worth of nourishment. As if on cue, it gave an almighty rumble.

Patience she thought, the word rippling through her mind like a raindrop in a murky puddle.

This word had become a familiar friend since she'd first arrived in this new county. Beforehand, she lurked solemnly in the waters of Sligo Town, but the meat had become too much of a routine for her. Due to this, she decided to travel easterly into the cosiness of Drumshanbo. She had considered Carrick-On-Shannon, but thought better of it, as there were too many witnesses, not to mention that the town was directly across from her feeding ground. Drumshanbo, on the other hand, was smaller, and very few resided firmly across from any body of water.

The boardwalk, she noticed, was somewhat new. She would watch the many people walk along it from underneath the floating boards during the day. Yet here the problem lay – she could not hunt during the day. For five days she wandered aimlessly on (and under) Acre's Lake, yet not a single soul ventured out to the lake once the sun retired after dusk. Of course, this was typical of winter. Feeding time was always a chore at that time of the year.

That particular night, she had decided to follow the floating boards out of pure curiosity. They didn't last long, as suddenly they converted into a natural walkway. She hadn't ventured too far, just under a small bridge that allowed vehicles to cross the canal. Ahead of her were high, grassy banks that framed the canal with leafless trees.

In fact, it was between those bare branches that she saw the boat.

Immediately, she dropped into the water, submerging herself completely from view. Not fifty feet ahead of her was a small white boat, typically used for lazy river cruises one would take with the family. The steering wheel and electronics were protected by a slighted hooded roof, whilst the back of the boat was out in the open. There, reclined on a portable lawn chair, was a man. He was bordering middle age, definitely overweight, greasy black hair that framed his chubby face, and a scruffy beard that covered his multiple chins. He was in an extremely relaxed state, a near empty bottle of beer clutched in his hammy fist.

A slight smile attempted to tug at the corner of her lips. Easy prey.

Perfect.

Gliding along the floor of the canal, she aligned herself so that she was moving alongside the boat. She let out a controlled sigh, and felt her body begin to shift. Her scales, from neck to foot, flipped upwards, changing her appearance of creature to a naked female human. As soon as the last scale flicked, she lunged upwards, breaking the water's surface, and landed effortlessly on the boat.

Startled by the sudden appearance of a beautiful woman before him, the man spluttered, the bottle slipping through his fingers and rolling onto the floor. His eyes travelled up and down her body, and she noticed the subtle hunger in his eyes. Her body was dripping wet, glistening, almost glowing. The man's mouth opened and closed like a fish, yet no sound came out.

Trying not to roll her eyes, she stretched her arms upwards, showing every one of her curves, before whispering in an airy voice, "Hello there."

"Uh, erm, ah, I-I-I ... hi," he finally mustered. She took a few steps towards him, smiling seductively.

"What's your name, handsome?"

Gaining a hint of composure, he stood up, his eyes never leaving her bare chest. "P-Peter," he rasped. "And yours?"

She didn't have one.

"Not important. What is important is what you think of me, Mr Peter."

"Uh..." Peter choked, clearing his throat. "Really... really great, uh, gorgeous." Suddenly, he dropped to the floor, searching for his beer bottle. He picked it up and turned it around in his shaky hands, reading the label.

"Whatever the hell is in this stuff, it's magic," he murmured to himself.

Growing both bored and impatient, she approached him, cupping his face gently in one hand. "Do you like what you see Mr Peter?" she fake gushed.

Licking his lips, Peter answered, "V-very much so."

She leaned forward, her lips brushing against his right ear. "Do you want to see my most secret part?" she whispered, her hot breath tickling his neck.

Not believing his "luck", Peter merely nodded frantically. Grinning, she pulled away from him, and watched the colour drain from his face as she bared her fangs, flicking her forked tongue across his face. Peter only had enough time to part his lips to scream before she simultaneously sank her teeth into his face and ripped his torso open with her talons.

Although painful, it was a quick death. Quick, but messy, as they all are. She was thankful for his obesity as she dined on his flesh and insides. It was only a matter of minutes before he was left as a pile of bones. She licked the last of his bones clean of blood, halting for a moment to debate with herself, before ingesting his skeleton as well. Finally, her stomach had no reason to noisily complain to her. Glancing around, she realised the floor of the boat had been stained a cherry red. She hurriedly lapped at the blood around her, leaving the boat cleaner than when she has first hopped on board.

Looking down, she smirked at the blood that clung to her body. Instead of washing it off, she merely folded her scales back down, returning to her reptilian state. She strolled to the side of the vessel and slipped back silently into the water. She began to tread on the bottom of the canal in the direction that the boat had come from. If he had come from down there, then that meant there were more humans downstream, and she needed a stable feeding ground.

As she walked, her eyes shot up to the sky. The stars beamed with joy, knowing she had listened to their bad, naughty thoughts. She gave a curt nod, acting as a silent salute to them.

The moon merely smirked.

Controlled

By Sina Krings, age 16.

Wednesday, 24.01.2018

The charcoal puddles splash their filthy water all over my legs. My jumper is dripping from the pelting rain coming down on the roofs of Dublin. I run blindly to the right in the dazzling blackness of a side alley.

I drop to a hectic trot to grant my calves a little ten-second break, then I must speed through the derelict alleys again. A gust makes me shiver, the splashing rain has turned into fat, drumming drops.

My side stings as if someone had rammed a dagger into it. My feet burn. The pulse in my temple pounds in the rhythm of my madding heartbeat. Foam gathers in my mouth.

Faster. Be faster.

I sense a noise behind me. But I am too afraid to stop or turn around so I keep scudding through the dark. Right, left, left again and...

Stop!

Panic takes hold in me. A dead end.

Walls, garbage cans, muddy old tarps and gloom just about discernible in the pale, wan light of an old street lamp.

What now? WHAT NOW?

Decide. Quick. Think.

The garbage. The cans are stacked in the corner of the alley under a tarp. They might just hold my weight.

Sweat runs down my forehead. My burning body pressed tight against the cool bricks. My fingertips scrabble for grip on them. Battered knees and scuffed elbows. The taste of blood in my mouth. No time. Everything hurts. I force myself up the last few centimetres. I heave myself over the railing of the rooftop.

Done!

For now.

I remain lying down for a moment and look up to the filthy sky. My drenched clothes stuck to my body. Full of sweat and soaked. My pulse calms, the pounding in my head weakens. Sirens blare in the distance.

Pain, stabbing, shooting pain broadens in me. I sit up. My leg. Blood. What now?

I hear voices at the house. They are here. No time. I brace at the railing, trying to heft myself. I strain the wrong leg. Pain. Tears sting me in the eyes; a short sob slips out of my mouth.

I lose sight for a few seconds. But I recollect fast. I venture a glimpse down. They stand there. Baffled. Good. They don't know where I am. Not yet.

I drag myself to the other side of the rooftop. A fire escape. I can identify a neon, gaudy yellow sign of a little shop about 100 meters away. Open!

You can do it! Yes? No?

Yes! I crawl over the edge, anchor my arms in the top step and let my body slide down. Pain. I breathe in sharply and clench my teeth. Tough it out. Slowly, step by step.

Done! I'm down. My legs threaten to collapse, to break down under me but there is no going back now. Hobbling, I run to the small shop at the corner.

Sweat. Blood. Fear. Adrenaline. But there is something else.

Hope.

I get over with the last few metres, hoping to witness the next day one more time. The sign is getting brighter and brighter. Shooting pain kicks into my head. I push the door open with a groan and fall with a loud crash into the shop.

I bob up. Too fast. My head is spinning; the pain in my leg is unbearable.

Not a human soul is here. Nobody is here! Coal-black benches and chairs that seem like nobody has been sitting in for an eternity. Dusty tables and blind windows.

This place is a shithole. Literally. I drag myself to the counter.

"Hello? Someone there? "

A sudden thud shocks me. I am about to turn around and leave as a figure is recognizable. A tall, powerfully built man builds himself up in front of me. I can identify him as he steps into the pale light of a single bulb. A broad grin spreads over his face.

"Oh, no," I whisper.

-----ZIP-----

-Game over-

"FUCK! FUCK! FUCK! FUCK!"

"Louisa! Stop swearing! Give me your phone now. You've been on it for ages."

"But, Mom. I need to get through that stupid level! I just keep on loosing it by running into the wrong people. I almost got it this time."

A Q&A* with The Patriarchy

By Bronwyn Keegan, age 16.

So tell me, why is a woman's biggest concern how a man perceives her?

"That's too much make up; men won't like it."

"That skirt's too short; men may like it."

"Don't sleep around with men you fucking slut."

"Give him a chance, don't be such a prude."

Why must I label every man on the street as a predator just in case of one?

Because that's all it takes,

One.

I do not wish to label all men as forceful because of one,

But it's hard not to when all of those "one" men on the street see all woman as their objects.

Why are women an object and why must men claim them?

We all have a body,

We all have the chance to share it,

But don't capture a body not set out for you.

For my body is a wonder

A holy grail unseen by many but adored by me

and that's all it needs so get your hand off of me.

This is not your home to lay upon

This is my being of human.

Although my spirit is bigger and a wonder to all, it chose this body and you are not worthy until I say you are,

So get your filthy hands of off me.

When will I get raped?

Because the odds aren't so high for my safety.

And when I choose to dictate my body and wear what I like, walk where I like and be who I like,

It's misread as an invitation.

As you see my confidence as a connotation,

For slut.

For whore.

That's what I'm here for,

Is your pleasure,

Your joy,

As that's what a woman is to you,

You sick bastard.

*Q&A: question and answer.

Inner Monologue On The Move

By Ollie Tuohy, age 17.

As I hurtle down the motorway

I can't help but think of you –

Thousands of miles away,

Your day only just beginning –

And wonder what it has in store for you.

Is it nice there? Sunny?

It's cold here. Below zero,

And I missed my train by a breath.

We were waiting for an hour until

This bus pulled up with its blue lights and warm.

I've got loud music in my ears and a good book,

But you stroll across my mind anyway

With a kind smile and hopeful eyes;

Promises of warm hugs that I've never had

And soft kisses under mistletoe.

A safe future;

Freedom from these restraints

That hold me captive

– playing a part –

But you offer an escape

And I grab it with both hands,

Or at least I would if you were close,

But the ocean stretches between us

And I can't will it away to nothing

No matter how hard I try.

1943

By Hazel Hopkinson, age 17.

It is snowing somewhere in Poland. Snowflakes drift listlessly through the icy night air, settling on top of each other to create a damp, glistening blanket. The bright, waning moon is somewhat shrouded by clouds, only its tip visible as it peers out across the barren land. Further on, across the cluster of rectangular buildings, the squat, wooden towers stare down on rows of cruel barbed wire fences. It is quiet, eerily so; but if a person were to linger long enough, they might become aware of the ominous hum of high voltage – the fence is a living thing, a hostile, murderous weapon. There is a smell of mildew, of disease and excrement, and beyond this, something else; something sickening and harder to distinguish.

Inside the perimeter of the fence, under the harsh glare of a bare bulb, the fresh snow has been disturbed, churned to a dark grey where it has been squashed into the ground by impatient feet. A young guard paces back and forth, sniffing every few moments and wiping his nose on the back of his gloved hand. He is enveloped in a damp, woollen greatcoat that reaches the middle of his shins, and he has turned up the collar in an attempt keep out the chill, to minimise the discomfort that is a night shift during the Polish winter. His right hand rests on the butt of a machine gun, the strap of which is slung loosely over his shoulder. It is heavy and awkward and he secretly hopes he won't have to use it. His face, or what can be seen of it beneath the shadow of his peaked cap, betrays a profound disillusionment that belies his obvious youth. He scowls into the darkness beyond the fence, and wishes he could go home.

Beyond the fence, across the frozen train tracks, a house stands silent on a low hill surrounded by trees. Inside, all is still; asleep in various areas of the front room are five uniformed officers, ties loosened, hair dishevelled, faces red from the effects of drink and frantic merriment. A pack of cards is spread across the coffee table in a disorderly fashion, several of them having spilled onto the cream coloured carpet alongside a fresh stain of expensive red wine. The air is smoky; cigarette butts are piled in an ashtray balanced precariously on the arm of a long white sofa. Three empty wine bottles grace the floor, one upright and the other two on their side. Against one wall stands an upright piano, lid open; above it, a framed photograph, hanging slightly askew, depicts a straight-backed man in army uniform, his dark hair combed to one side, his expression severe. On the adjacent wall there is a large red flag with a white circle at the centre in which is placed an angular black symbol.

Upstairs, a sixth officer is sprawled across a double bed, breeches undone, shirt on the floor. He is middle-aged; his stomach is portly and his hair is greying. Beside him lies a girl, no older than twenty, slim, naked, her lower half tangled in the stark white sheets, her red lipstick smudged across one pale cheek. She does not know the man. Various items of clothing are spread across the room; dress, stockings, underwear, a pair of petite, red, high-heeled shoes.

Back inside the fence perimeter and north a little are the clustered wooden buildings. Inside each are packed the emaciated bodies of up to a hundred unfortunate men, women and children – alive, existing, but barely – squashed shoulder to shoulder on the thin wooden bunks, numb from the biting cold. They have been segregated between buildings; the men and the women and children are kept separate at all times. There is little movement inside; the children do not fidget, nor do they cry – they simply don't have the energy. Few of them are asleep.

All is quiet, perhaps, to a human ear, but between the huddled buildings one may begin to feel the silent, virtual cries of the souls within, a harsh, cacophonous symphony with endless, delicate variation, a cry for help, perhaps, or for nothing at all but for the fact that it cannot be helped – the sound, beyond sound, comes out of its own accord.

To wander through such a place at a time like this would be a deeply disturbing experience, for though the death and destruction cannot be seen directly, it lingers in the atmosphere, hanging between the buildings like a heavy fog, curling and creeping noiselessly through every door and window, into the eyes, the ears, the nose, the mouth, into the mind, where it plants a tiny, noxious seed of darkness that will grow steadily, eliminating all reason and all hope. It will spread to the heart, where it will eat away any sense of affection, of fondness and forgiveness, of love. It will make the eyes glassy and the soul so cold that it eventually shatters into a million frozen fractals which tumble across the unforgiving ground, where they will stay indefinitely, the owner having been robbed of the strength required to pick them up and attempt, in vain, to fit them back together.

Although, against all odds, there are dreams and aspirations, yet lingering, however suppressed; one or two tiny flames still flicker, the mortal fog having yet to smother them; and there are memories of what used to be, in a different place, a different time, a different world. If one observes intently, they may just catch the soft focus image of a family sharing a meal, the scent of a new book, the muffled melody of a child's laughter, the tender feel of a final kiss lingering on the lips.

The moon has emerged; a final snowflake falls to the ground.

All is still.

Smart, Smarter, Smartest

By Evelyn Rochford, age 17.

Have you ever looked back on something and wondered "How different could things have been if I had only decided to do things differently?" That was the thought on every human being's mind, every day, of every month, of every year, since the animals rose up. Though nobody could pinpoint the exact day that it happened, no one could possibly forget their regret at not acting sooner, and nobody forgot the day we finally figured out what was to happen to us. Their intelligence was something we were just too arrogant and narrow minded to see, but oh, how we wished we had seen it now...

"Hush, master has put us to sleep. We mustn't wake him." whimpered Simon, cowering in the corner. His two colleagues didn't look up. They were too engrossed in their conversation.

Before the tables had turned on the human race, these three individuals were some of the most celebrated scientists in their fields. Now they were just like everybody else: locked away under the watchful eye of their masters. Edward shook his head.

"No, no, no... The evolutionary process was not supposed to allow this." Betty was studying a diagram she had etched into the dirt of the cellar floor. The basement of the master's house was dingy, filthy and rotten from neglect. They only kept their humans in it, there was no need to waste time cleaning it.

"Based on what we've observed, the animals have a long way to go with evolution yet. They aren't even nearly finished yet... Humans on the other hand..."

Edward swore and kicked over a box of old papers in the corner, the last dated 05 July 5519. The day the humans were finally overthrown. Edward ran a hand through his hair and shook his head. Then he walked over to Simon and crouched down beside him, wary of startling him. His anxiety had worsened over the past week and he flinched as Edward reached a hand towards him. Edward sighed, full of pity for this extraordinary genius, now brought low.

"Come now old friend, you know more about this than either of us. Give us the zoological point of view." Edward knew it was a long shot and sure enough Simon just wrapped his arms around his knees and put his head down. Once he began shaking, Edward knew there was no hope of achieving anything. He rose and turned away. It hurt that Simon's one true passion, the ones he dedicated his whole life to learning about, discovering and helping, had caused him to collapse into this fitful state.

A few months previously, the small band of scientists came up with a theory. Simon, the zoologist, had been studying the animals' behaviour. It explained how dogs learned to open doors and bark when they needed help. They had been watching humans for some time. Monitoring our advancement and dictating how they could do it better, all the while evolving with better eyesight, smell and hearing. Betty the biologist analysed the possibility the animals' brains were growing at a much faster rate than was previously believed possible. Based on her previous studies of animal biology she could confirm the differences. This was an alarming discovery. Finally Edward could see why the animals came to evolve this way at this time. He spent his whole adult life studying evolution and this was like nothing he had ever seen before. Camels evolved to store water due to dried out habitats, fish evolved to have gills, therefore enabling life underwater and so on... So why were all of the animals re-evolving now? Simple, the scientists could conclude that the animals had evolved to survive against the race of men.

It began when they learned to communicate between species. They learned that patterns could leave a message and scents. Two things the humans would leave unnoticed. Just animals being animals, it doesn't mean anything. This was our biggest mistake. Not paying attention to the little details that we believe ourselves to be so good with. We overlooked this as a form of agitation due to Global Warming. This is when the animals started forming alliances.

Wolves and bears decided they were tired of being lured from their homes and having their families brutally killed for simply trying to feed their families. They were being hunted even tortured for sport, so they planned a counterattack. Acting throughout the winter, they used the deep snows to their advantage. The humans trapped in their homes during the long dark months were completely at their mercy and before long the northern countryside was completely human free. Suddenly the people took notice. There was a huge scandal, people blaming other people about laws, rules and regulations and all the while the animals were plotting.

More creatures followed the lead given by the beasts of the North. Eventually all the farms, households and zoos were empty. The animals simply vanished. It happened so fast that nobody saw it coming. Again, we failed to notice their communication. The birds were given marked pebbles, which they dropped into the enclosures and gardens and pens of any animals who could dig. These included dogs, wolves, big cats and lizards. Places were allocated to groups of creatures and they began creating secret escape routes for all the other animals... They had to get everyone underground. To this day, the humans never discovered how they did it. It was so precise, so well planned and completely unpredicted. Surely the animals didn't just do this by chance. There was so much that could've gone wrong, but didn't, for it to be just luck. No, the animals had decided on a leader, one who had evolved the slowest, most effectively and the most dangerously of all the beasts in the world.

The crocodiles were feared by all. As one of the oldest creatures on the planet it had survived the fall of many ages of man and beast. It survived when nothing else could and had seen enough species be overthrown that it would be no problem to do it again. Only this time they would be in control. After the rise of the North, the crocodiles applauded the animals' work and decided to rise with them. They inflicted more damage than any other, avenging all of their ancestors who had been killed for their valuable teeth and scales, and all of their children who had been snatched when they were still in their eggs so that they could be made into beautiful relics for collectors. When the animals went into hiding they turned to the massive reptiles for guidance. They who had seen and lived through so much would surely have a solution to this problem. They taught the animals patience as they had been throughout the age of the dinosaurs, through the rise of mammals and the birth of the first men. The animals respected them and it was because of their great wisdom that the animals learned the power of patience.

Simon was sweating. He rocked backwards and forwards on his heels. Edward was pacing up and down the cellar, muttering something indistinguishable to the others in the room. He stopped suddenly and let out a desperate cry of frustration. "Simon! You have to help us!" Betty rose to try and calm him. "We need to understand the animals behavioural traits if we are to figure out how to escape from here! We cannot do that without your help!" Betty placed a hand on Edward's shoulder and steered him away from Simon, who didn't even look up. His hands were trembling; dark circles were clear under his eyes from stress and a lack of sleep. Dawn was fast approaching and they all knew what that would bring. The master would soon wake with his hungry sons and daughters eagerly awaiting their morning meal. Their other colleagues had met their fate this way and Edward and Betty refused to end like that. The master's Game of Dominance they called it. It showed the humans who called the shots these days. Betty looked up suddenly, her eyes full of light. "Edward!" she exclaimed and he spun round to face her. "Could it be possible... to reverse the process of evolution?" The room went silent.

As the crocodiles had promised, their patience paid off. The humans were in such a flap about the position of animals and they had been searching for so long that they began to miss the simplest pieces of evidence. The takeover was quick and almost too easy. The ferrets, mice, rats, snakes and other such small creatures were sent to monitor houses and other buildings. They sussed out all entrances, exits, windows, vents and locks. The birds were sent to collect weapons from the humans so they would have no defence and the wise owls were given the specific task of disabling all cameras. The domestic animals were sent back to their homes. Their owners were so relieved to see them that they didn't suspect a thing. The pets lured their people to the cellars, scratching and pawing doors and then locking them in with no way out.

The farm animals set their old barns and sheds alight. Now nowhere could hold them captive ever again. The animals were free. The humans were completely at their mercy. Each creature was allowed to decide the fate of their own human. The better-cared-for ones kept their humans as pets or servants. The prize horses and cattle started buying and selling their humans at the local marts, they kept them well fed and cared for until a wolf or other such creature decided to buy one. Some creatures however were not so merciful. They had a score to settle with humans. Taking example from the wolves and bears, the dogs, cats and reptiles headed to the large industrial companies, cosmetics companies, science labs and breeding farms. They rescued as many of their kin as they could; some had to be carried due to the severity of their injuries, but it was too late for others. Spurred on by the sight of their fellow creatures, they attacked, rallying many other species to their cause. By the end of the fray the few humans who survived were kept for hunting sport or on food farms for the predatory animals.

The deer kept game farms, selling the humans to wolves, lions and tigers, some of which kept their humans as performers as revenge for tortured lives in the circus. Any animal with a score to settle wanted to see the humans eliminated. An agreement was put in place and signed by a nominee of every creature species on the planet. It was decided that after the removal of the human race, no species would try to take complete charge again. They would lead a life of harmony as they did before humans. Throughout the entire rising the crocodiles stayed underground. They simply watched, waited and learned.

"Reverse evolution!" Edward squawked.

"SHUSH!" hissed Simon, who was now glancing about the room in a panicked manor.

"Just think!" Betty whispered "the animals evolved to out-smart humans so that they may lead happier lives without us. They're hoping to eradicate us, so that the world may be a better place." She looked straight at Edward. "But I don't think we are a race that is ready to go yet." If the animals believe all the humans are gone, they wouldn't need to evolve anymore." Edward shook his head, but Betty ploughed on before she lost him. " What if a few humans managed to escape before the destruction of their race and stayed in hiding, finding where the animals source of power is and saving the humans from extinction." The room was silent but for Betty's panting from speaking so fast with very little breath. Edward turned and stared into Betty's hopeful eyes. He couldn't be responsible for that last bit of hope going out.

For the next hour they sat heads together, throwing ideas out, over and over again. Over and back they went, dismissing and re-arranging until suddenly Edward let out a sigh of relief.

"So the evolutionary process COULD possibly be reversed when one species rises unnaturally against another!" Betty clapped her hands in excitement. They wrapped each other in a huge embrace. Exhausted from

190

little or no sleep over the last few days and from the thought they there was still hope. They were interrupted however by a strange disturbance from the corner. Simon had stopped shaking. He was standing across the room and staring straight through the other two scientists.

"Simon?" Betty whispered.

"I said..." Simon's voice was cold and distant, his mind far, far away "I said, that your theory is false." Edward and Betty glanced uncertainly at each other, unsure what to make of this statement. "The animals have always been smarter than us; we were just too dumb to see it. The bullies have become the bullied and we can't just deal with that. Plot all you want, but you stand no chance against their intelligence. They can predict our every move, this won't surprise them." Simon stepped toward his colleagues "They smell us before we are even in their presence," he took another step. "They see us even when we think we are all alone. Did you really think you would last out there unprotected by your master? The birds will see you, or the rodents and they will come screaming to our master. There is no hope!" Simon was close enough for them to touch now. "They taste our fears on a cool summer breeze," he was whispering now, so close that Edward could smell his rotten breath. His teeth reeked of the small scraps of food that got thrown to them, but it had been months since his teeth were properly cleaned. "They hear us before we even know they're there."

The door at the top of the stairs swung open and the room was flooded with light. Simon hissed and scurried to the dark corner. Betty and Edward fell backwards in shock and attempted to hide but it was no use. The master's children bounded down the steps and were on them in a heartbeat. One pinned Edward, snapping and snarling in his face. One grabbed Betty by the arm. She cried out but the wolf held her still. Two more ran to the corner and penned Simon. The last two stood either side of the master who stood in the door way. They were trapped. As the master stepped out of the glare his appearance became all the more terrifying. His silhouette had been intimidating enough. Now his steely grey, matted fur was visible and his long sleek tail which appeared to be dipped in darkness. His paws were as large as dinner plates and his claws like meat hooks. His large ears lay pinned back against his head and his razor sharp teeth were visible under the curl of his lip. His face was obscured by a deep scar that zigzagged over and back, a gift from a human that was most likely one of the first to be taken down by the pack. His glowing yellow eyes evoked terror, as though taken straight from the pits of hell.

The scientists had only learned a few basic Wolvish commands, never truly understanding their new methods of communication. It was clear however that the wolves had mastered the human tongue and had understood every word that was said. The Master commended Simon's knowledge of creature intelligence with a sarcastic bow and his children snarled in satisfaction. The sound was so eerily human that Edward shivered.

The scientists lay still, barely daring to breath, lest they draw attention to themselves. Who would be chosen for the weekly hunt. The master turned to his eldest daughter who stood at his shoulder. She would choose one of them. The master turned back to his hostages and bared his teeth before turning and heading outside. Without so much as a sound the signal was given. The humans scrambled for cover as the wolves moved. The she-wolf pounced, leaping over Edward and Betty and grabbing Simon by the back of the neck. In an instant she had dragged him up the stairs, leaving a trail of blood as he screamed and begged for mercy. As quickly as they had arrived the pack was gone. Simon would be let loose in the forest and then the wolves would enjoy hunting him down for the morning. The door closed and the room was in total darkness again apart from a thin sliver of light that was visible under the door. The eerie silence that followed was broken only by Betty's quiet sobs. Tears streaked down her face and Edward stood, mouth hanging open and staring at the spot where Simon had been sitting only minutes before. The room fell into darkness. The sound of a very large animal dragging its gigantic body across the floor was audible through the door. Edward's breath lodged in his throat at the sound that followed. A ground trembling snarl echoed through the room, the unmistakable sound of a crocodile. Only this was a new beast, much larger, more intimidating and much more intelligent than anything they had ever known. Too terrified to move, the scientists stayed rooted to the spot, unable to take their eyes off the door. They could feel their hearts in their mouths.

"I watched... I waited.... and I learned". The crocodile's voice was chilling, like nails on a chalkboard. A menacing sound that could only belong to something ancient. It sent a shiver up Betty's spine. "We were always smart, but then we got smarter and now we are the smartest." His voices dripped like poison from a vial. The air was tense as a bow string which fell just short of snapping under the pressure. The voice was like a grater on skin, it peeled them back piece by piece leaving the listeners raw and writing in pain. It hissed in a way only crocodiles can deliver, one which was delivered like a death sentence. "Miserable humans, I ask you this. Do you really think you are smart enough to know how smart we really are?"

The Truth Behind Trust

By Ciara Whelan, age 17.

How can I place myself

In someone else's hands

When they can so easily

Crush me?

A life is spent

Cultivating broken promises

People never intended to keep.

Am I suddenly expected

To blindly place my faith

In the hands of others

I have been led to believe are no

Different?

Is it possible

To know someone

To the full extent

Of real human connection?

Every fear and flaw and feeling that flows,

Every thought and theory and trauma they know

How history has shaped them,

How the future will shape them still.

I have been taught to believe,

No.

No one can ever truly know me:

The delicate map work of my mind

And how I am

Tortured by it.

The truth behind trust

Is that I have been fed so many lies

I will never truly know them

They will never truly know I.

Love's Last Dance

By Michaela Shaw, age 17.

We drove west at the turning of the seasons. We left the noise-riddled hub of the Isle and drove endlessly toward the coast. Large cities fell away to small, sparse villages and then, the sea. A clear glistening strip on the horizon. I roll the window down and let the sea breeze course through my lungs, filling them with an exhilarating coolness. We reach the edge of the world and spill over the ledge of a hill and into the final village. We pass a weather-beaten sign, half eaten by ivy. 'Somerset' is softly printed in old italics on the yellowing surface. Mellow, soft-coloured dainty shops and houses fly by. Children race each other breathlessly through the cobbled streets, their cries of delight travel weightlessly through the village.

The houses become fewer and farther between and finally we gently glide down an overgrown dirt track, coming to a skittering halt before a quaint whitewashed cottage, on the brink of the sea. Runaway roses and alliums weave their way around the house, a homely embrace. Stepping through a low door, I peer around the dimly lit house. The walls are scattered with oil paintings, slightly clouded with must. Black and white tattered photographs, faded to yellow in brown leather frames, line the mantel above the dwindling fire. The upholstery is a jumble of floral patterns, rimmed with frills and tassels. The clock stopped working a long time ago.

An old, gracefully delicate woman sits in a large purple armchair, the fire flickering lightly on her high features. A timeless smile breaks her intent gaze as she rises and draws me towards her in a warm embrace, a sigh leaving her lips, "My Mia". She smells of rose with a faint powdery underlying scent. Her grip is strong and firm, but familiar. My mother's eyes survey the room clinically; a sour distasteful twist in her features takes hold. She leaves very shortly after, a stiff compulsory hug is all she gives Granny Helen. She stalks to her car without a backwards glance to either of us, muttering furiously under her breath about some very important report she has to do at the office. After she leaves I let out a breath I hadn't realised I was holding. I head back inside and finally allow myself to really take in the house.

Nothing has changed in the past six years since I last saw my grandmother. I was eleven then, the frills and tufts of the décor were still as amusing then. The room is a clash of colours and patterns, a complete disarray of items, but somehow feels perfect and right. We spend the afternoon chatting about every mundane thing that comes to mind. Local scandal and school, weather and the audacity of children these days. Our family tends to stick to such peripheral topics. It has always been safer to do so. I made the mistake of asking about Granny's older sister once. Of course, back then I had never heard that she even had a sister. I spotted a weathered picture of her that day. A radiant young girl. All blonde ringlets framing porcelain features. I remember the eyes Granny wore just then, when I posed my multiple questions. The sad dry eyes, the usual glint had faded, replaced by a mournful dullness. I dropped it after that and learned to never ask about family matters again. Of course, that rule never extended to other members of the village. I learned later from a slightly slurred gossip in the local tavern that her name was Lily, Lily Taylor. She had been older than Granny Helen by a few years and had run off sometime in the winter of 1940. She had stolen off under cover of darkness and had never been seen, or heard of, again.

Granny is chattering on about how delighted she is that I'll be spending the entire summer here with her. She says it will be good for me, to get out of London, and as she says, "Renew the salt in my blood", that apparently is a Taylor family attribute. I land my scratched suitcase on the low bed in the dingy spare room. The room, despite it being a warm day, is cold and I move the bed out from its place against the wall, its iron frame making jarring screeches against the floorboards. A small warped door leading to a tiny crawlspace reveals itself. I inch my way in, along dusty cold flooring, past stacks of bed sheets, hoping to find something slightly less floral and riddled with ruffles to put on my bed. Praying that the old, mint coloured trunk at the very extreme of the passage will have saved some from the onslaught of must, I make my way laboriously over to its side. I lift the weighty lid and it slides aside, landing with a resounding thud. I search the reaches of the void and find only worn copies of Dickens and an accumulation of leaves of crinkled paper, all destroyed by scrawl. At the bottom, I produce a leather-bound journal, aged by sunlight and soft to the touch.

At the end of the evening, I curl up on the window seat, bundled in several heavy quilted blankets. The light has faded out and the surrounding hills have been dipped into an impenetrable ink. My phone has long since died; the entire cottage plunged into a natural darkness. I light a tall tapered candle and hunker down in my mountain of duvets. The wind whistles loud outside, rising to an impossible crescendo and then falling again, in a blissful sigh. The leather crinkles slightly as I open the cover and turn my squinting eyes to the cover page. 'Lilian Taylor', is inked in pretty, looping letters, one giving way to another. I open the next page.

January 12th 1940

The rations are becoming shorter now that the war is well and truly under way. Faith is failing in the village. There is less laughter in the taverns at night; worried glances are shared more frequently. Warm, friendly smiles are becoming more and more scarce, day by day. The good people of our village have been reduced to squandering for food and money. But this night, this very night, I feel a stirring of some of my old life. Some small glimmer of light. I met the most charming and gentlemanly man at the village gathering in the hall. James Turner. William and Jason, who live by the docks, have brought him home with them as their entire company is on leave. He lives in the east by the sea and joined the efforts two months ago, just as he turned nineteen. Tonight was the first time I had laughed since the war began. I had almost forgotten the sound.

The candle quivers gently against the page, illuminating the dates as the fly me by. As I read, I am cast into her life, almost seventy years before, when a war rent her world apart. I read countless entries, each one painting a more vivid portrait of her life. Soon after the first entry the war worsens and the man she writes entire pages about is whisked off to the front again, leaving her alone. I read for hours as the moon's ghostly gleam dances its way across the room, lending deep shadows to the furniture. Pages and pages flash before me, a kaleidoscope of memories flit behind my eyelids.

I can see the village as it once was. The waves crashing relentlessly against the resolute bay. The town hall swamped to the rafters with the village's congregation. All crowding around, stumbling over one another, craning to hear the latest defeat in battle all from one tiny radio of crackling static. The town's people come to life page after enchanting page. Old Jim Morgan, chasing hooligan children from his store front, frantically yelling obscenities as they barrel away, hooting triumphant choruses. Ladies gathered in groups, frantically confabulating with one another. Mr and Mrs Collins, at the end of a particularly deflating update, pulling out his violin while she ignites a verse of an old ballad, voice soft and comforting.

She recites her nightmares and her darkest worries. Committed to paper, but never to people. I know every deep saddening moment she endured. Every long night alone, cold and numb. Every letter James sent back from some far-off corner of the world. His letters steadily grow darker, less full of life as the days go by. She writes away the nights, pouring every feeling onto the page. Every fear. She talks most about her family. Her father, far away, working on the railways. Weeks passing without sight nor sound of him. Her two brothers have joined the fight, in some deluded dream of glory. Neither has been home in months. The three girls are left in their small village. Her mother stalks around by night, in numb, inconsolable silence, eyes long dried and heavily sunken. The two daughters, Lily and Helen, spend long evenings huddled by the dying fire, speaking in hushed voices, muffled by the cold darkness that hung over the world.

February 14th 1940

I have had the single greatest night of my life. The church had set up a grand dance for Valentine's Day. A pointless day I had always believed. The whole village came, all dressed in their finest attire. James, having been on leave for only three days, accompanied me. He says he is being sent to France next to drive the Germans out. He's sure he will be there for a long time. The music was amazing, the hall was radiating with mummers of joy. I danced all night with James to long sweeping songs. Jordan Smith played the piano so beautifully my mother, who was huddled in the corner, began to cry softly. The last dance saw James and I, along with everyone else, on the dance floor. Elegant couples moving across the floor in elated bounds all around us.

I'm reading the entries quicker now. Every page racing impatiently before me. Lily goes on for pages about that night. The music. The people. James. Committing every last detail to paper, never wanting to forget. I grasp for more, desperately needing more. And then everything changes. Delight turns to despair. She tells of a clear day in May. There came a knock on her door. William, James' best friend and comrade was ushered into the kitchen, being intently ogled by Helen. He seemed to choke on his words, unable to force them out. Pale faced, he holds up a shaking hand, tightly clutching a letter. Lily recalled herself sinking to the cold floor, already knowing what the letter contained. Everyone knew what those letters meant. Helen was shaking her wildly in a panic, trying fruitlessly to jar her out of her trance. With a pained look, William left, his farewell came in the form of one word, "Dunkirk", with a hollow, haunted shadow to his eyes.

I didn't know I was crying until I reached up to touch my face in horror, and my hands came away slick and glistening with hot, salty tears. A hollow ache had dragged its way into my chest, gnawing at me. I didn't realise I was choking out soft, pitiful sobs until the floorboards creaked. Holding up the remains of my candle in to the dark, the dwindling radiance cast its faint glow on my grandmother's face. She shared my own sad eyes as she took in the diary that was sprawled in my lap, open still on the last page. Her wrinkled hand found mine in the dark, clasping it firmly, giving it a knowing squeeze. I wanted to say something, anything to ease the pain that was so evident in her hazel eyes. But then I understood; nothing would. I no longer had to ask what had happened to Lily, like I once did when I was a child. I already knew. Sometimes the people you love leave scars on the places they were, long after they're gone. They become part of its foundation; every street, every wave that crashes against the shore, every time the sun rises, is them. Those memories are just too much for some people. Lily left because she had to.

From a breast pocket, slightly thread bare from use, she pulled an old yellowed black and white photograph of a girl laughing, blonde ringlets bouncing, clasping the hand of a sister, both smiling devilishly. Granny Helen rose slowly, weary and stiff and sat the photo in the centre of the mantel piece. On display for everyone to see, at last. It was no longer a secret that was hardly whispered amongst the family. It was finally just an old, sad story to be told.

Mohill Pride 2017

By Sadhbh Goodwin, age 16.

It's hard, you know,

Walking through a town that is not ready for your level of self-acceptance.

We had just finished shedding old skin

To reveal new rainbow plumage that we took great pride in.

The residents of Mohill didn't seem to understand this, and as we walked down small-town shop street

Their stares felt stale with disgust.

It's hard, you know,

Trying to shield your best friends from the words that fall,

Spat from the mouths of men, on their way home from stag parties

In Carrick-on-Shannon.

But you barely know enough self defence to look after yourself.

And when the force field breaks

And shards of words, like glass, breaks through

Splinters of slurs embed themselves in tissue-tender flesh and

I know nothing about pain theory, but

Sticks and stones may break my bones,

Words weren't supposed to hurt me.

On a scale of one to ten

How much does it hurt me?

On a scale of one to ten

How much easier would life be in monochrome?

On a scale of one to ten how much pride is left?

It's hard,

But there is pride left.

And I am learning

To take back the slurs

Reclaim 'Queer', I will wear it as a winter coat

To keep out the cold and cruel looks.

Give me 'Dyke', watch me as I mould it

Into armour, for when I need to go to war

Or the shops.

I will take all their words

Until nothing they can say will hurt me

And having pride is no longer hard.

Once Upon a Starry Night

By Nene Lonergan, age 17.

He led me down the path, kicking at splashes of orange streetlights as we stumbled, laughing. Over the railing, the water glimmered, leading out into the wide unknown. He stopped abruptly and I lurched into him, face meeting the softness of his jacket; more laughter in between repeated 'sorrys'. He let go of my hand then; it's a quaint thing, how he was a stranger to me until yesterday, yet my palm has moulded into the shape of his, and felt so empty without its clammy presence. I stifled a smile as he stretched out his arms, looking out into the sea, the edges of his form glowing from the light of the moon. It was late; so late. Like Van Gogh in 'Starry Night', we stood, isolated, on top of the sleeping town; the stuff of their sweetest dreams.

He turned around, the wind in his hair. My mother was right to have pointed it out. His eyes were incredible. Everything about him was incredible.

'I never thought myself the type to sneak out at' —he checked his watch— '11:59 to spend time with a girl I barely know.'

'And I didn't think I was the type to be invited to an eleven pm sneak-out. Guess we're both discovering things today.'

'Guess we are.'

I walked up beside him and leaned on the railing, our sides only inches apart.

'I'm leaving tomorrow, you know. We only came here for the weekend.'

'We're waltzing on thin ice.'

'With the horizon close to cadence.'

The words spilled out of me, as if in a trance. I mentally slapped myself. He didn't have to know I was that pretentious.

'…I don't want to stop dancing.'

My cheeks burned. How… obscene. He sighed wistfully, looking out to the sea.

'Isn't it oh-so-tragic, Lady Capulet?'

'The greatest injustice I've ever suffered, Monsieur Montague,' I smiled.

The moored boats bobbed in soft arms of the waves, oblivious to everything. He looked at me then, but in a way that's different from how everyone else looks at me. He looked at me like I was Helen of Troy, like I alone am the contents of Pandora's box. Like I could only imagine Michelangelo must have looked at the stone from which he will set an angel free.

And then he mumbled, methodically.

'And so, being young and dipped in folly; I fell in love, with melancholy.' I tried to restrain my reaction; tried not to burst into a thousand beams of light. He said love. He said love.

'Edgar Allan Poe… but surely you could do better?' Who was this seductress speaking out of my mouth and painting my grins?

'Hmm…'

'No pressure!' I quickly added.

'Between the salt and wrestling throes / I'm pierced with arrows of awful woe, / For here she stands in moonlit glory / Afflicting, elating, in all my stories.'

It should be illegal. It should be illegal for someone to do that. It should be illegal for someone to make you feel this way. Like you're at the summit, aurora borealis behind you, and they say 'don't turn around'. Good lord. Good mighty lord. It should be illegal. He should be illegal.

'Your turn now.' His hands were shaking as he shoved them into his pockets.

'Poetry isn't my strong suit.'

'I'll help you.'

'…He whispers to me in the dead of night / Forbidden words in forbidden rites…' I paused, trying to think of the next line. He caught my words, like he was waiting at the end of the waterfall, volleying it up in cold glittering sprays.

'But bear in mind, above it all / He knows, I know, that I will fall …'

At this point he was whispering in my ear, his hot breath on my neck. We're not touching, not technically; but his words drained through me like blood. Who knew something so simple could be so intimate. Who knew it was possible to make love through a conversation?

'And what of the dawn, in the case that I did?'

'Don't trouble with morn but seal my soul with your kiss.'

It was impossible to breathe.

If only I had the power to end my life then and there, feeling that way forever, frozen like that forever.

He broke the tension.

'Okay, that sort of just slipped out of me, but I've never— I mean I have no idea how to— I've never kissed a girl.'

'It's ok, me neither! I mean— not a girl but I've never, uh boys, uh…'

Hysterically, he started to laugh; the anxiety and release of it all made me do the same.

So there we were, wayward spirits, finding each other as randomly as leaves on a winding river; fancying ourselves a couple of Shakespeares and Dickinsons; reduced to clumsy, sporadic awkwardness, falling over ourselves at the silliness of it all.

And then he kissed me and the stars fell down.

Cardboard buildings and paper trees collapsed in the winding breeze; the sky spun, throwing sparks and moons and suns into whirling seas and for the longest second there was nothing, nothing but this, but me, but him; nothing but us. And as quickly as the birth of the universe, the eye-blink of a big bang, our feet returned to the ground and we were back on earth. I tried not to stumble, my head reeling.

God knows I wanted more. God knows I wanted to throw my hands around his neck and kiss him until we destroy ecosystems and galaxies, till the world erupts into a billion pieces; till we forget how we had ever breathed without each other.

'I'd kiss you again,' he said with his eyes 'but it would ruin the poetry'

Yes it would.

You get one.

One kiss for Snow White, one for Sleeping Beauty, one for the Little Mermaid to reverse the spell; one for teenage girls and boys whose lives will never again cross paths.

'I'll walk you back to the hotel,' he said with his mouth, and I hoped he would hold my hand again, but he didn't.

***

And so we went, talking about nothing at all. As if we didn't just co-operatively tear down the sky. Isn't the oxford comma a quaint instrument? What did you think of Gatsby and Daisy? All the while on a bricked road whose yellowness faded more and more with each step.

We're going back to reality, back to real life with real boys who can't differentiate Yeats from Heaney or quote you Edgar Allen Poe or call you things you've only read about in novels. Real boys whose words aren't snow globes with the entire world inside.

A heaviness came over me and gathered at my feet, a childish stubbornness in the face of inevitability; we've arrived at the hotel, outside Dante's gate.

There were so many things to say that I decided to not say them at all. He took out his notebook, ripped out a page, folded it, and gave it to me.

'If fate ever decides to be so good that we meet again, I will awkwardly wave at you from across the room.'

'And I will do the same.'

I saluted. He smiled.

And just like that, he was gone.

Once I had successfully tiptoed past my parent's room to the sanctity of mine, I threw myself into an armchair and carefully, I unfolded the page. He must have written it yesterday.

'To the faint of heart, to the meek of mind

Your glances strike sweetly but also unkind

It brings out of hiding dreams of romance

Small, pitiful, terrified

that you'd deny me without chance.'

And on the back, scrawled in blue ballpoint pen,

'Ross O'Donnell. 086 2278626'

Me and I

By Aaron Kavanagh, age 17.

Me looks to their work with glee,

Writing with the utmost positivity.

To I, the work of me is presented,

Who, upon reading, makes me resent it.

Therefore once the review is complete

The only option for me is to 'delete'.

Tell me why I shouldn't be so hard on me?

I has free reign to act however I wishes to be,

Even if how I acts is belittling to me.

After all, think of the dreaded they;

Think of the horrible things they could say.

No. I is merely helping here to assist,

Without I, me simply couldn't exist.

And for me, I honestly knows best,

I wants to help me stand out amongst the rest,

I is the worst critic of me.

That's how it's always been

And that's how it's always going to be.

The Boys of the Hudson River

By Lydia Flanagan, age 16.

Edward's pillow no longer smelt like him. It smelt like chemicals and soaps and washing powders; of over-earnest cleaning. He had never smelt like a mortuary after they received a fresh shipping of formaldehyde. He had never smelt like a washing machine left too long with too much powder. Yet that is what his pillow remembered him by only days after his demise.

He had smelt of smoke, his mother's perfume and of wet ink. His smell had been evicted from his pillow like the memory of him from the city he knew so well. It wafted around New York, looking for a place to rest until it followed the boy it had belonged, to the bottom of the Hudson River. There it floated around in joy and mixed with scents of mint, lemon, paper, grass, coal, pollution and roses. It delighted in finally belonging with the smells of the others boys that had been led to the bottom of the Hudson.

It was July the 16th, 1968. Edward Murphy was lounging around Greenwich Village. It was the hottest day of the year and he was taking advantage of it. The evening was so warm that it could have been midday. He perched on a bench, his jeans rolled up to his mid calves as if he was paddling. Clouds of smoke from street boys lying in doorways wafted slowly and the faded neon sign of 'Hartley's Finest Coffee' tried to compete with the fierceness of the sun. The buildings towered above Edward but failed to block him from the heat.

Edward's eyes were softly closed. A passer-by may have assumed he was asleep if it had not been for his every so often readjustment of his collar. It was sticking to him; the sweat was rolling down his neck and pooling at the collar base. It was too hot for Edward to keep sitting directly in the sunlight. He wasn't the palest of folks, but even he knew that tan people like him could burn, he only had to look across at the people strolling around him, with their red shoulders and peeling noses, to see it. He opened his eyes ever so slightly and leant his head forward. He watched the street boys lying in the shade of the doorway. One of them looked familiar – was it Mike from school? Edward hadn't gone to school since last March and he suspected Mike hadn't gone for much longer.

He made his way to the doorway where the boys lay, grateful for the movement which provided some cooling for him. He stopped uncomfortably in front of them. He recognised some of the other's faces, but not enough to strike up a conversation. He looked down at who he believed to be Mike. He was looking straight upwards as if he was making patterns from the clouds. Edward wondered how his eyes weren't watering; like Edward, he didn't have eye protection.

"Are you Mike?" Edward asked the unblinking boy. The boy's mouth turned up in the corners slightly. He repositioned himself so he was sitting and looking up at Edward.

"I'm his brother, Davey," he stared straight at Edward without blinking. His eyes were rimmed red. Laughter bubbled out of his mouth. "Mike got a girl pregnant last year and went to San Francisco."

He tilted his head ever so slightly to the side. "What's it to you?"

"I was a friend of Mike's and was wondering if he'd let me share his shelter." He stared at the ground while saying this, only looking at Davey for the last two words.

Davey didn't say anything, but nodded slightly and closed his eyes again, tilting his head towards the sun. He clasped his hands over his chest as if he was praying.

Edward awkwardly sat down in the doorway and shuffled around until he could get comfortable. He didn't care about the stares and whispers from the other boys, he only cared about the cool relief he was feeling. It was like a chilled hand on his forehead after being in a fire. Edward knew that in a few months when he couldn't move because of the rain he'd be wishing for this weather. But he didn't want the scorching weather now; the relief from the heat was glorious.

Davey sat up and rested on his elbow. He leant towards Edward.

"How would you like to make some money?" He grinned like a persistent salesman.

Edward shifted. He did need money, but if he knew anything about these boys it wouldn't be in an honourable way.

"I'd love to, but I want to keep my nose clean," Edward confessed.

Davey laughed. "Of course you do. Don't you worry; your nose will be so clean by the end of this that I'll be able to see my reflection in it." He continued grinning widely like he was about to reveal a huge set of teeth.

"What do I have to do?" Edward asked.

Davey began to describe a previous event at a book shop nearer to the coast. "Frank was only having a look at a book," He paused and pointed at a grubby looking older boy, "That's Frank."

Frank nodded his head towards Edward and he nodded back.

"He was only looking and they kicked him out of the store! So I'm thinking, it's not their right to kick boys out of bookstores. It's our right to look at books in bookstores. Right?"

Edward wasn't quite sure what Davey was saying but he agreed anyway.

"And if it's our right to look at books in bookstores, it's our right to fight for justice in bookstores. And to fight for justice for Frank we need to take the books that Frank was looking at."

"You want me to steal some books?" Edward asked incredulously. He didn't expect the money-making scheme to have anything to do with literature.

"Steal? What do you take me for? I'm a fighter for justice. You'll be fighting for justice. It's a matter of principle."

"I'll do it. What books?"

Davey's smile grew even wider.

"I knew you were a good man. It's a set of encyclopaedias. But I've scoped you out and you could definitely carry them with ease. Like a feather, like a feather. Isn't that right, Frank?"

Frank nodded silently.

"That right. Even Frank could lift them and he's the closest thing to spaghetti you could find outside of a grocery store."

Davey set out the plan for Edward clearly.

"Tomorrow we'll meet a few blocks up from the store, alright? Just before lunch. New boy, you walk around the store for a while until I get around the back. You get the encyclopaedias, hide them under your jacket and get out of there. The back entrance will be unlocked for staff to leave on their lunch break. Then we sell them and split it 70-30. Seem like a plan?"

"70-30! We'll split it 50-50," Edward complained.

Davey smiled his Cheshire-cat smile again, "You drive a hard bargain, but alright. 60-40."

The next day it was colder than it had been before. It was still warm enough for beads of sweat to appear on Edward's forehead as he leaned outside the pizzeria where he was waiting for Davey. He scanned the area around him. Tourists were strolling and pulling children behind them, business men were walking and pushing past people as if they were the only ones who mattered. Groups of people loitering were littered around the street. He caught the eye of one of them and he winked at him. It took him minute to realise it was Davey.

He sauntered over to Edward. "You finally saw me then? You're as blind as Frank is dumb. And trust me, you don't want to see Frank's spelling." He chuckled to himself until he saw Edward's serious face.

"Relax, new boy. Alright, if you want to be serious then let's get down to business."

He led Edward to the bookstore in question. He followed a step behind. He could feel his stomach turning at the thought of being caught.

The shop was tall, yet so skinny it looked like a puff of wind could have knocked it over. It towered over the boys imposingly. Edward swore that it tilted slightly to the left. The store was made of brick, with green shutters and a green sign. It had a single person door and an 'open' sign barely visible through the glass. The paint of the store was peeling slightly which made it look like it was a once highly reputable business that was falling into disrepair.

Edward looked down at his feet. He had stolen before, but only essential things like bread and cigarettes. He felt a hand bracing his shoulder, Davey loomed over him. Davey gave him a shove disguised as a pat and pushed him into the store.

Edward stumbled inside. The walls were covered ceiling to floor with books. He could see a desk with a staff member poking out from behind some of the hundreds of stacks of books. Gentle music was playing quietly from the staff member's record player.

Edward pretended to peruse the book selection, with every step walking closer to the back of the store where the encyclopaedias were. He saw the back exit and walked quickly towards it. His heart was beating like a train pounding down its tracks. He saw the encyclopaedias and began pulling them out. He nearly dropped them on the floor as soon as he had picked them up; it seemed that Davey had seriously underestimated the weight of the books.

Edward regained the balance of the books and slipped them under his jacket. He looked suspiciously over his shoulder. His jacket barely covered half of the books and they stuck out at an odd angle.

He shot a last fleeting glance over his shoulder and pushed open the back door. He ran head first out of it.

Edward was ecstatic– he had done it. He had successfully burgled a set of encyclopaedias bigger than most two-year-old children. He stopped suddenly and his breathing grew even more erratic than it had been beforehand.

In front of him was an employee smoking.

They both froze for a moment, unsure of what to do. Edward didn't know what the employee would do to him if he caught him. The employee didn't know what his boss would do to him if he let the boy escape. He recognised the books Edward had poorly attempted to hide and knew that they were even older and more valuable than Davey had told Edward.

In a split-second decision, Edward decided to make a run for it.

The employee was a second ahead of Edward and had him by the scruff of the neck by the time he tried to pass him. Edward squirmed in his grip and tried to wriggle out of his jacket that the employee was grasping so tightly. Edward slunk down in defeat once he realised that he couldn't escape. He had failed and wouldn't get his money.

He was beginning to accept his fate when he saw someone jump on the employee and flatten him to the ground. The figure sprang back up and ran from the scene. He looked back over his shoulder and called to Edward.

"Run, you idiot!" Davey yelled.

Edward didn't hesitate any longer and took off at a ferocious pace after his partner in crime, making sure he had the books firmly in his grasp.

Together they nearly knocked over several disgruntled street vendors and almost flattened a cat who dared to step into their path. They thundered up alleys, around roads, along blocks and through the streets. Edward didn't know where they were going but he trusted Davey to get them out of trouble safely.

Edward could see a body of water in front of him and he skidded to a halt as he realised he was approaching too near to it. It was the Hudson River.

He turned around to see if the bookstore employee was still chasing them. He let out a relieved sigh when he realised that he had given up, probably long ago. He turned to Davey.

"He's gone, should we go sell the books now?"

Davey cleared his throat.

"I can carry the books, they seem heavy," Davey offered.

"I can manage," Edward replied.

"Hand them over," He gritted his teeth into a smile, "You're tired, I can see that. Don't refuse a kind offer from a friend." He held out his arms.

Edward reluctantly handed the books over to him.

"Good," Davey said.

Davey moved closer towards the water and loosened his grip on the books. Suddenly, one of them tumbled out of his hands and fell with a splash into the river.

"No!" Edward screamed.

"Go get it!" Davey yelled.

"Me?" He asked, confused. Surely this was the sort of heroic act that Davey would typically love to be a part of.

"Yes, I can't swim," he looked at Edward's hesitant expression. "Now!" He commanded.

Edward waded into the river; the cold water made him shiver and recoil. He paddled out to where the book was and threw it to the shore. Davey caught it. Edward made his way back to the shore and tried to pull himself out of the water.

His efforts were fruitless as he kept sliding back into the cool depts. He tried again but couldn't get a grip on the slippery surface of the river bank.

"Davey, pull me up!"

Davey looked at Edward dead in the eyes and waded into the water.

"I don't think I'm going to do that."

"But-I thought you couldn't swim. Why are you getting in the water?"

"You know, you shouldn't trust boys you meet on the street."

"Why are you saying that? Davey? Davey!" He was panicking; if Davey didn't help him back to land he would eventually drown or get hypothermia.

The last thing Edward saw was Davey's grinning face. He didn't blink while he spoke.

"If it makes you feel better, you're not the first. You'll have company down there."

"Down there? What do you mean?" Edward was cut off by Davey plunging Edward head first into the water.

Edward thrashed around and tried to bring his head above the water, but Davey was stronger than he looked and kept him pushed down. Edward felt the icy water reach every part of his body and after a while he began to feel drowsy. His vision started to blur and fade in and out. He stopped splashing as his body grew limp. He tried to scream as the last remnants of life left his body, but water had filled his lungs.

Davey released his hand and climbed back onto the shore. He had had enough practice to pull himself up easily. He watched as he lost sight of Edward's body in the water.

Davey sold the books. And he got 100% of the profit.

Love

By Brooke Feldman, age 16.

A swelling heart,

An aching soul,

Trapped inside a prison of flesh and blood.

The greatest addiction known to mankind.

Love.

The everlasting search for safe vulnerability,

The twists and turns on dangerous roads that come with it.

What is this attraction to love we feel that turns us into co-dependent fools?

Falling into the abyss, even when we know better.

Yet, we always climb out only to fall back in again until finally the abyss closes,

And you are either above it or below it.

And you have no choice in the matter.

Swing

By Bronwyn Harding, age 17.

The chains, once shiny and new,

Now rusty and old, chipping away.

Used all day, every day.

Now barely used at all.

I used to swing so high,

And touch the sky.

Feeling like I could fly

Away —

Away from this new day,

Away from this darkness,

Just me, and my swing.

But going up, I come down,

Again.

And in that split second,

My heart races.

The moment everything pauses,

In that split second.

Before you swing down again.

I wish that second could last forever.

In that split second

I let go.

– And I fly.

Inis Meáin

By Arianna McKirdy, age 17.

How can I be happy here?

When my heart is filling a gap in the claí,

where the light shines through.

Everything is wild there, the claí,

which sprawls in every direction like bad handwriting,

The waves that throw themselves against the cliffs,

Which remain raw and defiant.

The sea air seeped through our skin

And pulsed in our veins

until we too were as wild as the rabbits

that dart through the machair

and the bramble bushes that explode

with blots of berries in Mean Fomhair.

The island people are tired of wildness.

They tie the legs of the goats to each other

So they can't jump the claí

and roam to their heart's content.

They'd do it to us too

if they could catch us.

The Grand Abomination

By Ben Martin, age 16.

"AND THE LORD OF DARKNESS WAS CAST FROM HIS
THRONE, AND THE NIGHTMARES HIDING IN THE DARK
WERE REVEALED BY THE HELLISH FIRES OF A NEW
TERROR"

The Year of our Holy Lord 977

The hallways screamed. That was the only way to describe it. With a dark
red colour permeating the air and staining everything it touched like some
noxious infection, the walls throbbed like a living being, textured with
flaking skin. On them were carved indescribable patterns the likes of
which made my forehead hurt, and the floor was strewn with small wax
figures. I stopped for a moment to pick one up, turning it over to reveal
the snarling insectoid vista of a fly. I was hurried forwards by the beings
that flanked me and began to stumble ahead once more. Tall and
seemingly made from the same malleable substance as the wall, with
crooked arms and loped gait they held onto ornate brass spears. The one
on my left had shrivelled skin that seemed too small for his anatomy, so
that muscle and gristle was visible heaving beneath. Where its head should
have been there was merely a twisted lump of flesh, crowned with long
fingers containing far too many joints that wafted in the blazing air. The
thing on my right was similar in stature, however his arms ended in
stumps, and his head was a twitching mass, with rows of human teeth
visible in the wound shaped slash of its mouth. I nearly tripped over
another wax figure, and they slashed at me with their weapons. I walked
on.

***

When I had arrived in this place days earlier, I had thought that this was
some foreign land or purgatory. The Irish, for Ireland was the land I
travelled through on a mission of bringing God to the pagans, were a

superstitious people. They believed that underneath the hills and fens were whole worlds made of dreams, populated by 'little folk' as the Irish called them. I myself would not tolerate such nonsense, and I had spent the past few days resting at St. Kevin's monastery to clear my head of them. The monks there had survived the pillaging of the Vikings, and they welcomed me and my work with hospitality. We ate bread in their dining room and talked of religious matters until the sun set. The monastery itself was very old, its stones worn and covered in lichen, despite the efforts of the gardeners the monks hired.

The monks had started to unnerve me however after a day or two, when I realised not one had stepped outside in the time I had been there, and at night they looked odd, with crooked shadows and lopsided grinning features. That and the fact that every single item of food they ate, which they produced from some hidden storehouse, so they did not have to leave the crumbling stone of their abode, was so profusely blessed it practically dripped holy water. I complained about it the first evening, but they explained that the food here 'requires it' and stated I would complain no more. I did as I was told as I presumed they viewed it insulting of me to question their ways while I was a guest.

The final straw was when, to sate my curiosity, I began to ascend the high tower in the centre of the complex. As I rose higher a foul stench grew until I could ascend no further, and I went back to my room defeated. When I reached my room, it was filled with the vacant faces of the monks as they crowded my bed. Dressed in their official robes and each holding an ornate candelabrum, the candles tinted red in the moonlight streaming in from my singular window, they stood still and silent while I berated them for this most unusual behaviour and I demanded to know its reasoning. They refused, apologised for disturbing me and left, leaving me alone in my room bar the blackbirds which had taken to roosting in the ceiling.

I left that morning, taking all my supplies, maps, and a bible I had taken from the monastery without the monks' permission. I prayed for forgiveness for stealing, however I doubt it mattered as the monks were dubious at best when it came to their practices. Atop my horse I set off into the Wicklow mountains, hoping to make it to the nearest town on the other side of the range within the next few days. With the hill my maps labelled 'Scarr' to the right of me, rising out of the cold winters ground to cast its shadow over Brockagh Mountain to the left, I started to follow a small river upwards.

Despite all its faults, blasted rain included, Ireland was truly a land of beauty. In the browns and greys of the mountainside backed with the bluest skies I had seen, I could see small dots of white grazing amidst the bright yellow gorse that engulfed the lower slopes and slowly melted into the greens of the forest I walked through. Green was everywhere you looked, and I understood why they called it the Emerald Isle, for its forests and pastures were somehow more appealing here than anywhere else. The woods I walked through was scattered with pine trees and mighty oaks wormed their branches through the canopy, colouring the brittle ground with dappled sunlight.

However, I was not here to admire the scenery, I was here on duty. The sunlight shone on my armour as my horse made its way slowly through the valley, and I thought upon the monks. They deeply troubled me, and I feared that had I not been investigating whatever lay at the top of the tower they would have killed me in my bed or perhaps performed some unknowable ritual. I had heard legends of their patron saint, who talked to animals and ate the sickness in children, and how he was said to have drowned a woman in the nearby lake. The few pagans left in the area believed the woman had turned into a banshee and that her screams could be heard rolling across the dark and bottomless waters.

That night, after the sun set below the black sheet of the horizon and the stars had spilled across the sky in all their glory, I heard a sound. The fire had long gone out and my supplies, wrapped in a leather bag, were resting across from me. I had eaten rabbit and then rested, reading scripture and planning my preaching before taking off my armour and wrapping up under a blanket. I had just begun to drift off when I heard the sound, and it took me a while to realise what it was due to my grogginess. It was my horse, whining in discomfort. I shrugged off my blanket and stood up, looking around. The tree where my horse had been tethered was across the campfire, and, thanks to the faint embers of the fire, I could see that the rope my horse had been tied with was cut.

Blasted ungodly pagans, they had probably stolen my horse to eat. I hurriedly dressed and donned my armour, wrapping some spare cloth around a stick and lighting it to form a torch. Making sure I brought my maps, so I did not get lost, I headed out to search for my horse. The forest was silent save for my feet through the undergrowth, and I could barely see anything. Following tracks made by my horse, I found myself at a ledge. Below me was a small rock face made of crumbling scree, covered in tangled branches and bushes. Very careful not to slip, for the slope continued for some time downwards, I made my way through the undergrowth towards the rock face. Leaning against a great pine tree to support myself, I noticed the ledge seemed to have been formed when a part of the slope gave way, creating an overhang. Within this overhang was where I saw it. A hole, a deep dark cave that must have been opened up by the fall, nestled between the twigs and damp soils of the forest floor. It was in here that the faint tracks led.

The roof of the cave was low, coated in a thin layer of tiny roots that stretched down from above like grasping fingers. The walls, lit by my torch, were made of mud and soil, black and brown turning to grey stone as it reached the floor. If the forest outside was silent, in here was somehow even quieter. The only signs my horse had been here were the marks on the floor and walls where it had been dragged along, with considerable force. Judging by the size of the cave I doubted the large animal would make it out unharmed and I felt pity for the creature and prayed for it as I walked. Suddenly, the walls opened out and I found myself in a relatively spacious area. I must have been far under the hillside at this point, so that not even the faint moonlight could reach me and all I saw by was the flickering of my torch. This must have been where the pagans had been hiding out, unnoticeable against the forest floor or the valley sides.

But there, far along the cave walls, which were unusually dry to the touch, was a softly glowing light. The sort of light an anvil makes after the flaming smiths hammer has just cracked down once more, or as the embers of a dying fire give their last breath. Holding my torch out in front of me I slowly made my way forward, wary of whatever this mysterious anomaly was.

As I got closer a boiling heat built up, so that I was sweating under my armour and when I tried to pull my sword it felt slippery in my grip. I was now close enough to see my horse, lying alongside the wall of the cave, backed by the strange light. I could see grisly wounds on the horse, and presumed him dead, before looking for the source of the light. The wall behind the horse was cracked and flaking, and it was through these cracks that the light was emitting. Strange formations, made of some pulsing black material, were crawling up the wall and draping across the floor and over my horse, and appeared to be releasing the intense heat. I had no idea what any of this was, however I could tell it was unnatural.

I had never met any godly or hellish beings, or had any holy visions before, but I was sure that the obsidian flesh sloughing from the walls within this cave was not of this world. I approached it carefully and put my torch close.

This was a mistake, as when I put the fire near the material, which upon closer inspection glistened and shone in the light while looking like clay or mud, it began pulsing with renewed vigour. I jumped back, startled, before rushing forward to try to retake my saddle from the horse. It was valuable and while I no longer had a horse, I would need it for when I reached my destination.

As I reached for the straps that tied the saddle around the corpse of the horse, I felt an immense force pull back and with my hand caught in the straps, I was pulled towards the wall at great speed. The black material was soft and unyielding, and I was dragged straight through, the incredible heat burning my face and scorching my armour. Unimaginable pain and scorching temperatures blasted me as I slid along the ground.

And then, as suddenly as it had started, the experience stopped, and I was no longer being heaved along. I felt coarse dirt and sand beneath me, being blown about by a soft breeze. Slowly I tried to open my eyes, which took a considerable amount of effort and I feared my face had been badly damaged by the heat. When I managed to open them however, I muttered a prayer and begged for my forgiveness.

The sky was wrong. From my position, laying on my back the first thing I could see was the sky and there was something about it that didn't feel right. Dusty grey and black clouds roiled and churned above, and ash fluttered down like snow from some unknown source. The air itself was heavy, thick as though laden with moisture, and I had to take deep painful breaths for it to work its way down to my lungs. All that greeted me was silence. I slowly began to sit up, closing my eyes again and groaning with pain. I must have broken bones, and the skin on my face and neck felt taught and hot. The heat in this place was also unbearable, and I quickly fumbled with the straps on my breastplate until I could take it off. The ground on which I threw the armour was a pale red soil, covered in a thin layer of sand constantly being blown by the breeze. Then I fully opened my eyes and looked up.

The ground around me was flat for as far as I could see, and a thin veil of ash-filled fog obscured my view. But beyond that an oddly curved horizon displayed a landscape that I will never forget. Mountains of indescribable size rose from the smog, each a jagged tooth of deep crimson rock and stone. Peaks capped with grey littered the mountain range, and the highest of them cut the clouds in two. Raised plateaus and flatlands curved between the mountains and valleys, some covered in what looked like forests made of pitch-black trees. It was both beautiful and terrifying all at once, and I quickly became short of breath.

Turning behind me to where I'd come from, I was faced with a steep slope of rust-coloured scree, with ribbons and veins of the strange black substance oozing between the rocks. I knew I wouldn't be able to survive going back through, so I whispered a prayer and set about finding an alternative way back to Ireland, for I was somehow as far away as I could possibly be. I managed to stand up shakily and look around. My breastplate lay on the ground, and the marks in the soil where I had come through were also there. My hand must have come free as I came here, for my horse was nowhere to be seen, and only another track in the dirt showed where it had been pulled along. I decided to follow, in the little hope it might lead to somewhere other than some beast's lair.

It wasn't too long following the trail that breathing began to become increasingly difficult. The air here was different and tasted foul and felt sluggish to move through. My lips and tongue were also parched, for the heat and lack of water were taking their toll. Even concentrating on the marks in the soil where my horse had been dragged was difficult, and my vision swayed with each step.

Surrounded by nothing but flat land and mist, with the occasional cliff or slope appearing either side and rising into the sky above, I was completely alone. The trail seemed to start descending at some point and I quickly found myself scrambling down one of the hillsides. Loose rock tumbled around me, and dark shaped began to appear from the mist. After a moment of panic, I realised they were just trees, needle-like and protruding from the ground completely straight. The bark was leathery and black like the hide of a beast and the rotten stench in the air intensified around them. The ground was covered in them and I realised I had entered a forest of some kind. Unnaturally silent, the ever-present mist seemed to soak up the sound so that even my own footsteps couldn't be heard, and the trees crowded around so that I soon became lost. There were no roots for me to trip over and the ground was still the same, so I could thankfully still follow the trail as it slithered through the trunks.

Now breathing really was becoming difficult, and I feared I would faint or die from lack of proper air before I left the woods, becoming just another pile of dust in this hellish place. Suddenly the world swayed and flickered and the next thing I knew was I was splayed across the ground. Heaving in gulps of air I tried to stand, and shakily crawled to my feet by clinging onto a nearby tree. It was fleshy to the touch. The path, which was there a minute ago, seemed to have disappeared and I turned around frantically in a panic. Where in god's name had it gone? Praying to myself for his guidance, I set off in a random direction and hoped it was right. However, I feared that god's goodwill could not reach this unholy land.

Thankfully after wandering lost for a while, still on the verge of fainting again, I managed to find the tracks. They led deeper and deeper into the forest, where the trees crowded in closer and closer until I noticed some were leaning to the side where my horse had been forcefully pulled through. Then suddenly, as I began to sway, my vision darkened once more. I feared I'd never be able to find the trail again, but then I saw something through the mist. Completely silent, a large lump I presumed to be my horse was slowly fading into the fog. Behind it, with long spindly limbs wrapped tightly around the neck of my former steed, was a disturbing silhouette with a long ribbed body and far, far too many legs. The unnameable beast disappeared into the fog, and I never saw it again.

Then my sight disappeared, and I felt myself fall into the emptiness of unconsciousness once more.

I awoke with a pounding headache and lungs burning for air. I wouldn't last more than a day here. The sky was still the same churning ashen grey, yet it seemed to be moving quicker. I then realised it was I who was moving. I felt tarp or cloth beneath me and felt a swaying motion as if I was being carried. Looking to either side showed me I was on some kind of stretcher, and the landscape I was in was more disturbing than the last. A thin trail wound through piles upon piles of rock and debris. Like some monumental desert, boulders and stones of black material spread out into the distance with crevices, canyons, pillars and cliffs permeating the archaic landscape. Some even looked like the ruins of buildings, but I dismissed that thought. What horrific civilisation could actually have ever lived in this ghastly place.

Then I looked ahead of me.

The hunched thing quivered with each lumbering step it took. The colour of dried leather, it was vaguely human in shape. Large and broad with patches of spiked or scaly skin, it was at least eight feet tall and two huge arms extended back out of a raged shawl draped across its shoulders, holding onto the front of my stretcher. Each hand had an unsettlingly large number of fingers, with two extra joints on each so that it looked like a spider was protruding obscenely from each. With the consistency of clay, shapes I would normally think of as muscle twitched and heaved beneath its skin, and its head swayed with each footfall.

The head itself I cannot accurately describe, I can only compare it to more worldly things. It was as if someone had taken the blade of an axe, draped it with loose folds of rotting skin, and then sprinkled a series of black and beady eyes along each side. These swivelled and blinked each of their own accord, some staring at me, others ahead. I followed their sight and my heart skipped a beat. A procession, which followed the trail and stretched to the horizon and upwards, made entirely of these daemonic beings. Some were tall and thin, with multiple gangly arms and heads little more than mounds of meat, while others were fat and broad, with strange protrusions jutting from their heads and waving in the air, while shards of red metal orbited along their spines, hovering. Now that I noticed, many had these oddly shaped anomalies circling their various appendages. God forbid, some of the beings even had the horns of a goat or a bull. All were wrapped in tunics or shawls, and they all marched in time with each other, creating an unending and incessant beating, a drumbeat for the hounds of hell. I now truly believed I had somehow fallen into the pit itself, and I wished god could show me an escape. The one with the axe-head turned, and what sounded like the words of some abysmal and antique language emitted from it, as if it was trying to speak to me.

I promptly fainted again.

Flashes of strange landscapes. Breathing is becoming harder and more laboured.

Bright red lights.

A flat field of grey dust, the horizon curving at the edges. Hundreds of workers toiling with picks and implements the size of a man, carving out the mud and rock. Beasts of burden dragging loaded carts, their pale white heads swivelling at all angles, blind and sightless, while their many jointed legs heave them along.

Darkness.

Flats receding behind, the ground is now a messy jumble of boulders and rubble similar to what I had seen before. Many different trails wound through like snakes, and above the sky was belching black smoke. Far in the distance there was a haze of fiery light, and in my sickness I thought I saw spires and towers stretching into the air and faint exotic smells and shrieking sounds on the hot wind.

More darkness. I fear the gaps in my consciousness are getting longer, though I don't have much time to ponder this before I slip into the comfort of nothingness once more.

Cresting a mountain. Piles of snow-like ash litter the thin trail and I do not look down. In the distance, surrounded by dozens of high walls and a blasted desolate plain I see an object too huge to fathom spearing the clouds, silhouetted by sanguine light.

Nothingness. How long have I been here? Does time still function? I do not know when I doomed myself by entering that cave in the now dreamlike Wicklow mountains.

Crossing the plain. There is nothing here bar the shadow of what I can only assume is an immeasurably huge citadel. From this distance it faintly resembles the tower of Babel itself, although surely it must be a coincidence. The ground here is parched and cracked as if there used to be water, but that water is long gone.

We come up to one of the walls. I do not know which. Our procession has been joined by dozens of others, each mingling and waiting for the massive iron gate to open. I see a wide variety of beings and animals, seemingly each unique from the next. One, riding on top of a creature with a disturbingly human face, has wings made of rotating shards and twitches them restlessly. Another towers above at least twelve feet, with a veritable army of grasping hands pouring from what I can only assume is its mouth. They all either look at me with some sort of curiosity, or ahead with what I think to be nervousness. They fear whatever dark thing lays squatted within that palace, or citadel, or tower or whatever it is. The walls around the gate are covered in eyes, and they blink in unison as it slowly swings open.

Blackness once more.

I am made to stand, and two guards come to guide me through the tunnels and hallways that worm through this place. I awoke inside and have no recollection of arriving; however my breathing comes easier inside, and I celebrate that as a little victory. The guards themselves are as disturbing as all the other inhabitants of this place, with the exception of their beautifully carved brass spears, and they prodded me every time I swayed or stopped. The walls and ceilings were covered in strange symbols that seemed to flow and spiral forwards. The image of a fly with a snarling twisted grin was everywhere, and I had a vague and terrifying idea of just who I may be facing. There are many different texts explaining the nature of hell, and while I refuse to believe that is where I am, there are some similarities. And if the fly iconography represents who I think it does, then I accept that I may not survive much longer.

We came to a door. A normal-sized door made from dark wood, which seemed out of place amidst the surrealism of everything I had just been through. I was prodded and stumbled forward, making my way through the door and closing it quietly shut behind me.

I turned around and found that my voice escaped me no matter how desperately I wanted to scream.

The chamber I was in was monumental, with arches and alcoves littering the stone walls, and a faint light filtering in from above.

And there, sitting upon a bare throne the size of a small house and carved from the same rock as the wall, was what I could only assume was the Lord of the Flies himself. Beelzebub, the usurper of hell, the grand abomination.

A humanoid figure with a ribbed chest and long, three-jointed insectile arms, he hunched forward on his throne studying me. His body was covered in shimmering carapace, glimmering with colour similar to oil, and he wore armour of red marble on his shoulders. Robes extended down, covering his legs and what I guessed might be a second pair of smaller arms twitched at his sides. Framing his form were giant wings, twisting and curving so that it looked like they could never lift his immense bulk, but I knew they probably could all the same. His head however was the only part of him not seemingly perfect. Two empty dead eyes, like an insect, swivelled and stared, and his mouthparts moved of their own accord like rows of fingers.

The imperfection I mentioned took the form of a huge scar twisting down from the left, a wound so great the horns there were missing and the halo was shattered. Bits of flesh and broken horn floated silently, orbiting his head like the red shards did on his underlings, giving him a true, if slightly lopsided, halo. When he finally stopped studying me he leaned back and spoke. His voice sounded like whispers in my ear, yet I knew it must really be deafening.

"Where do you come from, strange One?" it asked, "I have never seen your kind before. So whimsical and little. Delicate even."

I trembled and found myself short of breath again, but I managed to choke out a response. Why I was telling him I did not know, but for some reason I felt compelled to.

"I… I come from the Church. I travelled to a land called Ireland to spread the word of God and the fear of… of things like you," I stuttered, and the abomination showed signs of interest.

"Things like me you say?" it gave a rasping laugh, "Child, there are no things like me. The last thing as powerful as me was thrown down from the top of this tower while I took his Throne, little one. But do continue, your tales of this… God… interest me. "

Why was I speaking to this thing? Was it making me? I continued, "I found a way from my world into yours. Please, I did not mean to come here, please," and at that I fell to my knees in desperation. I understood none of this, meanwhile the fly just sat and looked thoughtful.

"Another world you say?" I nodded. "Well… this is interesting. Could you perhaps show me and my generals where you came through…?" I nodded again in defeat, unaware I had perhaps doomed my world. A cruel delighted smile spread across the fly's crooked face, and its empty eyes lit up with new ideas and the indefinable concept of evil was made clear to me in those twitchy orbs.

"We have a lot of work to do, you and me, my friend. Why don't you start by telling me everything you know about this brave new world of yours?"

The Blizzard of 1510

By Philippa Byford, age 16.

The blizzard covers my tracks almost the moment I leave them in the snow and the gales rock whole trees back and forth either side of me, howling like the hungry wolves that once roamed these dark forests.

I pull my shawl tighter around myself and duck my head against the next stiff gust of icy wind. It stains at the shoulder in minutes, but I keep going; to stop now would be suicide, and, without exercise to keep warm, I might as well lie down in the snow and die of my own accord.

Fight on, a voice shouts through the darkness of my mind. I squint against the loss of vision and my ears prick beneath my helmet.

"Rob…" I mutter into the shawl, before clamping my mouth shut.

Forget him, I say internally to my hallucinating brain. He's probably dead in a field somewhere. Even England's best soldier could not survive that ambush. Let alone a lone archer from the north east.

My armour clanks with every heavy step I take: the boots are starting to drag uselessly through the snow and the sword in its dull scabbard is a deadweight at my side, which makes me miss my knives all the more. The shawl is becoming useless now; I've wrapped it every which way around myself, particularly around my dying shoulder, and it is practically drenched in blood now.

"Bloody hell," I hiss as I pry the wool away from the wound. It stings like when John threw me into a patch of thistles and nettles, throbbing with every heartbeat and still bleeding. Snow gathers on the open skin, cooling the burning deep in my remaining blood. How had Rob managed to bandage Much's stump of an arm when he'd lost it? Trust me to forget.

Another gust of wind almost sends me falling back into the snow drifts. I grit my teeth against the biting cold and pull my shawl around my shoulders again. Damn this breastplate and its shoddy making. It's just my luck that it fell apart with one hit of a French arrow. Actually, just damn the arrow.

My knees buckle and I fall against the sheltered trunk of a nearby fir tree. I shiver all over and collapse entirely, straight into the icy blanket beneath me. It soaks the lower half of my tunic all the way through until my undershirt sticks to my skin. The sword lies at a funny angle, pulling my belt in the most unladylike fashion.

Ladylike. I scoff and rest my head against the tree, shaking all over as the blizzard picks up again. A lady doesn't steal her brother's armour and run off to fight invading Frenchmen with her heart's desire. Nor does she tie up her hair beneath a cap and fight the tyranny of a monarchy with a band of men, or wear their clothing and take a boy's name.

Will Scarlet. I'd thought it fetching at the time, a sure-fire way to become a living legend. Will had half a chance of becoming something, someone. Marian stood none.

Will Scarlet. I roll my eyes and close them. Perhaps, if I die here with no one around to say otherwise, Will shall die in Rob's battle. The stories they'll tell! Two friends, comrades, part of the same band, falling side by side.

I pull a face, keeping my eyes tight shut. Good God, how morbid! I open them again and slap myself awake with a crack of skin on skin. Is the hunger getting to me at last? Never imagined I'd be missing John's rabbit stew—

A flicker of light catches my attention from afar. I squint into the forest. There it is again: the soft glow of flickering candlelight in the distance.

I'm insane. This is a mirage. I chuckle to myself and brush the snow from my helmet, watching as it falls like an avalanche before my eyes. I push myself to my feet, peering into the darkness of the night and the blizzard. At least if I die now, I'll die seeing a log cabin or something similar, no matter how fake the image may be.

One foot in front of the other, I barely hear the crunch of millions of snowflakes beneath my brother's boots. Rob's voice cheers me on in my mind, battling with John, Much and Alan for my attention, something that never usually happens in day to day life. I smile and push on.

I drag myself towards the candlelight, leaning against the occasional tree until I rebuild enough strength to get a little closer. The candle flickers again in its glass case as I approach and I stand transfixed by its light a few feet away, only breaking my gaze when another gust of wind blows snowflakes down my neck thanks to my useless, loosening breastplate.

A small tavern, made of snow-dusted stone and a roof of thatched hay. I smile and head straight for the oak door. Maybe I won't be so hard done by if I die seeing this quaint little inn.

I push the door open and step inside, met with a wave of heat from the roaring open fire on the other side of the bar room. And silence. A long, hard silence.

The door slams behind me, silencing the howls of the blizzard. What seems like thousands of eyes stare at me as I shake the snow from my shawl into a nearby bucket and hang it on the cloak rack. The guard at the door stiffens slightly when he sees the splashes of blood on the melting snow, but doesn't say a word. All eyes in the room are on me. All except one pair.

The innkeeper watches me like a cat would watch a mouse as he cleans a wooden mug with a raggy old cloth. The man he's serving doesn't turn on his bench to stare at me, but takes a swig of his ale, the green hood of his cloak not falling from his face.

I shuffle through the crowds of drinking or nearly drunk men to the only available seat: a large armchair by the fire. I'm surprised no one has taken it yet, until I see the cracked window nearby and feel the occasional snap of freezing wind. The chair groans beneath me and all the eyes follow.

"Go back to your drinks," a low voice says, breaking the painful silence. I glance at the hooded man, but he stays hunched over his drink at the counter and takes another gulp of ale. "Leave the boy alone."

The men comply and I relax into the chair, staring into the flames and wondering just how long this mirage might last. It seems almost too real to be a trick of my mind, but isn't that why so many people fall for them?

"Mead," I say to a passing waiter as I pull my helmet off and let the cascades of dark hair loose down my back. The helmet clatters to the slabstone floor and I rub my soaked skin against the hide of deer that serves as a chair drape, leaving my cheek buried in the warmth of the fur. As I close my eyes, I hear the cries of battle ringing in my ears; commands being screamed from all directions, the shouts and gurgles of men as they're hit with enemy arrows—

And Rob's voice, louder than them all and right beside me, telling me to flee the battle when he found out I'd followed him there, to retreat up north.

I grit my teeth against the cacophony. Say this inn is real. Say I'm not outside freezing to death. What then? What's my next move? Nottingham is days away by foot and this blizzard is only a hindrance.

"Your mead, girl." I peer through my frosty eyelashes, met with the sight of a mug of drink and a gloved hand right before my nose. My eyes widen and I grab it, throwing some coin at the waiter's feet from my tunic pocket and gulping down the honey-made drink as if it's life itself. "Take your time with that, Scar. I need you healthy. I'm not carrying you home this time."

I stop drinking.

That voice.

That name. Only four people in this world call me Scar.

I stare up at the hooded man in horror. A pair of bright, ocean-blue eyes look back from the shadows, worried and strong. I stifle a sharp breath and some remaining mead runs the wrong way down my throat.

"Robin!" I splutter, choking on the alcohol. He snaps his hand over my mouth with a long 'Shhhh!' I cough like a sick, old man until it clears and flop back into the chair. That voice. I look again at those eyes, cracking something in my neck loudly.

"Rob!" I say again, in the lowest hiss I can manage. "How in God's good name are you alive?"

"Ignore that for now," he says, shaking the cloak I didn't see him fetching in front of the fire and tossing it to me. "Get out of that armour, Scar. There's a lot of distance between here and Nottingham."

A Grave Goodbye

By Hannah Murphy, age 17.

Nothing remains,

Only broken hearts and tearful eyes,

Red and puffy, staring at your name engraved

On a single slab of slate.

Nobody remembers.

Most don't know, others don't care,

Except for those avoiding eye contact

By bowing heads and thinking.

A stranger in paradise,

A nobody on earth.

Alone, except for the handful of prayers,

Whispered from the mouth of a mother

Who never held you in her arms,

But will hold you forever in her heart.

Dawn

By Danny Dermody, age 17.

My table stands confidently in front of me. It boasts last night's needles and roaches, as well as many more nights before. I pick up the fallen can, its contents I've just stepped in. I finish it off. I rise like the broken toy I am and stagger to the bathroom. The mirror watches my every move. Dead behind the eyes. I can see right through me. My ribs pierce me. My skin crawls at the sight of me. Every breath serves as another stab wound to my heart. Each day, week, month pulls me ever so close. The edge of darkness, I'm almost there. Clinging with my might to the end, not sure why I'm even trying anymore...

My mind goes back... to her... eyes as brown as chestnut oak, would judge you more than any barrage of words could. Velvet hair that could seduce anyone to her not so innocent soul. A delicate touch that could slow down a lorry. Badly done eyeliner shower her pain with black tears. She was a body of work. A demon disguised as an angel. She's gone, she left me, yet she remains. Nailed to my back like a crucifix, helping me march to my inevitable death. She's what I needed, as miserable as me. She was the record player that could play a broken record. We were a Ferrari. Great to look at but would spin out of control. Maybe too many times. We brought out the worst in each other yet it was the greatest time of my life. Drug induced comas, music only we could understand and too much trouble to handle. Truly living in the moment. Something I never did.

I never thought it would be. No one to care for. Living in a motel. No one thinks it will be them, do they. I was actually good in school. It was my college years when it went downhill. The wrong crowd. I suppose that's the cliché isn't it. Never their own fault. I never really had anything that made me tick. Other than the chaos. That's what attracted me to her I suppose.

We used to escape to places like these. High out of our minds. So much paraphernalia, it would make Kurt Cobain proud. We would just lay on the ground, CD's scattered like UFO's trying to capture the wild frontier, embracing the music. Our connection was something else. Those were the good times. Never mind the countless fights, breakups and screaming matches we had. She was an absolute psycho. The time we were out and a girl had a good look at me. Ah the poor lassie, she was beaten to a pulp. She was more protective than me and I loved it. Ying and Yang without the Ying. We were too similar, that was the problem, or so I like to tell myself.

Screw it! Now's a better time than ever to visit. The air outside is a crisp cold. Refreshing actually. The streets are empty. Isn't everything nowadays? The neon lights remind me of 70's New York. I light a cigarette. Seems appropriate in this setting. From one corner to the next is trouble. I blend in now. Like dogs, they smell fear. That's why they don't bother me anymore. I used to have something to live for. The trees and gates are intertwined to create barrier to keep me out. I open the rusted gate. It creaks. Thousands of people surround her, one story to the next. Easy to get lost if you don't know where you're going. I found my way easy enough "In loving memory of Denise Smith. Aged 27, loving daughter, sibling, aunt."

It kills me not to see wife there.

"Hi," my voice cracks. I'm sick of my voice already. I lay against the headstone. "So how have you been lately?" Ah this is too hard. I drop my head into my hands. Why is this so bloody hard? A warm tear rolls down my frozen cheek. "I've been in a bad place lately. AAAAGGGGGGGHHHHH". I stand up and balance myself against her. "JESUS, you couldn't have left a bloody note or something, would that have been so hard!" my teeth are so clenched they could challenge a pit bull. "But now you just killed yourself". I drop to the ground, a stream of tears turn into a sea. I roll back and forth, before I start clawing away at the stones that block me from my baby. I soon hit the concrete layer, and punch it. I scream with every emotion I've ever had since her death. Sobbing, I soon retain myself "I'm sorry I just can't... I just can't anymore, not without you."

Tonight's the night. The night it ends. The cross nailed to my back dissipates into a dark cloud above me it slowly starts to drizzle. I don't feel cold anymore. The drizzling turns into lashing. Maybe they're the thousands of tears I've shed. Maybe its god crying in disappointment. I don't care. I start running. Almost there. Just around the corner.

I arrive, swinging my leg over the railing of the bridge. Carefully dragging the other one behind. Once I'm over, I instinctively hug the railing of the bridge before I slowly turn around. The railing presses my back just below my shoulder blades. I look down. My heels are glued to the railing yet my toes hover over nothing. I look past my feet to reveal a chain link fence topped with barbed wire. All I can think is how far out do I have to jump off this bridge to avoid that fence. I just don't want to hurt anymore. "I pray to you god if you're real I'm sorry but please, PLEASE let me see her. Just one more time…" I take a deep breath. My arms rise above the railing like they've just become weightless and unburdened. I feel the edge of the concrete under the arches of my feet begin to shift. The wind blows in my face and through my hair; I drop a tear and a smile. I just feel free. I let go.

Early Summer

By Nicole Langan, age 16.

In early summer, given a light breeze and warm sun for a full week, we would wander off; we'd not go far from the house, the grass softly swaying in the gentle breeze. We swiftly moved as though we could fly, mother sent with a pair of boots and an apple each. Rolling in the fields amongst the daisies, leaving stains upon our knees and scars on our hands, scratched by branches as we ventured to the treetops to catch a glimpse of the swallows soaring above. Round fields and bogs we'd travel gathering flowers until our hands were covered with thorns from briars. We moved towards home with our hands full of flowers that had already begun to wilt in the heat of our sweaty palms, clenching the stems, smelling the sweet honeysuckle as the sun began to set. We went to bed the afternoon wondering would the sun ever shine like it did that week...

Woman

By Klaudia Ptasinska, age 16.

She is a Woman,

Her love will surround you like air,

Slowly carving itself into you,

Making sure you feel all of it.

Her love will flow through your bloodstream,

Like a never-ending river.

And one day, it will all become too much,

Her love will be too strong, too obvious, too embarrassing,

Not the way you want it.

So, you decide to leave,

Taking what she gave you and leaving what he had yet to offer.

But honey,

You forgot, that water eventually evaporates if it's not refilled,

And oxygen will turn to carbon dioxide after it leaves the lungs.

You can't keep the feeling of her,

 without having her whole.

You forgot,

That the absence of her love will leave empty holes all over you,

That you need her love,

The way plants need water and sunshine.

So, you decide to come back,

Your apology drowning in excuses,

But she stopped listening a long time ago.

You see, when you left,

You gave her the opportunity to absorb the love you rejected.

Letting her bloom, oh so beautifully, like flowers during spring.

 She is a Woman,

And she is not perfect,

But when you'll look at her,

you will see how her skin glows, so brightly

Like the golden stars in the night sky.

Her voice will remind you of the pleasant melody,

Composed by birds every morning,

While the sun paints an iridescent sunrise.

Her eyes,

will make you redefine the meaning of beauty,

And her smile,

Will make you realize,

That you lost the only thing that made you feel alive.

She will stand there,

looking at you with kindness in her eyes,

Her love tattooed on her soul,

shelled by her transparent body.

And it will be then that, you will regret ever taking her for granted.

My Summer Snow

By Róisín Kelleher, age 17.

Our love was as lively and vibrant as the summer months it began in, but almost everything in life is temporary.

Spring

I was having my routine morning coffee when I first met her. I sat in a pocket-sized cafe, nestled despondent among the vast city buildings. It was usually faded beneath the overcast sky, huddled in itself, fighting against the downpours that were almost expected at this point in spring. However, today was different. Blazing gold and orange shades bled like fire into the large windows, the usual dreariness absent. The first sliver of the morning sun made itself known, illuminating the modest, rustic-themed space. There was nothing too slick about Gloria's, no intricate fonts or white etching stained on the glass. You could've sent it back to the 70s or 80s and it wouldn't look out of place. There weren't any tables with fancy umbrellas or anything, most mornings it was just my Americano coffee and myself. It was for this reason that I came to this spot each morning before work, to lose myself in its silent beauty.

That all changed when she waltzed in. She was the kind of girl that people didn't notice. Not that she was boring; she was just timid, fragile, like a glass ballerina. She was an adult I suppose, but so young that she still had an exuberance of youth. Her pale face was framed with locks of fiery red, enhanced by her icy blue eyes. She wasn't tall or willowy, rather short, but well built, yet she walked with the confidence of someone a decade younger. Her nails were short and bitten, her eyes glued to the floor. She seemed to be trying to hide in herself, attempting to take up less space by hunching her shoulders and crossing her arms. Even so, I couldn't draw my eyes from her and that seemed to be the opposite of what she wanted. Her ivory skin was like silk over glass, sleek and soft, unblemished and radiant. She possessed an intelligent sort of beauty. There's no great story to tell, no long-winded romance tale that'll make you reach for tissues. It's rather simple, really.

To my surprise, her piercing cyan eyes fell on me. She darted them away as quickly as they had fallen on me, but not quite fast enough for me not to see. She sighed quietly, pretending to focus on the carved out letters of the menu.

"Get the Americano, you can't beat it." My own words surprised me, I was never one to make the first move, but there was something about her that had me captivated.

She smiled; the corners of her eyes crinkling slightly and she looked back at me and spoke, "Sounds good."

She bought a mocha and sat down opposite me and it just flowed from there. I was late for work that morning, for I had completely lost myself in conversation with her. She was almost a completely different person to the woman that entered a few hours prior. She was outspoken and witty, intelligent beyond belief. She slotted into my morning like a puzzle piece and I felt nothing short of whole. That was the first time I had laid eyes on her, but it certainly wasn't the last. I found she visited Gloria's a lot more often and my quaint morning safe-place soon became ours. The ageing seats of our café turned into nights eating Italian food for prices we couldn't afford. It went from once a week, to twice, to three times. Eventually, the key to my place soon became the key to our place and I couldn't have been happier, I was so hopelessly enthralled. It was soon after she finished her university degree that she fell into the twisted business that she called politics.

There was always a politician in her. She was argumentative and righteous, she had a heart of gold and she was as strong as an ox. Her confidence blossomed with me by her side, she was never without support. We had many a debate at our kitchen table and she had emerged victorious after every single one. We joked about it a lot but we both knew she could really do it if she wanted to. She was shy though, as smart as you could get, but she froze up in front of people she didn't know. She said she could never think straight when there were dozens upon dozens of faces looking up at her. Yet, she threw herself into it. She jumped each hurdle as she came to it and I had her back every time she fell. I admired her determination, almost envious of the fire in her blue eyes. I saw her overcome her greatest fears like they were dust in the wind and, soon enough, politics was her vocation.

Politics was a dirty game, but a game she always played well. She saw her country through the eyes of a mother on minimum wage, raising four children. She saw her country through the eyes of a young, single father, an immigrant or a refugee, young, or old. She saw the great United States through the eyes of the vulnerable and the voiceless. For that, she was both loved and hated. Her views were the opposite of those in power, contradicting the opinions of the rich CEOs and privileged politicians. But her success motivated me. I was never jealous, only proud of her but I wanted to achieve as she did.

I thought of medical school. When I was only fourteen, I lost my brother and the memory of him still bleeds the wound in my heart – little brothers can get you like that. And it's worse because I saw it all happen. It was a bitter winter, January of 2008 when I watched the life being stolen from his eyes and I felt the rhythm of his chest rising and falling come to a sudden halt. He might as well have taken me with him, for I was never quite the same after that. There'd be no more football in the park, no more birthday parties and he'd never see another American snowstorm. As I grew older, I convinced myself that his death was God's mercy. Ben's life was one part hospital and two parts medication anyway. That's what I told myself to heal the void left in me. I tried to stitch my torn soul with the lie that it was fair and fill the hole in my heart with oblivion and false ignorance. It became part of me as I grew; it was like a scar or a birthmark. And the only person who ever really managed to cleanse me of my torment was her. Her rose perfume reminded me of summer and it cast away my relentless winter thoughts. But she wasn't always there, it returned without fail. When I was younger, I promised myself I'd devote my life to being a doctor, to saving others as I couldn't save my brother. This promise to myself had become a distant memory, a silly, young thought, but she had awoken a part of me I thought was long dead. I saw my love become who she wanted, fighting even when she was well past exhaustion and it lit a fire in me.

Spring was a time for new beginnings and I felt as if I had found mine. She was love and she was fire, all in one. Our relationship thrived and grew like the budding April flowers and all I could see in the distance was hope. She was the root of my happiness and my success, she put the spring in my step. It was a time of transition. My usual perpetual emptiness was fading to nothing. It was not entirely gone yet but it was being overtaken by her adoring warmth. She held my Eastertide heart in her pale hands.

Summer

As spring grew to summer, she became my entire world. The physical parts of our relationship were nice, but she was someone to which I could show my soul, show my heart. And that was reflected right back to me. I was man enough to be a boy around her and she was woman enough to be a girl. We showed each other ourselves as ourselves, not as who we wanted to be or felt we should be. We were like two halves of the same soul. Her words brought out the pain I had buried in my bones and although it hurt, it helped them heal. She drew the poison that had become one with my blood so carefully and gently that all my toxicity evaporated like morning dew. She was the ice in my whiskey, taking the hard edge off of everything.

The first time we went furniture shopping for our apartment, she picked out everything. It's not that I wasn't interested; I was just more interested in the way her hair cascaded down her back and how she bit her lip slightly whenever she had to choose between two things. She asked me what I thought of the red mahogany coffee table in front of us and all I could think of was the red in her hair.

"It's beautiful, Alice. Just like you." She smiled as I wrapped my arm around her delicate shoulders and kissed her fondly on the forehead. I liked her company like that. We could be doing absolutely anything and I'd have the best time in the world if she was by my side.

Summer was the season where Alice and I became one. I had tunnel vision, Alice was all I saw. My universe began and ended with her. I could run forever, I could search for miles, but in the end, everything would lead back to her heart and soul. I woke up every morning with the music of her soft breaths filling my ears. I'd trace her lips lightly with my fingers and watch her eyes open sleepily. She'd pout slightly and I'd have to resist the urge to kiss them in fear I wouldn't be able to stop. I'd fight the urge to wrap us up in the warm, white blanket we shared and listen to her gentle breathing, watching the cotton sheets ripple like skipping tones and sharing crooked smiles. Her lips felt slightly chapped beneath my finger, but I didn't care, I gazed at them like they could map out ancient seas and my medical school plans and absolutely anything I could ever want to know. She turned me into a morning person. I woke up happy, excited to see the sunrise tenderly light up the room I shared with her. I have been on this earth long enough to know that these feelings would never be replicated. I knew I'd never look at anyone other than her and feel the way I do. This love, this feeling, it was just us. I could travel the seven seas and only be able to find true love where I left off; with her. It's not that no one else wanted me or wanted her, she was beautiful. But we were made for each other, born to spark and run the same course. When I embraced her, the world stopped still on its axis. Time ceased, along with rain and snow and wind. Her love was pure and generous, altruistic and free. It was the sort of love I'd prayed for and when she was in my arms, I was home.

And the summer sun only kept on giving. The contents of my dreams in a crisp white envelope sat terrifyingly on my red mahogany coffee table. The bold, black letters of 'YALE' were burnt into my mind.

"Sweetheart? Come here." I almost didn't recognise my own voice, shaking with my evident nervousness.

She wrapped her arms around my torso as she approached; her presence soothed me instantly and slowed my racing heart. She massaged my shoulders gently and on her tiptoes, whispered softly into my ear.

"Darren, open it." Her voice accompanied by a tight squeeze.

And I could never say no to her so open it is what I did and it became a memory I would hold dear to my heart forever. Those words of acceptance were like a chance at redemption. I wasn't able to save Ben but I could save people just like him, I could cure my aching turmoil. All I wanted to do was save a life, one was enough. I didn't care about the money or anything material like that, it was something much more than money to me.

Alice introduced me to feelings I'd rather die than let go, I'd rather wither away than to never feel them again. Her love was my valour and my virtue, she never left my side. She was like all the best parts of me in one.

Autumn

She didn't like autumn. She said that these days, her shoes had no grip. The sullen footpath was constantly wet and the threat of rain never ceased to loom in the evenings. Every morning was dim and cold and her walks to the bus stop always seemed so slow. But I couldn't stand to see her falter. The smile returned to her face when I told her that I had a newfound love for autumn because the leaves matched her hair and I've always wanted to kiss her in the rain anyway. As true as that was, I found that thoughts of medical school had pushed Alice aside. I was constantly trapped in Yale's four walls or I was captive in that of our bedroom, surrounded by heavy books and essays. She told me she didn't mind that we hadn't gone for Italian in months but I could see her heart break a little every time I told her no. I could see the effort she poured into our relationship, I could feel it as if it was an embrace but a part of me was absent. The energy I had devoted to making her happy as she made me belonged to something else now and I was hurting her. Yet, I loved her. I couldn't let her go.

The man I was would've slapped the man I am now silly. He would've condemned any man who ever had the audacity to give Alice anything less than the world. But as I looked in the mirror, that's exactly who I had become. I had thrown myself into medicine and I forgot to take her hand when I jumped. It was too late now. I was almost annoyed at her efforts, irritated that she would be so selfish as to expect my attention during my studies and I hated it. But I couldn't see past medical school. I couldn't see her valiant efforts or the time she devoted to me, even when I was undeserving. My mind could only see my studies and it killed her. I unknowingly began to let her go, for I couldn't bring myself to fight for her like she fought for me. She carried the weight of our relationship on her delicate shoulders. And I allowed it. I pretended not to notice that the light in her ultramarine eyes had been drowned out by the tears she cried almost every night. The spring in her step was no longer so apparent and I watched my summer rose slowly wilt with autumn in my fingertips.

I began to feel like I was on the outside looking in when it came to us. I watched Alice love a man so selfish he was blind, a man as cold as a crypt, but the man wasn't me, it couldn't be me. I felt like an observer, unable to change the dire situation unfolding in front of me. I had left Alice lonely; I was a million miles away. She gripped on so tightly, her hands were torn and burned. She dug her nails into the corroding strings of our relationship to give herself a better grasp, to hold onto possibility. I saw the tears roll down her cheek and it didn't hit me like it used to. I had to stay focused, that's what I told myself. School was all I cared about now and she knew it, still refusing to give up on me.

So I closed my dog tired eyes and I let her go in the hope that she would start to live again.

My decision was far from easy. I had gone from wanting forever with her to leaving her of my own free will. I wished she'd understood that I didn't end our relationship because I wanted to. I did it because I couldn't stand what I was doing to her, yet I had no control over it. Her pain was so evident it seeped into her words and her actions, sitting blatant in her eyes. She had started living like every breath she took stung. I was angry at myself for it, I didn't understand it, but I couldn't allow it. Our status quo had become tortuous; I was her medicine turned toxin. She needed my honesty and if anything, I owed her the truth. I knew that if we kept going, we'd break ourselves. She was still all I had ever wanted but time wasn't on our side.

I knew she'd be okay. She was a strong as the wind and as powerful too. She told me once that she thought empathy from others could only do so much. It would heal what it was capable of, but the rest? That was on you. It was courageous and independent; intimidating even when that desire for recovery is strong. It took a lion-heart to walk past fear and pain like it was a ghostly vapour, but I knew she had it in her. A very loud part of me told me that this wasn't really the end for us. That she could take this time to be herself, to heal the bruises I had left on her and when we were both better, we could come back and be stronger than we ever were. I wanted her to light the fire in her eyes again and I knew she couldn't when all I did was extinguish it.

Loneliness brought my life into another realm. It was once an abstract idea to me, an affliction of the old, but perhaps it wasn't so bad. I missed her dearly but I wanted this for myself, this time. A self-hatred had formed when she was by my side. Not because of anything she did, but because I hurt her, over and over. It seemed like only yesterday, the air was warm and the sun bright. I longed for that again, but it was energy wasted. The softness of spring and summer was dead, replaced by that cold breeze that told me winter wasn't far away. I felt empty ever since I had left her; there was a silence to my soul. My blood possessed a bitter chill, my brain frozen to a standstill; my thoughts were glassy and iced. Part of all of that was pain, but a pain I found I could endure. I slept through night after night without the anaesthesia of false hope. I knew that someday, spring and summer would come back again and that there would be light for us, but that wasn't my purpose now. I was driven by exams and studies and I was terrified to let myself think about anything other than that.

As the days faded, the nights closed in and the trees said farewell to their vibrant hues, a chill had crept into the air. Not the bite of wintry blusters, but just a nip to let me know a new season was at hand. A season without her had begun. The wide avenue was lit by the first rays of the day, shining through a thin layer of grey cloud like a stained glass window. No more were the trees their viridescent shades of spring and summer, but they shone in scarlets and gold. In just a few weeks they would stand unclad in the frozen air, bereft of their gaiety. Already the usual grey of the concrete sidewalk was adorned with their pitiful beauty. As I walked to the bus stop that morning in my black woollen coat, I deliberately stepped on each one to hear the crunch and just ahead, I glimpsed a leaf tumbling from its weary branch. It twisted and turned as it fell through the stiff air. I paused to listen for the sound it made as it joined its fallen brethren on the ground, but it was drowned out by the roar of city traffic. I began to realise my cracks would start to show soon, I would crumple just like the leaves I saw every morning and no one would notice, too caught up in their own hectic lives. I was scarlet and gold on the outside, hiding my increasing weariness. I saw a lot of myself in autumn's tired, greying days.

Winter

Winter was a hurricane stemmed from regret. The crisp white snows of November had smothered summer and long since laid it to rest. However, I wasn't a fan of being sad. I tried to see the beauty in winter. I'd watch the silver flakes descend from the grey sky and I'd admire their utter grace and elegance. I'd lie to myself. I'd ignore how they became one with the frozen, dark pathway and thawed into nothing. I'd pretend the sharpness of the cold didn't sting my fragile skin when they met. I'd spin a story in my agonised mind that the beauty of winter filled my heart's gaping hole. I sold my nights to lonely bars in the hope that it would change something – anything. I told myself that going out and forgetting about her would fix everything, but I'd end up isolated at the bar, drowning my broken heart in whatever spirits I could find. The pain was still there, the alcohol just numbed it for a few blissful hours. But I had left her for a reason. The few hours of serenity weren't worth the wave that would drown me the next morning. I completely threw myself into medical school after I was finished feeling completely pathetic. Gone were the hours spent at the forlorn corner bars, replaced entirely by relentless study.

And that worked for awhile. I didn't have time to notice how shattered I had become when all I did was work. But it was just like the snow; a lie, a facade fooling only myself. My fantasy would be so rudely interrupted every so often and my cracks would begin to show. I'd see Alice post a picture of her and a man who was far too close to be her friend. His hand would be comfortably draped around her slim waist, pulling her close. His eyes clouded with lust looking down upon her caused fury in me. Alice deserved to be looked at with nothing less than adoration. The adoration I failed to provide her with. I was filled with frustration and these were the moments in which I knew. My heart rate would double and my muscles would shake uncontrollably. Tears would leak from my half closed eyes and I'd hold my breath between pursed lips to hold back my grieving cries. It was times like this that brought out the shards of regret I had hidden in my mind. I wasn't strong enough to pretend it didn't hurt, that I hadn't made a fatal mistake. The fire she had lit in me was now a forlorn storm of heartache, remorse and complete fear. My heart was beyond torn and none of the medication I had learned about could fix that. It was only her.

What I had done to her hadn't really hit me until deep into winter. My mind was on my side, retracting all the bad things I had ever done and said to her and piling them into extinction. They were never a reflection of her, I knew that now. Only a mirroring of my inner demons; my own selfishness. She laid herself bare for me and I only saw what she failed to do. I had fallen into a state of permanent fatigue in which I couldn't be the man she needed. I wanted her to know that; to know that she was not to blame. In my misplaced entitlement, I gave her passive-aggression in the place of love. I withdrew to punish her, absorbed in myself. And she was gone now. I was plagued by nightmares of Alice with another. Someone who would give her endless warmth instead of cold, hard stares. Someone who would give her respect rather than demands, the kind of someone she deserved. I longed for her by my side. I planned out how I'd make amends with her and mend our broken strings. But what if it was too late? I had grown since I lost her, learned about what I want and what I need; what she wants and what she needs but I was far too fearful to approach her for the possibility of it being too late was immense.

I hadn't seen Alice in months when I decided to halt my pathetic cowardice. The floor of what was our home was stained with our inert love, the smell running past my mouth, leaving me choking on the air of my own space. My mistakes bled from my ears and dripped from my chin. My head hung heavy with the endless running thoughts of her, I was a man broken.

But I was finished watching her slip through my fingers. The fear was still lodged deep in me but as was my love for her. They were beasts within me and the one that thrives is the one you feed; I chose love. I had lived my mistakes, spent months immersed in my own regret and I was ready to change something. I didn't even need to ask myself if this time would be different; I knew it would be. I would give her my heart and soul if she'd be mine again, I'd love her like she was the last of my kind. We were two halves of the same whole. I was nervous, sure, but something told me that she'd see the change in me and agree to let me love her like I used to.

The clock read 2am as I settled down to sleep. For the first time in this wretched season, I drifted off without a pit in my stomach and without fearing my ruthless nightmares. I'd call her in the morning, we'd arrange to meet up that day and I could hold my world in my arms again. It was the first sound sleep I had gotten since autumn.

And a couple of days before we had arranged to meet, death came to Alice like the slow, rattling gasps that had taken my brother. She was at peace with her elbows perched on the stone wall overlooking the sea, breathing in the salted air. She didn't mind the long drive to the coast; she always said that's the only place where her mind would be quiet enough to let her think. And I would've bet my life that she was lost in her running thoughts when the Land Rover violently swerved out of control. The driver, a man in his twenties had leaned forward to the turn up the volume of his pounding bass music and in that moment, lost the opportunity to safely avoid the small sheepdog that had darted across the country road. Even if he'd been paying attention, he would've been hard pressed to make the manoeuvre. He said he barely had time to scream before the airbags knocked him sideways and back. The car on its sideward swerve skidded on winter's hidden black ice and tumbled over and over, stopping only in its collision with the wall Alice stood at. They told me her death was instant – like it was supposed to be a comfort. Like it meant her broken bones and punctured lungs didn't matter for she was just a number in their hospital morgue now and she hadn't even suffered. After all the hospital's losses, it's like they had no sentimentality left for people like Alice. The light left her eyes and for them, she was just another corpse left to be dealt with.

She was cold. The fire of life was reduced to ash; no more harm could come to her now. The heart that used to beat with such love and empathy lay still in her chest. I knew very well that death wasn't kind. It snatched anywhere it could, taking people who were far too young; far too good. It didn't pretend to care or weep. It didn't distinguish. It just stole, ripping the souls of people from where they belonged and it was unapologetic; unstoppable. The hooded vale of death had hung over my life for a very long time but it had only touched me quite this close once before; when I had lost Ben. Death had ripped away the parts of me I loved the most and now it dared to take her too, it dared to take everything. It laced our dear memories with arsenic, every single moment I looked back on ended with the reality that we could never have that again. Just as things had begun to mend for us, she had been prised from my desperate grasp. It didn't take me long to realise that the young man had not only taken Alice's life, he took mine along with hers. I was stuck in a place between life and death; too fearful to die and too weak to keep going.

This grieving agony was a feeling all too familiar; a feeling I couldn't conquer twice. I couldn't pull myself out of it this time and God knows I tried. The gaping hole was too great. What I once treasured was a memory now, nothing else mattered. She was a fading shadow lingering in every thought, in every aspect of my mind. Almost immediately after her funeral, I said goodbye to medical school and joined the league of piteous dropouts. I lacked the passion and drive for it now, I had lost everything. My life lacked any purpose now. My motivation was a cold cadaver and as was my career. The only way I can describe that feeling is heavy. I carried it around with me even though I never wanted to. I was too weak to shrug it off, too small to fight it. It was always there, casting a shadow over my life. It was hung on a thin, fraying thread and eventually, that thread snapped with the weight of knowing I'd never heal. Without the distractions of love and school and anything bright in my life, I craved happiness almost as much as I craved her presence. It was just out of reach, I was held back by my darkness. Her death led me to old habits and I turned to my own personal anaesthetic; alcohol.

Five Years Later

I looked older than my age; alcohol had robbed my final youthful years. My cheeks and nose were tinted red and my breath was constantly scented with spirits, I was determined to stay drunk until I died. All of my potential had turned to dust due to my own weakness. I had failed as a lover and failed as a doctor. My dreams were no longer mine, they were too far out of reach and I was too occupied by the bottle. I often wondered what Alice would say if she could see me now. I could've taken any path I wanted to but life was cruel to me. I had stumbled at her death but I didn't know I was destined to fall so far.

I had never once forgotten her, not in the last five years. Even amidst my many drunken blurs, she was always there. The alcohol did its job, I was numb to the core but it couldn't make me forget. Her icy eyes lived as vibrant in my mind as they were on the day I met her in Gloria's. Her long hair still burned like flames and her voice spoke as sweet as birdsong. The door that life held open for us was closed now; it had been for years but I still looked to it in search of peace. The anger never quite faded either. I hated myself for what I had done, what I had lost and given up. I had well and truly messed up. I wrote her a million letters in an attempt to cope after she died, each letter saying the same as the last. That I missed her and she should be here with me. That I was beyond sorry for hurting her; I had never meant to. I wrote that I missed her wily heart and the soul that I broke. I was missing an integral part of myself, a vital part. The grief came in waves that threatened to drown me, year after year after year. I was at the mercy of its whims and it hit me so ferociously at times that I was left nothing but an empty, cowering shell. I was numb and I had been for years now.

To enter the cemetery, I had to skirt around a pile of brown, frosted leaves. The innumerable flashing fragments shone in the brilliant wintry light, for that day there was no weather; no wind, no cloud, just subzero temperatures. Even the leaf stems lay white and sharp. Ahead the path glistened like white quartz, but it was only ice crystals on weary concrete. I found it odd; this beauty a mask over everything dead. And here I was to add to it with a bunch of pink roses in my gloved hand. I paused, my breath rose in visible puffs and then I remembered why I came. I needed to talk to her and this was the only way. I wasn't here for her, not really. I was here for me. Love and sorrow were twins. Love came first, sweet and strong followed by the sorrow of knowing I would never be with her in this life again. The proximity to her frigid bones and the gift of flowers would close the gap between us for a moment, and in that brief window of time I would feel her close again. To kill Alice and I, there would only ever need to be one bullet. Five years ago today, Alice embraced me tenderly, kissed me on the cheek and told me she loved me. And now as I stood lonely at her gravestone, I almost said it back.

In Youth We Learn

By Eileen Cloonan, age 16.

"In Youth We Learn"

That we are too young to understand

The dynamics of the world because

It was not built with us in mind

But for the world of commerce;

Where leisure lies indoors behind

Money machines and cashiers.

"In Youth We Understand"

That free Wi-Fi isn't really free, because

The password lies at the bottom of your coffee cup;

That free water doesn't exist because

The only way to drink is to build a raft

Of plastic bottles

And pay and pray for tide.

"In Age We Learn"

How to keep on top of the cost of living,

Because we wasted years in school, learning

How to measure angles in triangles

While our parents helped build a

Plastic spire that will never meet the ozone—

They sent smoke signals to God.

"In Age We Understand"

That money is the centre of living

And the root and route to evil.

That power-hungry leaders decide

What should mean most to us, because

Media is shaped

To shape our minds.

Our Turf

By John Shannon, age 16.

I feel it in my hands as I tear it from the soil

Its long dead roots lifeless have seen lifetimes

They resist weakly and relieve with a rip

I clamber and throw up into neat organised piles

Placing, stacking and steadying as I fortify their brown peat bodies

And lay them to rest; drying

Looking around watching my father stack and pile as age proves the skill I do not have

I watch on in envy, him always a foot in front

I stand relieved thinking if that skill could one day be mine

A hardened veteran

His pride is as clear and precise

As the mounds he leaves behind as evidence of his work.

And off we'd trod home when the sun like a lamp would dim

Boots laced and splattered with mud and mould

Flicking off as we'd walk

He'd pray for a dry one and turn to look up

Silently cursing

Our bodies aching as the soil had worked them

Yet the sting of pleasure would numb our woes as we returned

The next day, dried, crisp and sharp,

Our turf.

True Magic

By Aoife Lennon, age 16.

The first time it happened,

I was a small child.

the words on the page

surrounded me, lifted me, and took me away

to a tiny cottage on a mountain

where the breeze blew cool,

and a young girl frolicked with the goats,

miles from my little pink bedroom.

As the years went by, the adventures continued,

to a magical place at the top of a tree,

or to a castle full of sorcerers,

or to a hidden, underground fairy city,

and everywhere in between.

Through those words, I found friendship,

love, thrill, and excitement far beyond anything

I had experienced in my short life.

The characters shaped me, inspired me,

gave me courage to face the real world,

and I flourished in the images of magic and mystery

that the stories evoked.

Until, slowly but surely, the real world stole me away,

keeping me far from the fantasy places that I loved,

trapping me in the humdrum of day-to-day life,

like the young girl in my first storybook,

who was held in the bustling city

instead of her mountaintop paradise.

But sometimes, in a quiet moment,

I pick up a book

and lose myself again.

A Formula of Little Bits

By Siobhán Walsh, age 16.

I'm a little bit happy,

But I'm a little bit sad.

A little bit Mam,

I'm a little bit Dad.

I'm a little bit A's,

I'm a little bit B's.

A little bit 'le do thoil'

And a little bit 'please'.

I'm a little bit Rowling,

And a little bit Dahl,

A little bit Blyton,

And a lot more 'et al'.

I'm a little bit stories,

And a little bit art,

And a whole lot of wondering

How to tell them apart.

I'm a little bit lost,

But a little bit found,

A little bit dreamer,

A bit feet on the ground.

I'm a little bit earth,

I'm a little bit stars,

A little bit Pluto,

I'm a little bit Mars.

I'm a little bit magic,

But a little bit plain,

A little bit good,

But a bit of a pain.

So that makes me:

Eighteen percent stardust,

Twenty-four percent stories,

Thirteen percent earth, steel, and rust.

Eighteen percent good stuff

And twelve percent bad,

Fifteen percent Éire –

I am enough.

I'm a little bit of everything,

But these numbers they add up to be

One hundred percent human,

And one hundred percent me.